IM

D1081992

Celebrity Status

A Kate Huntington Mystery

Kassandra Lamb

A *misterio press* publication

Cover art by Rebecca Swift Artwork rebeccaswiftartwork.com

Formatting By Debora Lewis arenapublishing.org

Published in the United States of America by *misterio press*, a Florida limited liability company
http://misteriopress.com

ISBN 13: 978-0615722535 (misterio press LLC)

ISBN 10: 0615722539

"Fame is like a river, that beareth up

things light and swollen,

and drowns things weighty and solid."

~ Sir Francis Bacon

PROLOGUE

The watcher hunkered behind a tree up the hill from the barn. The back screen door of the house slammed. The woman–*his* woman–strode across the yard toward the barn, catching her honey-colored hair up into a hasty ponytail as she went. Her slim body was tucked into snug jeans and a crisply ironed, light blue shirt and, yes, she was wearing riding boots!

An hour of patience was about to pay off... maybe.

The golden voice that thrilled her fans called out, "Bobby?"

The groom ambled out of the barn and shook his head in answer to something she said. She headed for the paddock. Bobby returned to the barn and came out a few minutes later, leading a frisky bay horse. He wrestled the less than cooperative animal through the paddock gate, then handed the end of the long lunge line to his boss. She began to put the colt through his paces.

Damn! Why wasn't she going trail riding today? Maybe the last note hadn't been such a good idea. Had the things it hinted at spooked her?

The answer became clear a moment later. Bobby led another horse out of the barn. The sturdy gray gelding was limping. The groom leaned over and slid a hand down a front leg. The hand stopped and Bobby shook his head.

Looking out over the pastures, the watcher cursed softly through gritted teeth. The two mares in the distance were heavy with foals. There was no horse for her to take out on the trail.

A grim smile spread across the watcher's face as another idea materialized. There was more than one way to get his woman's attention.

Waiting until she and the groom both had their backs turned, the watcher edged away from the tree and blended into the shadows of the woods behind the farm.

CHAPTER ONE

Skip Canfield paused on the sidewalk and looked up at his home of the last three years. Warmth spread through his chest. The tension in his muscles eased.

The old Victorian could use a fresh coat of paint.

That would please his wife who seemed to thrive on such projects. His lips curled into a slight smile. He took the porch steps two at a time.

His mood sobered as he unlocked the front door. If only he could've left this damn case at the office! He shook his head. Time enough to deal with that later. He'd talk to Kate about it after dinner.

"William Robert Canfield, what *were* you thinking?" Kate's raised voice coming from the kitchen.

Skip leaned against the doorjamb in the kitchen doorway and took in the family drama. His young son slouched down in his chair, a pout on his face. A china bowl, tipped on its side, had spilled half its contents across the big oak table.

"Me no like peas," Billy said.

Hands on hips, Kate scowled at the child. "*Don't* do that again."

Maria muttered something in Spanish, too low for Skip to make out the words. She carried a plastic colander to the table and scooped the runaway vegetables into it. The peas, after a good rinsing, would no doubt show up in tomorrow's soup or stew. Having grown up poor in Guatemala, Maria gave frugality a whole new meaning.

Four-year-old Edie looked up and saw him. "Daddy's home," she sang out, blue eyes sparkling and dark curls bouncing as she wiggled in her chair.

She was a miniature version of her mother. After all this time, it still made Skip's heart swell to hear the little girl–who was not his biologically but was most definitely his nonetheless–call him *Daddy*.

He gave her a slow, easy grin. "Hey, Pumkin." He walked over and dropped a kiss on the top of her curly mop.

Looking across the table at his son, Skip had trouble maintaining a scowl. Kate's use of the boy's full name reminded him of how lucky they were this child even existed. Billy's middle name, Robert, was in honor of Kate's friend, Rob Franklin, who'd played a part in saving her life three years ago, along with that of the baby in her womb.

Chubby arms crossed in defiance, Billy eyed his father through the veil of light brown hair hanging down over his forehead. Skip ran long, slender fingers through his own unruly forelock. Billy might look like him, but personality-wise, the child was all Kate–energetic, intense and stubborn, but also kind and cheerful.

Most of the time. Lately, he'd been illustrating how the terrible twos earned their name.

Skip opened his mouth to add his own reprimand, but Kate shook her head. "Let it go," she said in a low voice. "I'm not up for a tantrum right now."

He looked at his watch. Why were they eating so early, and weren't they going to wait for him? Then he noticed the table was set for three rather than five.

Kate was smiling at him. "Two steaks in the fridge, in Maria's marinade, alongside a salad and a bottle of wine."

He started to grin back at her, then froze. Had he forgotten some special occasion?

Kate's smile widened at his worried look. "I figured we'd both been so busy lately, we could use some quiet time together."

"Darlin', that's the best offer I've had all day." Skip headed for the study to lock up his pistol.

Once back in the kitchen, he took his seat at the table, where only a glass of iced tea awaited him.

Edie stumbled through the blessing.

After several miracles in their lives, including the two little beings sitting at this table, Kate had decided their family should be thanking the good Lord more often. They'd also started attending the Episcopal church several blocks from their house.

As the kids chattered about their day, Skip watched his wife at the other end of the table. Kate had rested her chin on her hand. Her eyes were glassy. He couldn't always read her thoughts, but right now he had a pretty good idea what fantasies engaged her mind. She unconsciously licked her lips.

Time and domesticity had impacted very little on the intensity of their attraction for each other. He knew she considered herself average, but he saw her as the most beautiful woman he'd ever known. And he'd known his share, ever since a late growth spurt in high school had taken him from the class runt to a six-five hunk in one short year.

Edie wound down her description of her day at preschool. Skip jumped into the lull, letting a touch of his native Texas creep into his voice. "I really hate to break the mood, darlin'."

Kate's head jerked a little. Then her cheeks turned an attractive shade of pink.

Skip suppressed a grin and said in a sober voice, "I need to talk to you about something later."

Her face fell, but she rallied and gave him a soft smile. "Maria's going to do b-a-t-h-s," she said in a low voice. "Early."

Skip nodded and made I'm-listening noises in response to his son's convoluted tale about petting somebody's dog.

When the children had finished all they were likely to eat–Billy was now finger-painting on his plate with his applesauce–Maria announced it was bath time. The children protested but the short, plump nanny herded them out of the kitchen and up the stairs, singing out in her heavily accented voice, "Early to bayd, early to rise, and de early bird gets de worm."

Maria, the cousin of Skip's business partner, Rose Hernandez, had immigrated to the U.S. four years ago. Her English was much improved over the dozen words she'd known then, and lately she'd developed a fascination for American sayings. She could produce one for almost every occasion.

Once she and the children were well up the stairs, Skip said, "I have a client I think could use your services. You know who Cherise Martin is?"

Kate tilted her head. "Isn't she that up-and-coming pop singer? She and her boyfriend are all over the tabloids at the checkout line in the grocery store."

"Yeah, that's her. She's my client."

"Wow, so you're private investigator to the stars now."

"PI and bodyguard. Normally I'd assign a couple of our men to her. I have Ben on duty when she's home, but I go with her whenever she's out in public. Big-name client wants the boss, not the underlings. That's why I've been working such odd hours lately."

"I didn't realize she lived around here," Kate said.

"Closely kept secret." Skip got up to clear the table. "Cherise Martin is her stage name. Her real name is Carol Ann Morris. She owns a fifteen-acre horse farm in that name, out in Howard County."

"So what does this have to do with me?" Kate asked, as she put away leftovers.

"She's been receiving weird notes from an anonymous fan. Love notes on the surface, but they have a sinister tone to them. Rose is looking into that. I think the stress is starting to get to Cherise. I'm not sure she was real well wrapped to begin with, and now she seems to be coming unglued."

She grimaced. "What did you tell her?"

Kate had opened a private psychotherapy practice shortly after Billy was born, rather than returning to her job at a counseling center. He knew her main reason for going private was to have more control over the clients she saw. He wouldn't push Cherise on her if she didn't want the case.

"Not much yet." He put the last of the dishes in the dishwasher. "I just asked if she might want to see somebody to help her cope. She seemed open to the idea, so I told her I knew somebody good and I'd check it out for her. Didn't mention yet that the somebody is my wife."

"I'm not sure I want to become a celebrity therapist. I have no desire to be the next Dr. Phil."

"I had the same hesitation about taking her case, but nobody around here knows who she is, so our privacy is protected along with hers."

"Well, I can talk to her once at least," Kate said. "And assess whether or not I could work with her. Do you think she'd accept that caveat, that neither of us is committed to continuing unless it feels right?"

"Yeah, I think she'd go along with that."

"And, Skip, you definitely need to tell her I'm your wife."

He nodded. Kate still went by Huntington professionally, since that was the name under which she'd established her reputation as a therapist.

"That might feel weird to her," Kate said, "in which case, I can give you some referrals for her."

The kids bounced down the stairs, dressed in their PJs and giving off the fragrance unique to freshly bathed children. Kate gave each a hug and a kiss.

Then Skip led them back upstairs to do story time and tuck them in.

~~~~~

Kate set the table again–for two this time–with a tablecloth, candles and a single red rose in a small vase. The fickle May weather had turned cool enough that her plan to eat out on the porch had been revised, but she figured Skip could handle the chill long enough to grill the steaks.

Skip came back into the kitchen.

"Now then, Mr. Canfield." She went over and wrapped her arms around his waist. "Can we get back to *my* agenda for the evening?"

"That sounds like a splendid idea." He leaned down to kiss her, the gold flecks in his hazel eyes sparking at her.

She'd intended they would eat first, but her hands had other ideas. Of their own volition, they slid up under his shirt and started exploring his broad chest. His skin quivered under their touch. He broke off the kiss and sucked in his breath.

He wrapped an arm around her to draw her tighter against him, and bent to kiss her again. His free hand went exploring as well, searching under her knit top for the hook to her bra. He found it.

When his thumb flicked across a nipple, she gasped and swayed on her feet. He broke the kiss, grinned down at her, then swept her up into his arms.

It was ten o'clock before they got around to grilling the steaks.

~~~~~~~~

The woman had made her appointment as Carol Ann Morris, but once she was in the office, she told Kate she preferred to be called Cherise. "I've gone by that name for so long now, it feels more natural than my real name," she said with a small laugh.

Kate asked some questions to get a feel for the woman's personality and overall mental health. The blue-eyed blonde was even more beautiful in person than in the images Kate had seen on television and in magazines. Her body language, relaxed and poised, expressed a level of confidence unusual in a twenty-seven year old.

"Where are you from?" Kate asked, segueing into the next phase of the intake interview.

"Georgia. I grew up on a farm just outside of Atlanta."

"You don't have a Southern accent."

Cherise flashed a perfect white smile. "Hours spent with a voice coach. A Southern twang is fine if you sing country, but my fans expect me to sound like the girl next door, so standard English was drummed into me."

Up to this point, Cherise had answered her questions directly and without hesitation. But each time Kate tried to find out more about the young woman's history, she was expertly deflected with a superficial response. She finally cut to the chase and asked about the strange love notes.

"They come through the mail. No return address, no signature. My assistant puts aside any fan mail that's anonymous or sounds the least bit threatening. I now realize how wise Sarah is to do that. Otherwise we might not have made the connection with the earlier notes. The first three were just anonymous declarations of undying love. But then the tone changed. They started sounding like veiled threats."

Cherise showed the first signs of agitation, sitting forward and clasping her hands nervously in her lap. "This last one, that came two weeks ago. It sounded like this guy, whoever he is, was going to try to kidnap me." She shuddered. "That's when I called Skip's agency. He looked through Sarah's file and made the connection with the earlier notes. Same style of writing."

The young singer sat up straight again. "That man's a real sweetheart, Kate. You're a lucky woman."

"I know," Kate said with a small smile, then intentionally changed the subject away from herself. "How does your boyfriend feel about the notes?"

After a flash of confusion, Cherise's face cleared. "Oh, you mean Johnny. He's not my boyfriend. That was our publicist's bright idea. We're just partners, singing partners that is. And Johnny writes a lot of our songs. He's secretly engaged to be married. I don't know what Jim–that's the publicist–is going to do when the wedding date gets closer. I guess he'll fake some dramatic breakup between us and pretend Sharon's caught Johnny on the rebound. They've actually been dating for over a year."

By the end of the hour, Kate wasn't totally sure about taking the case, but she couldn't pin down why she was hesitant. She suspected she'd only seen the public persona of Cherise Martin–who didn't seem to be coming unglued at all.

With a mental shrug, she decided to commit to only a few sessions, to teach the young woman some stress management strategies.

As they were winding down, Kate said, "I'd like you to sign a waiver of confidentiality, Cherise, so I can talk to Skip about your case. I wouldn't tell him specifics of what you say to me, but it would be helpful if he can keep me informed about the threatening notes."

Cherise narrowed her eyes. "I thought therapy's supposed to be private. It's okay if he tells you what's going on, but not the other direction."

Kate paused, the niggling feeling of uncertainty a bit stronger. "I understand that it might feel weird, thinking we're talking about you, but it would strictly be on a need-to-know basis. If that's not comfortable, however, we can see how things go for now."

"Well, I don't see how there would be any need to know." Cherise's voice had a sharp edge.

"As I said," Kate responded in a soothing tone, "we'll see how things go. There may not be such a need, and if there is, then we can readdress the issue at that point." She stood, to signal the end of the session.

Cherise remained in her chair for several seconds, elegant legs crossed. Finally she rose. "Please call my assistant," she said in a haughty tone, "to schedule my appointment for next week. She keeps my calendar." Handing Kate a card, she walked toward the office door.

This woman has major control issues. Or is she just spoiled and used to getting her way?

Kate kept her voice neutral. "Next appointments are usually scheduled at the end of each session."

"Well, Sarah has my schedule. I have no idea when I'm free next week."

Kate wasn't about to get in a verbal tug of war with a new client, but neither was she willing to spend valuable time each week chasing down Cherise's assistant to make the next appointment. "How about if I call Sarah and we'll set up several appointments for the next few weeks?"

"That would be fine." Cherise turned and opened the office door.

Skip was lounging against the opposite wall of the waiting room. He straightened to a stand and smiled at Kate over the woman's head.

Was it her imagination or did Cherise's back stiffen?

Kate resisted the urge to roll her eyes. Once the outer door had shut behind them, she muttered, "You're welcome."

~~~~~~~~~

On Sunday morning, church was more crowded than usual. Kate and Skip were running late when they dropped the kids off at their Sunday school rooms. They made it into the sanctuary just before the priest and choir started down the central aisle. Squeezing into the end of the first pew they came to, Kate knew she would have trouble paying attention during the sermon with Skip's thigh pressed up against hers.

As the congregation sat down after the opening prayers, she tried to focus on holy thoughts. Halfway through the Bible readings, she felt Skip's pocket vibrate.

He pulled out his cell phone as discreetly as possible and looked at the caller ID. His jaw tighten, a sure sign he was not happy with what he saw.

Taking her by the elbow, he moved her to her feet and led her out the back of the church. "Probably less disruptive this way," he said, once they were through the doors. "I've got a bad feeling I'd just have to come back in and tell you I have to leave. That was Cherise." He was punching buttons to call the client back.

As soon as he said his name, Kate could hear screeching from the other end of the line. "Cherise, calm down," Skip said, but the screeching continued.

Finally, he broke through the hysteria enough to get her to put Ben on the phone. He listened for a few seconds, then said, "Rose and I will be there in less than an hour."

Kate frowned, unhappy at the intrusion into the one day of the week they both tried to reserve for family time.

"Call Sarah and see if she can come over," Skip said into the phone. "Maybe she can get Cherise to calm down." He disconnected. "There's been another note. This one was delivered to her farm."

Some of Kate's annoyance dissipated. "That's not good. But can't Ben handle it?"

He stepped over and wrapped an arm around her shoulders. "It was delivered skewered on a bloody knife. Lying beside one of her barn cats on her front porch. The cat had been stabbed to death."

Kate was grateful for his steadying arm. "Holy shit," she whispered, then crossed herself in apology for cursing on the church steps.

"Go on back in. I'll get Rose to pick me up. And say a prayer that we catch this bastard soon!" He punched a speed dial number as he ran down the steps and across the parking lot.

Kate watched him retrieve his .38 from the locked glove box of the family van. Then he loped toward the street to meet his partner.

She shuddered and went back into the church.

CHAPTER TWO

Ben Johnson answered Cherise's door. Skip and Rose stepped into the vast living room of the renovated farmhouse.

Cherise raced across the floor and flung herself at Skip.

Resisting the urge to back up, he gently grabbed her wrists before they could circle his waist, and come in contact with the gun tucked into the back of his waistband under his sports jacket.

"It's okay, Cherise. We're not going to let anything happen to you." He steered her to one of the three white leather sofas that made a giant horseshoe in front of the stone fireplace. Not comfortable with sitting beside her, he crouched down in front of the sofa. He wasn't sure if she was throwing herself at him–literally this time–out of habit or if she was truly coming on to him. Either way, he didn't want to encourage her.

He breathed an internal sigh of relief when Cherise's personal assistant came into the room. "Sarah's going to take care of you now," he said. "I need to talk to Ben for a minute. I'll be right back."

He stood up as Sarah sat down beside her boss, a glass of water and a pill in her hands. Skip hoped the pill was a tranquilizer.

He moved over to where Rose and Ben were conferring in low voices. Rose gave him a succinct summary. "She wouldn't call the cops. Ben's bagged the knife and note separately. But she insisted that the farm manager remove the cat."

"Where's the note?" Skip asked.

Ben was slightly shorter than Skip and built like a grizzly bear, with thick dark hair and a beard to complete the image. "On the table," his deep voice rumbled as he tilted his head toward the kitchen.

"Stay with her," Skip told him. "This guy may still be lurking around here."

He and Rose headed for the remodeled 'country' kitchen that had all the most modern appliances and gadgets imaginable.

They stared down at the note, made even more menacing by a bloody gash down the middle. The author had left room for the knife thrust. There was a wide space between the words in the middle of the page.

Dear Cherise, or should I say, Dear Carol, There's no point in hiding from me. You know our love will win out in the end. See you at Merriweather.

"What's that mean?" Rose asked. "See you at Merriweather."

"She has a charity concert there in two weeks." Sarah's voice came from behind them.

Skip turned to the PA. "Sarah, I need something from you."

The plain-looking brunette nodded, her brown eyes serious behind wire-rimmed glasses.

"I need a list of everyone who knows Cherise's real name and knows about this farm. And a list of anyone who is a current or previous romantic partner."

Sarah's lips curled into a small smile, or was it a smirk?

"Or sexual partner," Skip added, since that wasn't always synonymous with romantic partner. "I know she's resisted giving us that information before, but now we have to have it if we're going to keep her safe."

Sarah's face sobered. "How soon do you need it?"

"Yesterday," Skip said. "And on those lists, indicate if someone was a cat person, or hung around the barn when they were here. How friendly was that cat?"

"The other two barn cats are half wild, but that one was very people-oriented. He liked being petted and was the only one who would let you pick him up." The young woman's eyes welled with tears. "Cherise loved that cat. She called him Sweety Pie."

"Okay, let me know who on the lists would know that he's the most approachable of the cats."

"I'll get on it right now," Sarah said. "Are you going to stay with her?"

Skip looked at his watch, then at Rose. "One of us will, for this afternoon at least, and we'll get a couple extra men on for tonight."

Sarah nodded and left the room.

"I'll stay," Rose said. "Mac's busy at the restaurant anyway. Take my car and go home. I'll have him pick me up later, or Ben can drop me off."

Guilt struggled with his desire to get back to his Sunday with his family.

"It's okay, partner. Mac's interviewing for a manager today. He wants to go full time with us."

Skip chuckled. "So, he's decided being a detective is more fun than serving up crab cakes huh?"

"Oh yeah."

"Thanks, Rose. You're saving me from sleeping on the couch tonight."

"Sure, that'll happen, not." She flashed one of her rare but dazzling smiles that turned her plain face into a vision of beauty.

He felt the heat creeping up his cheeks and silently cursed his tendency to blush easily. "She doesn't talk about it to you all, does she?" He was referring to both Rose and Liz Franklin, Kate's two closest female friends.

"Of course not, but it's pretty darn obvious. You two can't keep your hands off each other, even after three years."

His face got hotter.

She laughed, then slugged him in the arm, making him wince. Short but sturdy Rose packed a wallop.

"Glad to see you two are still able to party, despite the horror of current events," Cherise said from the kitchen doorway, her hands on her hips. "And who the hell is this woman anyway?"

Skip opted to ignore her tone. "Cherise, this is Rose Hernandez, my partner. Rose, meet our client, Cherise Martin."

"Ma'am." Rose nodded at her.

"Rose has been investigating the notes, trying to identify the source of the fancy stationary and checking into the postmarks."

"This guy's covered his tracks fairly well," Rose said. "Postmarks from four different cities all sent to your L.A. condo, then forwarded here. Doubt he was actually in those cities. He may be getting friends to re-post the letters to you, or bribing someone at a commercial mail service to do it."

"That's *all* you've figured out." Cherise looked Rose up and down. "Frankly, I'm not as impressed with Canfield and Hernandez as I once was. *This* is your partner?"

Skip resisted the temptation to point out they hadn't had much to go on until now. "Trust me, Cherise, size is not everything." He rubbed his bicep. "Rose is a former police officer and she's as tough as they come. I've seen her take down guys twice her size. And personally I wouldn't want to have to arm wrestle her. Not at all sure who would win."

"I would," Rose said, her expression neutral.

Skip gestured toward the big kitchen table. "Let's sit down and hash out where we're going from here. How many of your staff were on the premises today and/or yesterday evening?"

Cherise took a seat. "Not counting Sarah, three. The groom, Bobby Hall, lives in a small apartment on the back of the horse barn. The housekeeper, Bonnie, is off today but she was here yesterday. And Harry Bailey, he's the farm manager. He's usually not here on Sundays but he said he had to talk to Bobby about something."

"Is Mr. Bailey still here?" Rose asked.

"I don't know."

"Can you stay a little while?" Rose said to Skip. "I want to talk to Hall and Bailey."

"Yup, do it."

Cherise turned to him, tears in her eyes. "What does she mean, for a little while? You can't leave me alone!"

"We're not going to leave you alone. Rose is going to stay for the rest of today and we'll get some extra men to help Ben tonight. He's been a bodyguard for ten years and–"

"I want to hire you," Cherise interrupted, "as my chief of security, full time."

He stifled a sigh and chose his words carefully. "Well, essentially that's what you've done, for the time being at least."

"No, I mean as a permanent position. Even after this crackpot is caught, there's bound to be others. I think I need a security staff."

"I appreciate the offer, but I have a job. I like being my own boss."

"I'll pay you twice what you're making now. And give you free housing. There's a nice three-bedroom for sale right down the street. I could get it fixed up for you." She jumped up. "I'll have Sarah contact the agent and make an offer, then get my decorator started on it right away."

Skip held up his hands. "Stop, Cherise." Then softening his voice, he said, "Sit down, please. I know you're upset but I think you're over-reacting a little. We can keep you supplied with guards 24/7 for a lot less than it would cost to have a full-time security person like me. I'm flattered by the offer, but I'm not interested. For one, Kate would never agree to move out of our house. She loves it. And I don't want to disrupt my kids. Take them away from their preschool and their friends."

"Okay, so you don't have to live here, but I'd still like you to be my security chief. Would you think about it, please?"

"Yeah, I'll think about it, but don't get your hopes up. Like I said, I like being my own boss." He was tempted to tell her that money wasn't much of an incentive since his wife was a moderately wealthy woman, thanks to the sizeable insurance policy her first husband had bought two years before his death. But he decided that would just prolong the argument. Hopefully, once Cherise settled down, she'd forget the whole idea.

"So let's get back to the plan here," he said. "I want to hire extra people if that's okay with you. Have two outside and one inside for a while. Rose and I are going to step up the effort to track this guy down. And as upsetting as this was for you, now at least we know this guy's not just some random fan. He's somebody who knows you and knows about this farm. That narrows the field considerably. Now what's the deal with this concert at Merriweather?"

"I'm going to call my agent and cancel that."

Skip thought for a moment. On the one hand, he hated to see this guy get the satisfaction of controlling Cherise's life that way. It would probably egg the bastard on. But on the other hand, Merriweather Post Pavilion, an open air theater in Columbia, Maryland, was surrounded by woods, making it a security nightmare.

He nodded. "That's probably for the best."

It was after two by the time Skip was able to get away from Cherise's farm. She'd gone ballistic when he repeated that Rose and Ben would be staying, but he would be going home.

Rose walked out to the car with him. "I've gotta hand it to you, partner. You keep your cool with her really well. I'm grateful you're the hold-the-client's-hand person on our team. 'Cause I wanted to tell her to get a grip." Rose shook her head so hard her tight bun of black silky hair threatened to shake loose.

Skip chuckled. "She is a tad wearing on the nerves, isn't she?"

Serious brown eyes looked up at him as they stood beside the car. "I'm glad we ended up partners. We're a good... *complement* is probably the best word for it."

Skip wasn't quite sure what to say. For Rose, this was a significant display of emotion.

"Yup, good ole easy-goin' Skip reels in the clients," she continued. "Charms 'em and keeps 'em happy. Then I step in and do the real work." She flashed him one of her glorious smiles.

He grinned back at her. "I'm glad we're partners, too. You're the best, Rosie." He quickly jumped back when she tried to slug him in the stomach. She hated being called Rosie, which of course made her friends that much more inclined to do so when they wanted to tease her.

It took Skip a moment to figure out how to stuff his big frame into the driver's seat of Rose's car. Once he was in, the seat pushed back as far as it would go, he congratulated himself again on the decision to buy new vehicles when the agency had started doing well. This car and his own truck had all the bells and whistles, including a hands-free phone. And the new Ford Expedition had even more head and leg room than the Explorer he'd driven for years.

He squirmed in his seat, wishing he had some of that leg room now.

His mind drifted back to Cherise. He decided not to tell his wife about her attempt to hug him, nor about the job offer.

~~~~~~~~~

Once Skip had filled her in on the events at Cherise's farm, Kate sighed. "I should probably call her, make sure she's okay."

"I wish you wouldn't. She's already taken up enough of our day. She can call the answering service if she feels the need for your support."

"You talked me into it, or out of it actually."

"Wasn't exactly a hard sell, was it?" Skip teased.

Kate opened her mouth, then remembered she had no waiver of confidentiality. She closed it again.

He read her thoughts, as he had a habit of doing. "I know. She's becoming a bit of a pain. I'm sorry now that I referred her to you."

"That's okay. I could have told her no, but I didn't. And I've certainly worked with more difficult clients."

"Where are the kids?" Skip asked, looking around.

"Edie's at a friend's birthday party. We need to pick her up," Kate consulted her watch, "in an hour and a half. Billy's napping."

"How long ago did he go down?" The gold flecks danced in his eyes.

"Just a little bit before you got home." Knowing where he was headed with this, she was tempted to resist. She had chores she'd planned to do while Billy was napping. But something told her he needed to reassert something–she wasn't sure what–after dealing with Cherise.

Actually she wouldn't mind reasserting a few things herself. She suspected her handsome husband wasn't telling her all the ways that Cherise Martin was becoming a pain. He tended to take his good looks in stride, along with the frequent come-ons from women, but she couldn't help feeling a bit jealous at times.

She knew it was a primitive territorial thing–how dare these women think they could mess with her man? But she trusted *him* completely. He could have had just about any woman he wanted, and he'd wanted her. He'd even patiently waited several months, while she'd held him at arm's length, insisting it was too soon after Eddie's death for her to date.

Heading toward the bedroom, she let out an exaggerated sigh. "I just have so much to do today, so many chores. First I need to change the sheets on our bed."

"I'll help you with that, darlin'," Skip said, following her down the hall.

She giggled. "With your help, I'm sure we can get it done in *twice* the amount of time I could have done it alone."

He caught up with her and wrapped his arms around her waist from behind. "I'm thinking it should take three or four times as long." He kissed the side of her neck.

Her knees turned to mush as heat shot through her.

"After all," he said, "we've probably got an hour before Billy wakes up."

CHAPTER THREE

Following a Wednesday tradition of many years, Kate and her closest friend were meeting for lunch at Mac's Place, across from the Towson courthouse. It wasn't quite the same, however, now that the owner was seldom there. Kate and Mac Reilly had grown up together. Their parents had been best friends. It seemed weird to come into his restaurant and not have him stick his head out of the kitchen to greet her with, "How ya doin', sweet pea?"

Kate was already ensconced in their favorite booth when she spotted Rob Franklin's six-two frame coming through the door.

Lowering his significant bulk onto the bench across from her, he let out a sigh. "Feels good to sit down. I've been in court all morning."

They had started out as work buddies, with Rob handling the legal messes that Kate's psychotherapy clients sometimes encountered. Over the years, the relationship had evolved into a friendship, first between them and later between the two couples. Then Eddie was killed and his murderer had tried to kill her and the Franklins. Being stalked by a killer had taken their friendship to a whole new level of intimacy.

Now her friend was watching her. "How're you doing, Kate?"

"Fine," came out of her mouth, as she grimaced.

"What's the matter?"

"Oh, it's not a big deal. I just had a session right before lunch with a somewhat difficult client."

"Need to talk about it?" Rob asked.

"I'd love to, but I can't. She's a celebrity, pretty high profile, and a bit spoiled." Kate changed the subject. "So how are things in your world?"

While waiting for their usual order of crab cake sandwiches, with seasoned fries on the side for Rob and a salad for Kate, they chatted about the latest adventures of the Franklins' daughters. The oldest, Shelley, was in her third year in an archeology doctorate program, and Samantha was a junior at Johns Hopkins University in pre-med.

"Wow, your girls are gonna be doctors," Kate said.

"Yeah, who'd have ever thunk it, especially Sam. For a long time there we weren't real sure she'd make it out of high school in one piece." Rob shook his head. "You'll be dealing with that eventually, you know."

"Don't remind me. Billy's full-blown terrible twos right now. I don't want to think about that same attitude in a six-foot-tall teenager."

"Or taller, considering his daddy." Rob grinned, as the waitress delivered their food. He swiped the pickle slices off her plate to add to his own stacked on top of his crab cake.

"I've been meaning to do an intervention with you," Kate teased him, as she spread tartar sauce on the bun of her own sandwich. "Find you a treatment program for pickle addictions."

They ate in companionable silence for a few minutes. Then Kate's mind drifted again to Cherise. Her facial expression must have shifted accordingly.

Rob put down his sandwich. "What is it? Something's bothering you."

"It's this case. I really wish I could talk to you about it. It's somebody Skip referred to me. And what's really bothering me is not my involvement with the client, but his. He's providing bodyguard services personally, because it's a VIP..." She trailed off, wishing she could tell him about the threatening notes and the dead cat. Until the subject had been discussed in Cherise's session this morning, Kate hadn't realized just how much she herself was spooked by the cat incident, although she'd hidden those feelings from the client.

"Skip knows how to take care of himself." Rob covered her hand with his own. "I've never met anybody more capable of handling himself in a tricky situation. He keeps his cool, does what needs to be done."

Kate knew he was right. Skip had saved both of their lives three years ago, by keeping his cool. She turned her hand over and gave his a squeeze, then let go to pick up her fork. She looked down at her plate, stabbed at her salad. "It's just that I couldn't handle..."

When she didn't finish the thought, Rob said, "I know that. And so does Skip. He's always careful."

Kate poked at her salad some more, without actually eating any, while she got herself under control. Finally she looked up, having blinked away the tears in her eyes. "I know it's irrational, to be this scared for him. His work really isn't all that dangerous, and he's good at it. Heck, when's the last time you heard about a bodyguard getting hurt in the line of duty? As he's pointed out to me several times, bodyguards are there as a deterrent and their mere presence keeps the bad guys from trying anything."

She stabbed again at her plate.

"Kate, I don't think you have to kill that salad. It looks like it's already dead to me."

She gently poked the back of his hand with her fork. "Leave me alone, Funny Man. I'm trying to sort something out here."

He grabbed her hand and disarmed her. Then held the hand between both of his big paws. "Kate, I don't need a degree in psychology to figure out why you'd be afraid of losing him."

Kate shook her head. "It's not just that Eddie died, but how he died. It was so sudden, and so senseless. One minute we were going along, just being ordinary people, doing boring mundane things. The next minute... Hell, Rob, I think I'd be scared silly if Skip were a shoe salesman. Eddie was a tax accountant, for God's sake. How safe can you get? The only people he had reason to be afraid of were IRS auditors."

Rob patted her hand.

"A friend of mine," Kate said, "a psych prof at the university, she talks about what she calls healthy denial. I sat in on her lecture on PTSD and depression once. She told her class that depressed people are often more realistic than the rest of us. They realize that bad things really can happen to them. They've lost their healthy denial, the ability to assume that when they leave the house in the morning nothing bad will happen to them that day. That assumption is what allows us to function on a day-to-day basis, without being constantly afraid and depressed."

"But in your case," he said softly, "you have that denial for yourself, just not for Skip."

She nodded, her eyes filling again. "Every minute, every *single* minute I'm away from him, I'm afraid somebody's going to walk up to me and tell me he's dead."

Rob handed her his handkerchief.

She dabbed her eyes with it. "The only time I know he's safe is when he's in my arms. It's the only time I can relax."

~~~~~~~~~~

Driving back to his office after lunch, Rob was trying to decide if he'd been helpful or not. He'd been at a loss for what to say. He'd wanted to offer advice, to fix the problem. But he'd learned the hard way, after many years of marriage and friendship with two rather intense women, that the female of the species often didn't want you to fix it. They just needed to talk it out. So he'd tried to be a good listener.

It didn't feel like enough.

On the sidewalk outside his building, he paused to call a number on his cell phone. He almost disconnected while the phone was ringing. He'd never violated Kate's confidences before. Was this such a violation? He wasn't sure.

He got Skip's voicemail. "Hey, it's Rob. This case you're both on. She couldn't tell me much about it, but for some reason it's got her spooked. She's scared for you, my friend." Rob hesitated. "Don't tell her I called."

Rob was walking into his office when his phone beeped. He looked at the display. *You have a new text message. Do you want to read it now?*

He was technologically challenged. He'd never figured out how to send text messages and wasn't real sure he ever wanted to. But this was easy enough. He hit OK and the message popped up.

Thx. Will b careful.

~~~~~~~~~~

Cherise was not able to cancel the charity concert. Her agent informed her over the phone that Jim Bolton, the publicist, had thrown a fit at the thought of cancelling so late in the game. The charity–a local version of the one that tried to fulfill the dreams of terminally-ill children–had already incurred expenses. If Cherise backed out now, it would be extremely bad publicity, instead of good.

When Cherise told the agent, Jannine Welsh, why she wanted to cancel, Jannie threw a fit of her own. "What do you mean you've been getting threatening notes from somebody? And you didn't even *tell me,*" she yelled in her ear.

"No, I didn't. Because I was afraid Jim would try to turn it into a publicity stunt, and then every other wacko in the world would have played copycat. And don't you dare tell him."

"Okay, okay, you're right. Jim would find a way to leak it to the press," Jannie said. "So I won't tell him, but he's also right. You can't cancel. It would totally blow your image as the sweet wholesome gal who loves puppy dogs and kids."

"Actually I'm a cat person and I can't stand anybody under nineteen," Cherise said acidly.

"I know that, lovey, but the world doesn't, and we want to keep it that way. So you have to do the concert. But we can shorten your part by a few songs, just one long set, no intermission. I'll look into adding another warm-up act. And maybe Johnny could end with a solo, while security is getting you out of there."

"I'll talk to Skip Canfield about it and get back to you. But I'm not promising anything unless he's sure he can keep me safe."

"Who's this Skip dude?" Jannie asked, suspicion in her voice.

"He's my *personal* security chief. I hired him and his firm a few weeks ago."

"His firm?"

"He and his partner run a private investigation agency, and they provide bodyguard services."

"Ooohh. Bodyguards, as in hunks?"

Cherise smiled at the phone receiver. "Yes, and Skip is the hunkiest of them all."

Jannie chuckled. "Is he married?"

"Sadly, yes," Cherise said. "But a girl can still look." She giggled and disconnected.

~~~~~~~~~

This was a first for Canfield and Hernandez. Skip had called a staff meeting. Rose, Mac, and 'Dolph' Randolph, a retired police detective, were gathered in the agency's conference room. Three of the newly hired guards were at Cherise's farm, so that Ben could be at the meeting as well.

"Cherise Martin wants assurances from us we can keep her safe before she'll agree to go ahead with the charity concert at Merriweather," Skip began.

"When is the concert?" Dolph asked, chewing on the end of his bushy ginger mustache. It and his rust-colored hair were both heavily salted with gray. At eleven in the morning, his dress shirt and slacks were already rumpled, the shirt gaping a bit around the buttons where it fit too snugly over a slight paunch.

"A week from Friday. Memorial Day weekend," Rose said.

Ben and Dolph groaned in unison.

"Probably a capacity crowd," Ben finished the thought for both of them.

"Probably," Skip said. "Cherise has given us an unlimited budget, so here's what I have in mind. We hire as many big bodies as we can find. Cherise is going to be the President of the United States. Nobody gets within twenty feet of her. Rose, I'd like you and Mac to be in the crowd, near the front, screaming and acting like just another couple of fans, but you're watching and listening for anything out of whack."

Rose made a face.

"I know," Skip said. "Acting like a screaming fan isn't your cup of tea, but it's the best use of our resources." Neither she nor Mac had been seen in public with Cherise so they were the logical ones to be undercover.

She nodded.

"Two, three rows back. One of us on each side. 'Bout fifty feet apart," Mac said, in his usual clipped sentences.

Skip eyed the short, wiry man, who looked scruffy on his best day. Working hard to keep the chuckle out of his voice, he said, "Better make sure we introduce you to all the hired muscle, Mac, so they don't think you're the stalker."

"We going armed?" Rose said.

"Most definitely. But nobody draws unless the guy shows a weapon," Skip said. "Don't want anybody getting arrested for assault with a deadly. I'll take care of contacting the Howard County police and Merriweather's private security people to coordinate."

"Hopefully this won't turn into a train wreck," Dolph said, shaking his head.

Skip's jaw tightened at the thought of three different groups of men, with testosterone and adrenaline surging through their systems, trying to coordinate security in a crowd of crazed fans. "Hopefully not," he fervently agreed.

After the meeting, he and Rose conferred in his office.

"Sarah sent me that list of boyfriends," Rose said. "I've put them in order, most likely suspect to least likely. See what you think?" She handed him a sheet of paper.

"Oh, ho. Top of the list. Ex-boyfriend from nine months ago. Is he the last guy she dated?"

"No, she's gone out with a couple of guys, off and on, since then. But they haven't made it to tell-them-about-the-farm status. One's in L.A., the other's in New York. Seem to be fairly casual relationships, from what Sarah told me. This Lansing guy, the breakup was messy. And he'd practically been living at the farm for a while."

She shook her head in frustration. "I can't believe Cherise refused to tell us about these guys up front. They should've been the first thing we checked out, instead of me trying to chase down postmarks and fancy paper stock at stationary stores."

"Cherise claimed, when I signed her up as a client, that she'd only had a couple relationships and they'd ended amicably months ago. She was convinced it was some crazy fan."

Rose snorted. "There are seven guys on this list, and that's only going back about three years."

"You run a background check yet on this Lansing guy, to see if he's got a record?"

"About to. Then I think we should go talk to him together. If this guy's into sticking knives into kitties, he may not take a compact woman like myself too seriously."

"Since you're going to be undercover at the concert, I better go by myself," Skip said.

"Unh, uh." Rose shook her head. "Kate would kill me if I let you go without back-up."

"I'll take Dolph then. But run this guy through the system first. If his prints are on file, we might get a match with the partials from the knife."

"Wouldn't that just make it all too easy," Rose said as she left his office.

No such luck.

Two hours later, Dolph and Skip were knocking on Timothy Lansing's apartment door in a ritzy rehabilitated building, overlooking the Inner Harbor in Baltimore City.

The interview was not all that informative. After a half hour, they had learned only two things. Lansing did not have an alibi for the previous Saturday night or Sunday morning, claiming he had stayed in for a quiet night at home.

And he thought Cherise Martin was an unadulterated bitch.

He claimed, however, that he'd kept her secret regarding her true name and the farm. "I'm not about to give her any free publicity."

"Not even if one of the rags offered you good money for such juicy tidbits?" Dolph asked.

"Does it look like I'm hurting for money?" Lansing said, gesturing at his luxuriously furnished living room.

They were no sooner out of the apartment than Skip was saying, "Run his finances."

"One step ahead of you there, son. What do you think I was doing on my laptop on the way over?"

Skip laughed. Dolph was the oldest employee of the agency but by far the most computer-savvy.

"Wait a minute. How could you do that without an internet connection?"

"New set-up," Dolph said.. "Plug a card into your computer and it uses the nearest cell phone tower to connect to a wireless service."

"So what about Lansing's finances?" Skip asked as they walked to the lot on Light Street where they'd parked.

"Not as well off as he pretends to be, but he's not in any major trouble either. Modest trust fund. He plays around on the stock market, usually ahead of the game by the end of the day. Nothing jumps out on his credit cards–"

"Hey, wait," Skip interrupted, "how'd you get into his credit card accounts?"

"Do you really want me to answer that question?" When Skip didn't say anything, Dolph continued, "Only thing interesting is a recent purchase from Tiffany's in New York. Makes me wonder if he has a new honey, in which case he wouldn't be chasing after our gal."

"Unless he just wants to pay her back for being a bitch," Skip said.

"There is that," Dolph agreed.

On the way back to the office, Skip called Rob to ask if they had enough to get a restraining order against Lansing. He gave him the background on the case.

"This is the case Kate's worried about?" Rob asked.

Skip hesitated, unsure of how the confidentiality thing worked here. But he trusted Rob's discretion. "Yeah. You think we can get a restraining order?"

"Chances are slim any judge would grant one. All you've really got on this guy is that he's her ex, he doesn't have an alibi for the time frame in question, and he doesn't like her. Which is understandable since she dumped him."

Skip grimaced. "You want to give it a shot for me anyway?"

"The client doesn't have her own lawyers already?" Rob asked.

"Probably, but she's given me carte blanche to handle security, so I'd rather have you do it. I know you'll give it your best, not just go through the motions."

"Okay, I'll see what I can do, but I'll be shocked if I succeed."

~~~~~~~~

A little after five, Rob called Skip back. He got voicemail and left a two-word message, "No go."

Then, without thinking it through, he called the house. Maybe Skip was home by now.

Skip wasn't, but Kate was. "Hey, Rob. To what do I owe this pleasure?"

"Uh, actually I was looking for Skip."

"He's not here. What's up?" she said cheerfully.

Rob hated to deflate her good mood by bringing up the case she was worried about, but he couldn't think of a way out of it. She'd think it odd if he just said to have Skip call him.

"Uh, that case you two are sharing, well, it's my case now, too. Skip asked me to try to get a restraining order against their prime suspect. Tell him we don't have enough evidence at this point."

There was a long silence on the phone.

"Kate, are you there?" Rob finally said.

"I can't believe he involved you in this case." She sounded royally pissed.

"Well, it's not really a major involvement. I tried to get a restraining order and couldn't."

"But now this guy who's stalking her can get your name, because you're on record as her attorney. I just have such a bad feeling about all this. And I'm furious with Skip for dragging you into it."

Rob paused, weighing his words. "I don't quite get what's the problem here. We all refer cases back and forth all the time, when appropriate. Why's this one different?"

A moment of silence. Then Kate said, "This is the first time the client's refused to give me a waiver when I'm sharing a case with you or Skip. It's kinda like participating in a conversation with a muzzle on my mouth. If it was a normal case, that would just be annoying, to not be able to talk freely with you two. But... See, right now is an example. How much did Skip tell you about what's happened lately?"

"You mean about the cat?"

"Yeah. The dead cat is what has me so spooked. Somebody who kills animals is a real sicko, maybe even a full-blown psychopath. I need to get Cherise to give me that waiver."

"You might point out to her that it's in her best interest for everyone who's trying to help to be able to talk freely to each other."

"Yeah, well... I'm not so sure she wants us to be able to 'talk freely.'"

"What does that mean?"

She blew out air on the other end of the line. "I can't tell you. But that in-her-best-interest strategy might work. I'll try it."

Again, Rob found himself wishing there was more he could do.

CHAPTER FOUR

Skip turned his wrist to see his watch as he drove east on I-70, back to Towson.

Damn!

He was going to get caught in rush hour traffic.

He'd gone to Cherise's farm to spell out the security plan for the concert. Once that had been accomplished, she'd resisted letting him leave. Why was the woman so clingy?

Anxiety was understandable, especially after the cat incident. But her reactions seemed over the top. He shrugged. What should he expect from a woman who'd been pampered and idolized her entire adult life?

He'd opted not to mention his visit to Lansing and the failed attempt to get a restraining order. Reporting on what you hadn't accomplished didn't always get a positive response from clients.

Crap! Were those taillights up ahead? If he got snarled up in a backup, he'd never get home in time for dinner.

He went off the next exit to take the back roads.

Skip might not have been so eager to get home if he'd known what awaited him. The atmosphere in the house was quite chilly.

Kate was trying to act normally during dinner, but he knew his wife well. Something was wrong.

When the kids were finally settled for the night and Maria had retreated to her third-floor apartment, he took Kate's arm as she walked past him. "Come sit with me." He tilted his head toward their favorite spot on the sofa.

She stiffened. But then she followed him to the sofa.

"What's the matter?" Skip asked, once they were settled there, his arm around her rigid shoulders.

Kate turned her head to look up at him. "Why did you involve Rob with Cherise Martin and her crazy stalker?"

"I just asked him to try for a restraining order. Are you telling me I'm not supposed to refer clients to my friend anymore, when they need a lawyer?"

"Not this client, no."

"Why not?"

Kate just stared at him with anxious eyes. Then the angry tension in her face collapsed in on itself. "I'm sorry. I'm being unfair. I just have a really bad feeling about this whole case. And now Rob's involved. My God–" She broke off, dropped her gaze to her lap.

Skip gathered her up against him and rested his chin on the top of her head. "Nothing's going to happen to me, or to Rob."

"You can't say that." Kate pulled back in his arms. "I know you're careful and good at taking care of yourself, but..." She dropped her gaze again, swallowing hard. "Nobody ever imagined what would happen to Eddie," she said in a soft voice, "least of all him."

Skip's mind searched for a way to comfort her. A small voice in his head said she was being irrational. But was she really? She'd experienced senseless violence up close and personal. Her paranoia was understandable.

And there were no guarantees in life. One of them was going to die from something someday.

He put a finger under her chin, tilting her head up so he could look into her eyes. They were the washed-out gray they became when she was worried or stressed.

"Please believe me. I will never put anything above my safety. I plan to see my kids graduate from college, get married, and have children of their own. You're not gonna get shuck of me 'til we're old and gray, darlin'."

She gave him a small smile that didn't reach her eyes. But her shoulders relaxed and she snuggled against him.

~~~~~~~~~

On the following Monday, Cherise's session went much better than the previous two had. As usual, the young woman was meticulously groomed, but no amount of make-up could hide the dark circles and strained look.

Kate decided to try to get more of a history out of her client, who was now frightened enough she was letting down her guard. She soon had the woman talking about her parents.

"Daddy was a big handsome devil," Cherise said, a touch of the south creeping into her voice. "He was so full of life. The farm was really just a hobby. He was in real estate, based in Atlanta, but he traveled all over the country, making deals. Mama used to say he had the Midas touch."

"You talk about them in the past tense," Kate observed in a soft voice.

"Mama's been gone now for over a decade."

After a pause, Kate asked, "And your father?"

"He's still alive, but I don't see him much."

Another pause. "Is he retired?"

"Oh, no. He'll die with his boots on. He's still flyin' all over, doin' his wheelin' and dealin'."

After a bit more gentle probing, the story finally came out. Life was only idyllic on the surface on that farm in Georgia. Cherise's father was a womanizer, and a heavy drinker.

"Mama was a typical Southern belle, soft and gentle," Cherise said.

Kate refrained from commenting that a lot of the Southern belles she had known had a core of steel under the soft veneer.

"She did what she'd been raised to do. She ignored Daddy's behavior, until it got to the point where he was flaunting it in her face. They had a huge fight one night and he left."

Kate waited a beat, then asked, "How old were you?"

"Twelve. I only saw Daddy off and on after that. He refused to come to the farm, even to pick me up. Sometimes he'd send a car to take me into Atlanta to have dinner with him."

This time, Kate let the silence draw out.

After a moment, Cherise continued, "Mama was weak. She couldn't handle it, the rejection. She started taking all kinds of pills to help her sleep, and then to help her wake up, and then to help her not be too awake, if you know what I mean."

All of Kate's mixed emotions about this woman melted away as she listened to her story. In a soft voice, she asked, "How did your mother die?"

Kate watched the misty look on Cherise's face turn hard. "There was a fire, one night when I was sixteen. I couldn't get through the smoke and flames to Mama's room. She was so passed out from the dope she never woke up, which was a blessing, I suppose. She died of smoke inhalation."

Kate murmured sympathetic noises.

"I thought Daddy would come home after that, but he didn't. He stayed in Atlanta and left the staff to take care of me. I was already singing by then, had started to get a name for myself. My agent at the time suggested I apply for emancipation. You know what that is?"

Kate nodded. Sometimes young people under eighteen were granted the legal status of an adult by the courts, under certain circumstances.

"I discovered Daddy had deeded the farm over to my mother, and I was her only heir. I sold it and never looked back."

"Do you still see your father?"

"Now and again. When we happen to be in the same city at the same time, we go to dinner. And he always sends me flowers the first night of a concert tour."

Kate glanced quickly at the clock sitting on the small table next to the cushioned client's chair. Cherise caught the look and frowned.

Kate leaned forward. "With the time we have left, I'd like to teach you some stress management strategies."

She started with some relaxation techniques the young woman could use to help her sleep better. The client was adamant that she wasn't going to take any sleep aides, not even melatonin, a natural hormone. Considering her father's drinking and her mother's drug abuse, that was an understandable attitude, even if a bit all-or-nothing.

"I also want to work on how to manage your thoughts," Kate said. "Self talk is a powerful thing. If you're telling yourself that something terrible is going to happen, then you will be a basket case, and your anxiety might actually make you less alert to your surroundings, less able to think quickly should a bad situation develop.

"So you need to monitor your thoughts a bit. I'm not saying suppress your fear. That isn't healthy either. But when your thoughts start going down the 'scared to death' track, you need to stop them and start reminding yourself of all the precautions that have been taken, that Skip and Rose and their people are going to keep you safe, et cetera. That will help you stay calm so you can respond quickly to their instructions."

Cherise had been nodding throughout Kate's little speech, and she even went along with a few minutes of role-playing to help her get the hang of shifting her negative self-talk toward the positive.

With a few minutes left in the session, Kate brought up the issue of the waiver of confidentiality. Cherise immediately refused.

"I'm afraid I'm going to have to insist, or I won't be able to work with you anymore." Cherise started to interrupt but Kate held up her hand. "Please hear me out. I have good reasons for asking for this. I need to be able to tell Skip anything I think may be relevant to keep you and him safe. And it's just really weird for us now. He can talk about what's going on, but I have to monitor every syllable."

Cherise waved her hand in a gesture of dismissal but she said, "So why exactly would you need to talk to him about our sessions in order to help keep me safe?"

"Let me give you an example. If I can tell Skip the exact words you just practiced saying to yourself to calm down, then if he sees you starting to freak out, he can repeat those words to you. They'll be much more powerful than anything else he might think of to say, because they directly refute the negative things you tend to say to yourself when you're scared."

"Okay," Cherise said. "I'll sign a waiver, but only for you to tell him things that would help keep me safe."

Kate walked to her file cabinet and got out two blank waivers. On one of them, she filled in Skip's and Cherise's names on the appropriate lines, and "to enhance Canfield and Hernandez's ability to investigate and protect against threats" on the reason line. She figured that would give her a fair amount of leeway.

She handed that form to Cherise along with a pen. "I also need a waiver to discuss relevant information with Rob Franklin," she said.

"Why would you need that? You don't even know the guy."

"Actually Rob and I are good friends. That's how Skip knows him, and knows that he's one of the best lawyers in this area. And again, I would only tell him things that would help him do his job," Kate said, adding to herself, *or things he needs to know to stay safe.*

Cherise reluctantly signed the second waiver.

Kate waited until the client was completely out the door before allowing herself a sigh of relief.

~~~~~~~~~

Over dinner that evening, Kate said, "I got a release from you-know-who today so after little ears are settled down, I have some things to tell you." Skip just nodded and went back to listening to his children's rather disjointed accounts of their day.

When he came downstairs after story time and tuck-in, Kate took his hand and led him into the living room. "First of all," she said, turning sideways on the sofa to face him, "Cherise tends to be narcissistic."

Skip let out a small chuckle. "If that's psychobabble for self-centered, I'd already figured that out."

"Think self-centered on steroids. It's not that narcissists don't have any empathy. They're just so self-absorbed that they don't think about others' needs or feelings. If she's presented with an option that will keep her safe but might jeopardize others, she won't give it a second thought. She'll take that option. Say the stalker has a gun and opens fire on all of you. She might jump into her limo and order the driver to take off before any of you could get in the car."

"Duly noted. Her driver Friday night will be one of my men," Skip said.

"I can also imagine her shoving one of your people *toward* a knife-wielding attacker, to save herself. Although she probably wouldn't do that to you. She likes you. Also she's likely to give you a hard time about anything that doesn't make immediate sense to her."

"Oh, she's already done that on a couple occasions."

Knowing her laid-back husband well, Kate added, "You may need to be somewhat forceful with her at times, not let yourself worry about whether or not she's going to fire you."

"I'm not sure I'd be all that broken up if she fired me at this point. This case is starting to feel like it's more trouble than it's worth."

"Last but not least," Kate said, "I've taught her some techniques for keeping herself calm in a crisis, but she may not remember to use them when the time comes. The words I told her to say to herself are,

'It's going to be okay. Skip has things under control.' So those are the words to use with her, even if it's blatantly obvious that you *don't* have it under control.

"She's a bit of a control freak, and knowing what I now know about her childhood, that makes sense. She survived by taking control of her own life at a very young age. But she seems to trust you, so if she believes you have things under control, she should be more manageable."

Skip nodded. "Let me run one of our suspects past you and see what you think. He's her latest ex-boyfriend. Broke up about nine months ago, after he'd been staying with her at the farm most of the time."

After Skip had filled her in on Timothy Lansing, Kate said, "He doesn't quite sound like the type to carry a torch this long. Too self-centered himself."

"I'd agree with that, but he was definitely still quite angry with Cherise," Skip said.

"Yeah, but notes from him would be much heavier on the threats and much less about love, I would think. Even if he was still in love with her, he would probably deny that he is, even to himself. And cover up those feelings with anger."

"Could he have sent the notes and killed the cat just to mess with her head?" Skip asked.

"The cat sounds more like him than the other notes. Do you have any other suspects?"

"A whole list of them. Rose is slogging through it, but so far they've either had an alibi for the time period when the cat would have been left on her porch, or they just aren't ringing any bells with Rose for other reasons."

"Keep in mind that narcissists–and the type of people Cherise would hang out with are likely to be cut from that same cloth–they're often quite excellent liars. And the line between narcissist and full-blown psychopath is a thin one. Your guy may not look like the kind of wacko who would send threatening notes and kill cats. He may come across as charming and completely harmless."

Skip grimaced. "So in other words, he could be anybody."

CHAPTER FIVE

The family had just sat down to dinner the following evening when a purring noise came from Skip's pocket. He took out his cell phone and grimaced at the caller ID, then put it back in his pocket.

Edie was lobbying hard for a pony for her next birthday. "I'll be five years old, Daddy. I can take care of a horse."

"Whoa there," Skip said. "A minute ago it was a pony. Now it's a horse?"

Kate suppressed a smile. "We never should have given her that rocking horse her first Christmas."

Skip's pocket purred again. He ignored it. "I think five is still a bit young. We will revisit the question when you are say, seven, and in the meantime, we'll look into some riding lessons. You may discover you don't even like real horses once you get to know them."

Edie bounced in her chair. "Really, Daddy? Riding lessons!" She clapped her hands. "Can I name the horse I ride?"

Skip laughed. "I doubt it, Pumkin. He or she will probably already have a name. And you might not like horses as much as you think you will. They poop a lot, and part of taking care of them is picking up after them when they poop."

"Poopy, poopy," Billy sang out.

Kate shook her head, but the corners of her mouth quirked up in spite of herself. "You had to get him started."

"Billy, not good word to say at dinner," Maria admonished the two-year-old.

"Daddy say it," Billy protested.

"Yes," Kate said, "and Daddy is going to be *punished* later for saying it." She avoided eye contact with her husband. She knew he was grinning, contemplating what his punishment might be.

His pocket purred for the third time.

Kate sighed. "You'd better call her back, before she works herself into a total snit."

"Oh she's no doubt already there." He got up, leaving his dinner half eaten, and headed for the living room.

"Finish your dinner, kids," Kate said. She stood and followed him.

"Be there shortly," Skip was saying into his phone. "Call Rose and fill her in."

"You have to go out there?" Kate asked, trying to keep the annoyance out of her voice as she followed Skip into the study.

"Last call was from Ben." He unlocked the gun safe and removed his .38, along with its waistband holster. Unbuckling his belt, he threaded it through the holster.

"There's been another note?"

"Not exactly. A piece of jewelry this time, engraved. 'Our love forever, til death do us part.' And this points toward our boy, Timothy. Jewelry was in a Tiffany's box, and we know he purchased something from there recently."

Telling herself there was no immediate danger, Kate wrapped her arms around him. She expertly avoided the gun that was now at the small of his back, under his loose shirttail. "Be careful, sweetheart," she whispered, then kissed him hard.

He gathered her close against him and kissed her back. When they came up for air, he said, "I always am, darlin'."

~~~~~~~~~

At the farm, Cherise once again rushed across the room. This time she was too quick for Skip. As she flung herself at him, her hand collided with his gun. But instead of pulling back, she let out a soft, "Oh," and actually stroked the gun butt through his shirt.

His jaw tightened. He gave her a fake smile as he gently disentangled himself and led her to one of the sofas.

He remained standing and glanced in Ben's direction.

"Rose and Dolph are on the way to canvas the neighbors," Ben said. "Housekeeper found the box in the mailbox, but it hadn't been mailed. It was on top of the envelopes, wrapped in shiny red paper. No address or postage. I opened it with a kitchen knife. Nobody else touched anything, except the outside of the box. It's all on the kitchen table."

Cherise grabbed his hand and tried to pull him down beside her on the sofa.

He crouched in front of her instead. She hung onto his hand and he saw no way to get it loose without being blatantly rude.

"It's going to be okay," he said. "This may turn out to be a good thing. It may give us a major lead."

"I can't stand this, Skip. This... this pervert is ruining the farm for me. This was the only place I felt safe. And free. The only place I could walk around outside without worrying about who might be watching." She threw herself forward and Skip had no choice but to catch her in his arms. He almost fell over but managed to regain his balance. Standing up, he drew her up with him, then nudged her down onto the sofa again.

"Listen, I've got this under control." He sat down on the sofa at right angles with hers. "This could lead us to the stalker and give us the evidence to get him arrested."

"Oh, no, I'm not sure we should do that. It'll get in the news then, and others may try to do the same thing, and the location of the farm may come out."

"What would you have me do instead, Cherise? We have to involve the police once we know who it is, or there's no way to get him to stop."

"Couldn't you just talk to him, intimidate him into stopping?" She looked at him, her eyes wide and brimming with tears.

"I'm not a thug. I don't threaten to beat people up if they don't behave."

"I bet you'd do more than threaten if it was Kate being stalked," Cherise said, a touch of acid in her voice.

Skip stiffened. He paused to choose his words. "That's irrelevant. We need to address the matter at hand."

He was interrupted by two sharp knocks on the front door, followed by Rose's muffled voice, "Hernandez." Ben headed for the door.

"I want more people staying here," Cherise was demanding as Rose and Dolph trooped in. "I want *you* here, Skip. I only feel safe when you're around."

"I understand that you're spooked." Skip tried to keep his voice gentle. "We'll put extra personnel inside and out, but I can't stay. I have to go to Tiffany's in New York to check out who bought the bracelet."

"Send Rose. I want you here!"

Skip considered trying to explain that he was more likely to be able to charm information out of a salesperson at Tiffany's than Rose could. He decided to save his breath.

"Look, Cherise. If you want me to be in charge of your security, then you have to let me be in charge. Otherwise, you're going to have to hire another firm to take over. I'd be happy to recommend a good one."

She looked at him in horror. The tears were back. "You can't abandon me!"

"I have no intention of doing so, but you have to let me do my job. I'm either in charge of security or I'm not. What'll it be?"

She paused a second, eyes narrowed. Finally she said, "You're in charge."

"Okay. Rose and Dolph are going to ask the neighbors if anybody saw who put the box in your mailbox." Again, he paused to choose his words. His gut was telling him not to name Lansing as their prime suspect just yet, not until they had something more concrete. He wouldn't put it past her to hire somebody else to beat Lansing up. "If we can get a good description of this guy, then we'll know who to be on the lookout for at Merriweather on Friday."

"I'm cancelling that damn concert. I don't care if it is bad PR."

"I wish you wouldn't," Skip said. "We've got the security set-up there under control, and this will be a great chance to catch him in the act and stop him cold."

After a brief pause, Cherise nodded.

"I need to talk to Rose and Dolph for a few minutes." Skip stood. Cherise grabbed his hand as he walked past her. "I'll be right back," he said, pulling his hand free as gently as possible and gesturing to Rose and Dolph to join him in the kitchen.

Once there, Rose flashed him a megawatt grin. "Looks like she's got the hots for you, partner."

Skip ignored her comment. "You got your fingerprint kit with you?"

Rose nodded. Skip pointed toward the wrapping paper, box and bracelet lying on the table. "Ben tried to keep the handling of them to a minimum. Nobody touched the bracelet."

"Except, hopefully, the sender. Oh, looky what I see," Rose said. "Scotch tape! Might just get us a lovely print off of that."

"Dolph, are you willing to stay here tonight, along with Ben?" Skip asked.

The older man nodded, then grinned. "Afraid of her, aren't ya, son?"

"Okay, both of you, stop."

They didn't. They were grinning at him like twin Cheshire cats.

"Alright yes, she scares the shit out of me," Skip hissed at them in a low voice. "Are you happy now? Can we get back to work?"

"I don't know. Are you happy, Rose?" Dolph asked, his face deadpan.

"Yeah, I think that's about as good as it gets." Rose also kept her voice low. "Skip Canfield, the man who has faced down killers without blinking an eye, is scared of a hundred pound girlie girl."

"Cut it out." Skip shot them both a scowl. "Tomorrow, Dolph, I need you to do two things. Get your hands on a good photo of Lansing, maybe in back issues of the celebrity rags from when they were dating. A good head shot. Make enough copies so everybody and his uncle can have one Friday night. Then take another warm body for back-up and go see Lansing again. See what he was up to this afternoon, but more importantly, try to get something with his prints on it."

"Are we going to try again for a restraining order if we get more proof it's Lansing?" Rose asked.

"I'm thinking not until after Merriweather. Hopefully he'll make a move and we'll catch him there. If not, then it's restraining order time."

"Those things aren't worth much more than the paper they're written on if the guy's a nutcase," Dolph pointed out.

"Yeah, we'll actually be hoping he violates so we can get him arrested and throw the fear of some serious jail time into him, if he persists. Anybody object if I go home now and kiss my sleeping children?"

"Not us, but Cherise might," Rose said.

And she did. When Skip informed her he was leaving, she once again rushed him and threw her arms around him. He reached back and pried her hand off his gun butt, then held her away from him by the shoulders. "Cherise, you're okay. You're safe. I've got things under control." Silently he thanked his wife for those words.

"I'm going to send in another guy to stay with you and Ben until Dolph's finished canvassing the neighbors. Then Dolph's going to stay tonight, along with Ben. He's one of our best operatives, Cherise. Only the best for you. But I've got to investigate who's doing this. And get some ducks in a row for Friday. Coordinate with Howard County cops and Merriweather security." He'd already done that, but he wanted her to think he planned to spend the evening working her case, rather than kissing his kids and making love to his wife.

"I'll call you tomorrow," he promised, and was finally able to pull loose from her and get out the door.

~~~~~~~~

Skip got up well before dawn in order to catch the seven-thirty Acela train to New York. He arrived at Tiffany & Co. on Fifth Avenue just as they were opening the doors. Making a mental note of the fare and tip he had given the cabby so he could add it to his expense report later, he donned the Stetson he had dug out of the back of his closet, along with his Western-style suit. Entering the store, he sought out one of the female sales staff.

"Howdy, ma'am," he said, as the young woman greeted him. Laying the hat on the counter, he poured a considerable amount of Texas into his voice—for some reason that often charmed the ladies—as he told the saleswoman he was looking for a bauble for his wife.

"My friend, Timmy Lansing, said he was in couple a weeks back. Got himself a gold doodad for his girlfriend. Showed it to me 'fore he gave it to her. Had some real nice engravin' on it. Thought I might get one of them fer the missus."

The saleswoman showed him quite a few gold bracelets. He kept shaking his head, even though he had recognized the one Cherise had received. Finally he said, "Don't suppose you could look up what ole Timmy got, now could you?"

"Certainly, sir." The young woman turned to a computer monitor on a counter behind the display case. "Two weeks ago, you said."

"'Bout that, as I recollect," Skip drawled.

"Hmm, well, Mr. Lansing did make a purchase two weeks ago, but it was a pearl necklace. However, I seem to recall he was in more recently than that." She hit a few keys. "Ah, here it is. He was in just this past weekend. Bought a gold bracelet, number 165490." She pointed to the tray of bracelets they had just perused. "This one, sir."

"Ah, now, darned if that isn't it. Guess I didn't recognize it without the fancy engravin' on it."

"Uh, sir, this is a rather inexpensive bracelet. We stock them mainly for the kids, you know, to give to their girlfriends."

"Well now, how much is it exactly, ma'am?" Skip asked.

"Only two hundred dollars. I can show you something much nicer that your wife would be sure to be thrilled with."

Skip was trying to hide his shock that this young woman considered a two-hundred-dollar bracelet inexpensive. He was also trying to fathom what teenagers could afford a little bauble like that for their girlfriends. Even the rich kids in his hometown would have considered two hundred dollars a bit on the expensive side.

"Well now, that sure doesn't sound like Timmy," he drawled. "Never thought that boy was such a cheapskate."

"Oh no, sir. He bought a pair of diamond earrings the same day. He probably just liked the bracelet because he could get a fair amount of engraving on it. It will hold up to fifty characters and spaces."

"Yes, ma'am, I'm sure that's why he got it. 'Our love forever. Til death do us part.' Darn romantic of ole Timmy, that was." The saleswoman glanced back at the monitor and nodded.

Yup, Lansing sent the bracelet. Got 'im cold.

Skip considered trying to bribe the woman for a printout of the transaction, but decided she would probably take offense. Easy enough to subpoena it later, if need be.

Out loud he said, "Hmm, diamond earrings. Now there's a thought." He'd been contemplating whether or not to buy the bracelet and get it engraved with something, just to complete the charade, but... "My sweet Kate has a diamond necklace but I don't believe she has earrings. What do you have in those sparkly little devils?"

Forty-five minutes later, Skip was in another cab headed back to the train station. Tucked away in his inside jacket pocket was a pair of solitaire diamonds, set in platinum, in one of Tiffany's trademark robin's egg blue boxes. They had cost him a month's salary but he'd had to have them. He was fairly sure they were a match, in clarity and color, for the diamond necklace he'd given Kate their first Christmas together.

~~~~~~~~~

Kate and Rob were halfway through their lunch when her cell phone rang. She pulled it out of her purse. Rob expected her to turn it off. She hated it when people talked on cell phones in restaurants.

She glanced at the caller ID. "You mind?" she asked. "It's Skip. He's in New York today."

Rob shook his head.

She answered the call. "Sweetheart, I'm at lunch with Rob. What's up?"

She listened for a couple moments. "About four-fifteen. My last client cancelled."

Her cheeks turned a soft rosy glow. She glanced over at Rob. "It's a pretty day. Maria won't mind taking them to the park... Okay, see ya later."

"Hmm," Rob said. "I'm not sure I should've been listening even to your end of that conversation."

When her blush turned a deeper red, he laughed out loud.

"I guess we should be acting more like old married folks by now," Kate said.

"Lord, I hope that day never comes. May Skip Canfield still be making you blush like a schoolgirl when you're eighty, my dear."

Kate's cheeks turned pink again. "The client thinks he's spending the night in New York so we should have a peaceful evening for a change. I have a waiver from her now, so here's a thumbnail sketch. She's fairly narcissistic. She's not completely lacking in empathy but other people's feelings and needs don't normally show up on her radar screen. Be careful if you have any more dealings with her. Keep in mind that she'll be looking out for herself, first and foremost."

She grimaced, then took a sip of iced tea. "Okay, enough about you-know-who. Back to the party plans. If we're doing this the week after Liz's birthday, won't she be disappointed when not much happens on her birthday?"

"She said she didn't want a big fuss. This from the woman who announced my fiftieth birthday to everybody we know by inviting them all to that big bash."

"Come on, you loved every minute of it."

"Once I recovered from the heart attack when you all jumped out at me." Rob chuckled. "Anyhow, the girls and I are taking her out to dinner on her actual birthday. She'll feel sufficiently feted. And then the next weekend we're just coming over to your house for a cookout, and, lo and behold, your backyard happens to be full of thirty or forty of our closest friends."

"Heaven help us if it rains. We'll never get all those people in my house. Did you send out the invites yet?"

"Fran insisted on taking charge of them. I told her it wasn't appropriate for me to expect my admin assistant to do that. She pointed out that I didn't ask, she offered, and she's doing it as a friend, not an employee."

"That woman's been hanging around you too long. She's starting to argue like a lawyer."

"So can you and Maria take care of the food? As in you buy it and she cooks it, I mean," Rob teased. Kate was a notoriously bad cook. "Keep track of what you spend and I'll reimburse you."

"No way. I'll pay for the food as my contribution. You just concentrate on getting Liz there without her becoming suspicious."

"Ha! Easier said than done. I swear she's clairvoyant."

"I think we've got everything covered." Kate grinned and rubbed her hands together. "If we pull off surprising her, it'll be the coup of the century."

Rob glanced at his watch. "Gotta go. Partners' meeting this afternoon." He dug a ten and a five out of his wallet to cover his half of their lunch. Kate had long ago insisted they split the tab, rather than wrangling over the check each time.

He stood up. "Let me know if there are any glitches in the plans." With a sly smile, he leaned over and kissed Kate on the forehead. "And I'm paying for half the food for the party." He made a quick exit before she could argue.

~~~~~~~~~

Having caught the noon Acela express back, Skip beat Kate home by an hour. By the time she arrived, the kids and their nanny were already on the way to the park. Maria had a twinkle in her eye and a twenty in her purse to buy dinner at McDonald's afterwards.

Skip had bought roses from a street vendor outside Baltimore's Penn Station. He stuffed them into a vase. When he heard the front door open, he hastily placed the vase next to the champagne bottle, chilling in an ice bucket, and the small Tiffany's box on the kitchen table.

Kate came around the corner and stopped in her tracks. Taking it all in, she put hands on hips and said in a mock stern tone, "Okay, Skip Canfield, what have you done?"

"Nothing," he exclaimed indignantly, then grinned at her from across the room. "Just a few tokens of my love for my beautiful wife, *and* appreciation for the best psychological consultant in town."

She put her briefcase on a kitchen chair, shrugged out of her suit jacket and stepped into his embrace. After a long tender kiss, she leaned back in the circle of his arms. "Best psychological consultant, huh? I tried to convince you that Lansing wasn't your man."

"I know, but the stuff you told me about Cherise, it really helped me manage her better last night. And I'm not sure Lansing is our man, or at least not our only man. I think you're right about him not really fitting with the tone of the notes. He's just not the lovesick type."

"No, he's more the pissed-off, get-even type. I'm wondering if you and Dolph might have inadvertently planted the seed in his mind last week for a way to seek revenge on his ex."

"Yeah, I had thought of that. He also bought a couple other baubles at Tiffany's recently, so I think he does have a new lady friend, or maybe several. But either way," Skip continued, as he let go of her to pull the champagne out of the ice bucket, "I felt like celebrating. This is a break-through in the case, and I've got a real strong feeling that Lansing, or somebody, is going to make a move at the concert this Friday, and then we'll have him cold." He popped the cork and quickly grabbed one of the flutes off the table to catch the bubbles foaming out of the bottle.

"Champagne, Skip? It's only four-thirty in the afternoon. We still have to deal with the kids later."

"Not until bedtime. Maria's taking them to McD's for dinner, then she's doing their baths. I bribed her with a raise."

"Boy you are feeling flush tonight, aren't you?"

"You ain't seen nothin' yet, darlin'." He handed her a glass of champagne, then raised his own glass in a toast. "To me, the luckiest damn Texan alive!"

Looking up at his Stetson, knocked askew by their passionate kissing, Kate giggled. "I take it you used the Texan persona to charm the ladies at Tiffany's?"

"Yup, and Skippy has not lost his touch. She did her share of charming as well. Talked me into a little something." He put his glass down on the table and gently tugged on the silver chain around her neck. The diamond nestled in the hollow of her throat winked up at him.

"Something to go with this." His voice dropped to a husky whisper as he imagined kissing that spot where the diamond glittered, and then trailing kisses downward.

He shook his head, completely dislodging his hat. Snagging it as it started to fall, he dropped it on the table. His hand kept moving, scooping up the Tiffany's box to give to her.

Kate opened the box and her eyes went wide. "Oh, Skip! They must have cost a fortune."

"Only a small one, and nothin's too good for my gal." He took the open box from her and held it up next to her necklace. "Yup, perfect match." Handing the box back, he wrapped both arms around her.

She leaned back to look up at him again. "They're beautiful, Skip, and I will treasure them as I do the necklace." She had a funny look on her face.

He loosened his hold on her. "Do I detect a 'but' on the end of that sentence?" When she didn't answer right away, he said, "I told the woman not too flashy, more understated but elegant. You don't like them, do you?"

"No, no, I love them. It's just, I don't know..." She looked up at him, her expression serious. "Where is all this coming from? This isn't really like you. Roses and champagne and expensive gifts for no reason."

Skip tried to cover his disappointment at her reaction. He pulled out two chairs and gestured for her to take one of them, then sat down himself facing her. "I guess being in Tiffany's kind of went to my head a little, but I really felt like celebrating what we have. I don't know how to explain it." He paused, searching for words. "I see all the things Cherise has, everything money can buy, and she's got nothing. No lover, no family. The only thing she knows how to love is a cat."

He took both of Kate's hands in his. "And then I'm up there in New York, checking out this Lansing dude, and he's buying expensive presents for some woman. But I know damn well he's only getting sex out of the deal. And he's so shallow he probably thinks that's all there is."

He lifted one of her hands toward his lips and bent his head to kiss her palm. She sucked in her breath.

"I couldn't wait to get home and shower you with whatever I could think of that would let you know how much I love you–you and the kids and the life we have together." He turned her hand slightly so he could kiss the soft skin on the inside of her wrist, and heard her gasp again.

He looked at her through the veil of soft brown hair that had flopped down onto his forehead. There were tears in her eyes, but she was smiling at him as she pulled a hand loose to brush back his hair. He groaned at the gentle touch and started to pull her toward him.

"Better not," she said, "or we'll get naked right here in the kitchen. We should move this to the bedroom in case the kids and Maria get home before we come up for air."

"Good idea."

CHAPTER SIX

On Friday morning, Rose, Dolph, and Ben were sitting in Skip's office refining the plan for that night.

"I've arranged for a limo with bulletproof glass," Rose said. Kate had told her she had a gut feeling this case would go sour on them, and Rose's gut was agreeing with hers.

"Not that we think this guy is going to start shooting," Skip was saying, "but bulletproof means it's also fist-proof and brick-proof. Ben, we'd like you behind the wheel."

"No problem," Ben replied.

"In addition to the records from Tiffany's," Rose said, "I lifted a fingerprint from the tape on the package so we know Lansing sent the bracelet. But we're not sure he sent the other notes. So keep your eyes open for *anybody* who's trying extra hard to get past us."

"The hired muscle will create a corridor for us," Skip said. "Ben and I will be on either side of Cherise. Dolph, you bring up the rear. If anybody tries something, then takes off, Mac, Rose and/or I will go after him. You two stick with Cherise, no matter what."

Dolph and Ben nodded.

"While she's on stage, you two are right there in the wings on either side, ready to move if needed." Skip reached into a box behind his desk and handed out small two-way radios. "Compliments of Mac Reilly. We need to get some of these, Rose."

"I think Mac'll donate them if we make him full-time," she replied.

"That's a deal." Skip turned to Ben. "Once in the car, you don't go, no matter how loud Cherise is screaming. Not until I say. If I'm not inside, I'll bang three times on the roof. That's the signal to go without me, 'cause I'm about to chase down a bad guy."

Rose shook her head. "Not without back-up you don't, Skip."

He grinned at her. "Compact Rosie here is only afraid of one thing on this planet—my wife's wrath."

"You call me Rosie again, Skippy, and *you'll* have reason to be afraid," Rose fired back, but she flashed him a quick grin.

"You or Mac will be with me." Skip's tone was now serious. "We'll do our jobs but nobody's risking their hides here. Got it?"

Everybody nodded.

Getting into Merriweather Post Pavilion wasn't a big deal. They arrived at six-thirty, for a concert that started at eight, and Cherise wouldn't go on until almost nine. The fans that were already there were bunched up at the entrance.

Rose and Skip took Cherise in the back way.

A few members of the press lurked there. They weren't happy that they couldn't get a good shot of Cherise. A couple photographers yelled at Skip when his big body always seemed to be between her and the cameras.

Rose gritted her teeth and muttered, "Damn paparazzi." She had an uneasy feeling in her gut about this whole set-up.

But Skip called back good-naturedly, "You can see her on stage, ladies and gentlemen." He never broke stride, his hand firmly attached to Cherise's elbow.

The first glitch was no bathroom in the tiny dressing room. Only Rose and Skip were able to squeeze into the room with Cherise and her assistant. The others had to stand out in the hall. After hanging up Cherise's costume on a free-standing clothes rack, Sarah went looking for the manager, one of the bodyguards in tow.

"I'll stay with her," Rose said to her partner, then to Cherise, "You don't go to the ladies' room without me."

Skip nodded. "You slip out into the crowd about ten minutes before she goes on. I'll send one of the guys to go sit in your seat, to ward off any squatters, until you get there."

He looked at the doorknob. "Geez, the door doesn't even lock."

Stepping out into the hall, Rose looked around. Sarah was coming toward them, a nervous-looking redhead in her early forties beside her. The redhead started wringing her hands, then caught herself.

Stopping next to Rose in the open doorway, she addressed Cherise. "I'm so sorry, Ms. Martin. We had a pipe burst in the main dressing room area, just an hour ago. Made a total mess of things. This is the room where the extras usually wait. It's the best we could do on short notice."

Cherise didn't look happy but before she could object, Skip said, "Sarah, can you stay in the dressing room during the performance, make sure nobody messes with it?"

Sarah nodded.

"Mac, you got any radios on you?" Skip called out.

Mac appeared behind the PA's shoulder, holding up a small black box. Skip nodded at Sarah and Mac handed her the radio.

"You give a shout if anybody comes around," Skip said. "Don't hesitate now. Better a false alarm than no alarm." He gestured to one of the extra guards they'd hired for the occasion. "You stick to Sarah like glue."

Skip turned back to Mac. "I'll get someone to save your seat as well. Go look at that pipe, make sure it wasn't sabotaged. I'm going to go check out the crowd. Rose and the guys will be out here in the hall, Cherise. And I'll be back before it's time for you to go on."

Skip strode away, down the corridor behind the stage.

Cherise stared after him and sighed.

Rose narrowed her eyes at her. "He's married, Cherise. *Happily* married."

Sarah maneuvered past her and into the cramped room to help her boss with her makeup and costume. Rose closed the door and leaned her back against it, scanning the hallway for anyone who looked out of place.

~~~~~~~~~

Twenty minutes later, Mac joined Skip where he was standing at the back of the open-air amphitheater, watching the people who were streaming into the seats below him. Dusk was gathering around them. Skip eyed the surrounding woods warily.

"Plumbing problem looks legit," Mac said. "But hard to tell for sure."

Skip nodded. "Thanks. Take your seat. I'll go check on Cherise."

Everything went smoothly from there. Too smoothly.

Once his charge was on stage, Skip took up his position again at the back of the crowd, watching, and praying that someone would make a move.

But no one did. The fans screamed. Many of them jumped up and down. Some even stood on their seats, which was not popular with the folks behind them. But no one attempted to get near the stage where Cherise and her partner, Johnny Troop, were singing their hearts out.

As they started on their last song together, Skip quickly moved from the hillside behind the crowd to the side of the stage where Ben was waiting. Skip nodded to Dolph, in the wings on the other side, signaling that he should join them.

Cherise crooned her final note. She bowed, threw kisses to the crowd, then bounced off stage as Johnny, perched on a tall stool with his guitar, launched into one of the few songs for which he was lead singer. A recording of Cherise's voice backing him up was playing.

Ben on one side, Skip on the other, they moved their charge into the back hallway just as Dolph caught up with them and took up the rear. The extra guards hired for the evening once again created a wall of big bodies on either side, although surprisingly few people were wandering around backstage.

Cherise stopped abruptly. "I can't stand this make-up. I've got to get it off."

"No time for that," Skip said. "We've got maybe eight minutes to get you out of here, before the fans notice you're missing."

"It'll only take two of those minutes to wipe this gunk off, and I need to pee."

Skip figured it would take less time to indulge her than it would to stand here and argue. He grabbed her elbow and hustled her in the direction of the dressing room.

Rose jogged up to them. "What's going on?"

"Lady's gotta pee," Dolph said, just as Mac joined them.

Skip stuck his head in the dressing room door. The room was empty, the only change from earlier the lavish bouquet of flowers on the small dressing table. He practically shoved Cherise into the room. "One minute for gunk, one minute to pee, then we're out of here." He closed the door.

The men stood in the hall. "Just like her to screw with the set-up," Mac growled quietly.

A scream shattered the air.

Skip shoved the door open.

Cherise stood in the middle of the room, one hand over her mouth, eyes wide. She pointed toward the flowers. "I... I thought they were from Daddy. I leaned over to smell them."

Skip took a stride closer to the flowers. Just under the top layers of blossoms was the tip of a bloody knife, a chunk of raw meat jabbed down on it. A note was skewered on top of it, the paper turning rusty and greasy in places. The fragrance of the flowers couldn't completely mask the putrid smell of decaying flesh.

He squinted to make out the words on the note.

This is what you've done to my heart.

"Rose, stay here. I'll be back." Skip grabbed Cherise's upper arm and hauled her out of the room.

Sarah was coming down the hall. She looked at their faces, Cherise's pale with tears streaking her stage make-up, and Skip's grim. "What happened? I only stepped away for a minute, to go to the ladies' room." Her voice trembled.

"Go in and stay with Rose," Skip ordered. He looked over Sarah's shoulder at her guard. "You're with me." He gestured with his head at another guard. "On the door. Don't let anybody in there unless Rose or I okay it."

Ben on one side, Skip and the guard on the other they propelled Cherise down the hall. Dolph covered their backs. By the time they got to the exit at the end of the corridor, Johnny had finished his song and the fans were getting restless, wondering why Cherise wasn't back on stage for a last curtain call.

The hired muscle waited just outside the door. They formed a barrier on each side and Skip led Cherise around the perimeter of the crowd toward the car.

"There she is," somebody yelled. People surged in their direction.

The men forged a path and Ben and Skip propelled their charge down the middle of it. As they neared the car, Skip said to Ben in a low voice, "Go get it open and started, but be prepared to ward off unauthorized passengers."

Ben let go of Cherise's elbow and jogged briskly ahead of them.

The cameras flashed. "Cherise, look this way."

The fans screamed. "Cherise, we love you!"

Skip reached for the door handle just as a reporter stepped in front of them and the flash of his camera temporarily blinded them. Dolph stepped around them and elbowed the guy out of the way. In a second, Cherise and Dolph were in the back of the limo.

"Go!" Cherise yelled.

Ben, behind the wheel with the engine idling, ignored her.

"Go, damn it!" she screeched, just as Mac dropped into the seat across from her. She reared back. "Who the hell said you could ride with me?"

Skip stuck his head inside the car. He wanted to point out that now was not the time to get choosy about who guarded her. He drummed up a soothing voice instead. "It's gonna be okay, Cherise. I've got things under control."

He slammed the door with one hand while pounding on the roof three times with the other. Ben moved away from the curb, and Skip turned to push his way back through the crowd, Sarah's guard still with him.

"Any idea where those flowers came from?" Skip asked.

"No, sir. I didn't see no deliveries but I didn't go in. Just stood in the hall, 'til the lady said she needed the restroom."

Back at the dressing room, Sarah's eyes were red and puffy.

"Says she was only away from the room for a couple minutes," Rose said. "Should we call in the cops? That looks like a real heart to me."

"Couple minutes would be all it would take," Skip said. "And any staff hanging around wouldn't give a thought to someone delivering flowers." He leaned over to examine the bloody mass of flesh without touching anything. "Too small to be human."

"Unless it's a child's," Rose said.

Skip's stomach clenched.

Sarah covered her mouth with her hand. Tears leaked from her eyes.

"Sit tight," Skip said. "I'll find Sergeant Robinson. He's the head of the Howard County team."

While Robinson's officers were interviewing the Merriweather staff, trying to determine if anyone had seen the flowers being delivered, Skip was in the back of a police cruiser. He had just disconnected from filling Kate in on the evening's events when his phone rang in his hand.

"We're at the farm," Dolph said without preamble. "Everything's secure, but the lady's still a bit hysterical."

"Can you handle her? I'm on my way to the police station. We had to bring them in. Heart could be human, although I doubt it."

"Yeah, I can manage. Been married thirty years. Had lots of practice ignorin' a screaming woman."

"Better not ignore your wife too much or you won't make it to thirty-one," Skip said. He heard a low chuckle on the other end.

"Should we be concerned about Troop's safety?" Dolph asked. "The world thinks they're lovers."

"He refused a bodyguard before. We can ask him again. But I suspect this is one of Cherise's real boyfriends, and they'd know the romance with Troop was fake."

"When you get done with the police, go home and go to bed, son. You did good. Lady's safe. That's what counts."

"Gee, thanks, Dad," Skip said.

Another low chuckle. Dolph disconnected.

Skip was signing his formal statement at the police station when Robinson returned from Merriweather. The sergeant strode across the bullpen to the desk where Skip was sitting.

"Why the hell weren't we informed that Ms. Martin was being stalked?"

Skip suppressed a sigh. "I told you she'd been getting threatening notes."

"And why weren't we called in from the get-go?"

"Because my client refused to involve the police." Skip glanced at his watch. It was after one in the morning. "What exactly would you all have done if she'd called you?"

"We'd have investigated."

"Only if you'd known the vic was Cherise Martin. If Carol Ann Morris had called and said she was getting sick love notes from some anonymous admirer, what would you have done?"

Robinson deflated and sank into the nearest empty chair.

"Sent an officer to take her report," Skip answered for him. "Told the vic to be extra vigilant and beefed up patrols near her farm."

Robinson scrubbed a hand over his face. "I'll have a uniform take you home."

At the house, Skip locked up his gun, then slipped quietly into the bedroom. He put his cell on vibrate, set it on his nightstand, and sat down gently on the side of the bed. He didn't even bother to get undressed, just nudged his shoes off and stretched out, trying not to disturb Kate.

~~~~~~~~~

"Daddy, wake up!" Persistent little fist pounding on the door. "Cartoons, Daddy, wake up!" Skip usually watched Saturday morning cartoons with the kids, and Billy apparently wasn't happy that they weren't following that routine today.

Skip opened one eye and looked at his clock. Seven-fifteen. Ugh. Five and a half hours sleep might be enough to get by on any other Saturday but he had to work again that evening, and couldn't risk falling asleep then.

Kate's voice, coming to the rescue, "Billy, I told you not to disturb your father. He had to work very late last night." One last knock, then his wife's voice receded from the door. "Come on, little man, I'll watch cartoons with you guys this morning."

Skip rolled over and buried his face in Kate's pillow. Breathing in the smell of her, he tried to go back to sleep. But his mind wouldn't shut down again, even though his body was longing for more rest.

He was thinking about the new case he needed to work tonight. He'd been tempted not to take it, but couldn't bring himself to say no. The woman had sounded pretty scared and desperate over the phone Thursday morning, and she'd been referred by a former client. Good word-of-mouth could become bad word-of-mouth all too quickly if you turned down business referred to you by former customers.

When Skip had met with her Thursday afternoon, he'd found out why she was so freaked out. The thirty-six-year-old divorcee was discovering little things missing from her house, and other things slightly disturbed, almost every time she went out. The first time had been when she had been on a date and her children, six and eight, were home with a sitter.

Elise Thomas had assumed the sitter had taken the pieces of jewelry she'd left out on her dresser–a necklace and earrings she had considered wearing, then decided against. She hadn't used that sitter again.

But then it had happened two more times, when all of them were out of the house. Once during a weekday, while she was at work and the kids were at school, and then again the previous Saturday night when she and the kids went to their weekly dinner with her folks.

None of the items taken were all that valuable. The sense of invasion and fear were the main issues.

So tonight, while Elise and the kids were once again at Grandma and Grandpa's, Skip was going to watch the house to see who showed up. Despite Elise's protests that the divorce had been amiable, Skip was betting on the husband.

He was not looking forward to facing down an angry man bent on revenge against his ex-wife. But better he be the one in that confrontation than Elise Thomas. The petite strawberry blonde looked like a younger version of Liz Franklin, only four-ten and probably no more than ninety pounds. Skip was afraid her angry ex might do the mother of his children serious harm, perhaps without even meaning to, if she caught him in the act of invading her home.

Giving up on sleep, Skip stumbled out to the kitchen, lured by the smell of coffee brewing.

Kate apologized for letting Billy get away from her and wake him up.

"S'okay," Skip muttered as he wrapped his arms around her and buried his face in her curly mop of hair.

She hugged him back, then chuckled as she leaned back in his arms. "Sweetheart, I did promise to love you for better or worse, but you might want to consider taking a shower and changing your clothes soon."

He looked down at the rumpled brown shirt and khaki slacks he'd been wearing for the last twenty-four hours. "I'll have you know, darlin', that is the manly sweat of honest labor you're smelling, but I will go wash it off if you promise me two things."

"What's that?"

"You bring a cup of that wonderful coffee to me in the bedroom." He paused, then gave her a wicked grin. Nuzzling her neck, he added, "Right after you bribe Maria to take the kids to the park for a while."

"That sounds like a lovely deal."

Skip awoke with a start. He was lying across the bed stark naked, right where he'd flopped face down after his shower. He shook his head to clear it. Damp hair fell onto his forehead.

He rolled over and groaned. A mug of coffee–now cold, no doubt–sat on his nightstand.

He dressed in fresh clothes and feeling sheepish, went out to the kitchen.

Kate was sitting at the table. She greeted him with a smile and pointed toward the coffee maker. "I've been keeping it warm for you."

They heard the slamming of the side door of the van followed by little feet pounding up onto the porch.

"Guess I missed my opportunity." Skip dropped a kiss on the top of his wife's head as he walked by her, headed for the caffeine.

"We'll make another one soon, I'm sure."

Skip returned her grin as Edie and Billy came tumbling into the room, chattering at top volume about the fun they'd had at the park.

While he ate a late breakfast, the kids, made hungry by fresh air and exercise, had an early lunch.

Skip paused between bites of egg. "I may need to take another nap this afternoon," he said to Kate, "and I don't mean that the way I normally would. I have a surveillance job this evening and I need to be alert."

"On a Saturday night?" Kate didn't look happy. "Couldn't you assign it to somebody else?"

"I'm afraid we're stretched a little thin right now." Skip grimaced. "We've been getting a lot of new cases lately. The word-of-mouth is starting to get around town." A flutter of excitement competed with the anxiety in his gut. It was great to be successful, but what if they couldn't keep up with the demand for their services?

"Well, that's called good trouble," Kate said with a smile. "I'm not surprised you guys are so popular."

"Yeah, but the work's coming in faster than we can hire more people, or get them trained. Mac's now full-time, and I've finally convinced Ben to train as an investigator, but it's still not quite enough hands on deck right now. So I'm doing this job tonight myself, just a surveillance gig." He wasn't about to tell Kate any of the worrisome details. "I've got to leave about five, to find a good spot to watch from, should be home by ten though."

Kate nodded. "I'll hold down the fort, sweetheart, but tomorrow is definitely going to be your day of rest."

He would recall her words the next day, when his Sunday turned out to be anything but restful.

CHAPTER SEVEN

Skip made a second circle around Elise Thomas's block, trying to look like he was searching for a particular house number. He didn't want anyone calling the police to report a suspicious character casing the neighborhood.

That clump of trees between her house and her neighbor's seemed to be the best spot to have a good view of the back door and also most of the approach to the front of the house. He'd have to make a circuit around to the other side periodically to make sure no one was sneaking onto the property from that direction.

He parked three blocks over and called Elise. "Hi. Skip Canfield. I've found a good spot to watch the house from, but it's on the boundary line with your neighbor to the left. Do you mind if I knock on their door and tell them what's going on? I don't want them to see me out there lurking around and think I'm a prowler."

Elise was silent for a moment. "Try not to give them too many details if you can help it. I'm kind of a private person, don't really like my neighbors knowing too much of my business."

"I can relate. I'll be as vague as I can. Give me about half an hour, then you and the kids can go."

"Okay, we usually get home around nine-thirty."

"See you then and, hopefully, I will have nabbed your bad guy for you."

Skip walked over to Elise's block and up the sidewalk to her neighbor's front door. He was raising his hand to knock when the door opened and a teenaged boy came barreling out. As a kid shoved past him, Skip got a quick impression of pimply, pale face under greasy dark hair, baggy tee shirt and drooping jeans.

A man in his late forties came into the doorway. "By eleven, Jack, or you won't be going out next weekend at all," he yelled after the kid. The boy ignored him and turned left, toward the main drag two blocks away.

"Kids today," the man said, shaking his head. "They'll make you old before your time."

"Mine are still preschoolers," Skip said.

"Enjoy them while they're cute, sir, cause that's what they morph into eventually. What can I do for you?"

Skip introduced himself, showing the man his private investigator's license, then said, "Your neighbor, Elise Thomas, thinks you all might have a prowler. She's hired me to watch her house for a few nights and see if I can catch him."

"Hmm, I haven't seen any strangers in the neighborhood lately, but I don't blame Elise a bit. A woman living alone with her kids. I'd be nervous in her shoes if I thought someone was hanging around."

Skip politely turned down the man's offer to help, then pointed out the hiding place he had chosen. "I'll be making a circuit around Elise's house every fifteen minutes or so. Didn't want you to see me out there and think *I* was the prowler."

"Gotcha. Happy hunting."

Elise and the kids left at six.

Despite the catnap he'd gotten in that afternoon, by eight, Skip was wishing he'd brought a thermos of coffee. By eight-thirty, he was making his circuits of the house more often, mostly to keep himself alert.

By nine-fifteen he was resigning himself to the idea that he would be spending another Saturday night doing this. When Elise got home he'd suggest she get the locks changed, and invest in an alarm system to keep her and her kids safe between now and then.

At nine-thirty-five he was on the far side of the house when he heard car doors slamming in the driveway. Elise and the kids were home. He decided to make one more circuit around back before going to the front door to talk to her.

Skip came around the corner of the house just as the lights flicked on in the kitchen He froze. The light revealed the silhouette of a man standing outside the kitchen door.

Skip braced himself to give chase, but the guy didn't run away. Instead, he moved into the shadows beside the door.

Skip eased slowly along the back of the house, trying to decide if he should draw his gun sooner instead of later. Better to keep his hands free perhaps, until he saw what he was up against. He eased a little closer.

The man had his back to Skip and was peering around the edge of the window in the door into Elise's kitchen.

When Skip was close enough to reach out and touch the guy, he heard the sound of a key slipping into a lock. He lunged for where the door knob should be and clamped down on a skinny wrist with his right hand. The guy swung toward him and the light from the window glinted on metal. Skip's left hand was up in the air in an instant, grabbing the guy's other wrist.

He was staring into the face of the pimply kid from next door.

Skip had the kid face down on the ground, both arms twisted up behind his back in the next second. He was wishing he'd thought to bring restraints when he saw what was lying next to his right knee. He sucked in his breath.

He couldn't use the coil of rope to restrain the kid, though. It was evidence.

The kitchen door opened and Elise let out a stifled scream.

"Call the police," Skip said. "Then find me something to tie this guy up."

"Jack?" Elise said, recognizing the side of the kid's face that wasn't mashed against the ground. "You can let him up. He lives next door. My babysitter is his girlfriend."

"That would explain how he got his hands on a key," Skip said, without moving. "He had a knife and a rope this time. Looks like he was going to take a lot more than jewelry."

Elise blanched. She dug a ball of heavy twine out of her junk drawer and brought it to Skip, then picked up her kitchen phone to dial 911.

At a little after eleven, Skip called Kate from his truck, on the way to the police station. He told her the case had gotten a bit more complicated than expected, but all was under control and she shouldn't wait up.

At twelve-forty, after signing yet another official statement, he was about to part company with the detective handling the case. "Would you make sure my name stays out of this if possible," he said. "My wife's a worry wart. If she finds out I go around tackling knife-wielding rapists, I'll be flippin' hamburgers for a living."

The detective nodded. "Been there, done that. Now I'm divorced."

"Not an option," Skip muttered under his breath, as he headed out the door of the police station, sketching a little wave in the detective's direction.

At home, Skip once again slipped into the bedroom, sat down gently on the side of the bed and nudged his shoes off. Putting his cell phone, set on vibrate, on the nightstand, he reached over and set his alarm clock to go to church with his family. He sat for a moment, debating whether to just lie down or get undressed first.

He really didn't want to sleep in his clothes another night. While undressing, he thought about the night's work. He was dog-tired, but it was a good tired. This case had been a lot more satisfying than all the mess lately with Cherise, even though they'd bill Elise Thomas for a fraction of what they were making on Cherise's account.

Easing between the sheets, Skip let out a small sigh and drifted off to sleep.

~~~~~~~~~

Kate was late for church. The kids had been particularly cranky and resistant to going, but she wasn't about to have them running around the house disturbing their father. Last night, she'd waited until he was asleep, then tiptoed around the bed and turned off his alarm. He'd earned the right to sleep in this morning.

She hastily parked the minivan, then hustled the kids to their Sunday school rooms. She barely noticed the people who were climbing out of several cars and vans, assuming they were other latecomers, as she raced across the breezeway to the church itself.

She slipped into the sanctuary from the vestibule just as the processional hymn was ending. Mary Peters, sitting at the end of a pew, smiled up at her and slid over to make room.

"The Lord be with you," Elaine Jackson's powerful voice echoed off the walls of the sanctuary.

"And also with you," the congregation dutifully responded.

Elaine, the fifty-something, black rector, looked quite imposing in her white robe and bright green chasuble. "Let us pray," she said.

Kate had trouble staying awake as the prayers and the readings droned on. She hadn't slept well the last two nights, waiting for Skip to come home. But when it came time for the Prayers of the People, she perked up. She offered her own silent prayer of thanksgiving that her husband was safe.

She was drifting off again when Mary nudged her. Sym Peters, Mary's husband and the head usher, was standing beside Kate indicating it was time for her row to go up to the altar for communion.

She knelt at the altar rail. Elaine firmly pressed a paper-thin host into her outstretched hands. "Kate, the body of Christ, the bread of heaven," the priest said.

Kate mouthed, "Amen," thinking again how nice it was that Elaine said each person's name as she gave them the bread. The chalice appeared in front of her and she dipped the host halfway in the wine. "The blood of Christ, the cup of salvation," the chalice bearer droned.

"Amen," Kate said under her breath and put the wine-soaked host in her mouth. She pushed up from the altar rail to move quietly back to her seat, head down, contemplating the blessings in her life.

There was a flash of light. A voice called out, "Mrs. Canfield, look this way."

Her head jerked up. Standing in the open double doors between the church's vestibule and the sanctuary were a half dozen men and women, some holding cameras.

Another flash of light captured her confusion.

"Get out of God's house!" Elaine's voice boomed from behind her.

The ushers formed a line and moved past Kate. They were all middle-aged or elderly men, but with righteous indignation fueling them, they started shoving the reporters and photographers out of the vestibule and through the outer doors.

Kate stood frozen in the aisle of the church, trying to process what was happening.

A voice called out. "Mrs. Canfield, did you know about Cherise Martin?"

A feeling of dread spread from the pit of Kate's stomach outward. She raced down the aisle after the ushers' receding backs. "My kids," she cried out to Sym.

He took her elbow, then extending the other arm like the football quarterback he had been many decades before, he rammed through the crowd of yelling reporters and headed for the building that housed the Sunday school classrooms. Another usher followed in their wake, his arms spread to hold back the swarm. The remaining two ushers stood guard at the sanctuary doors.

A voice cut through the clamor. " Are you going to divorce him?" Another voice yelled, "How are the children coping?"

Kate snatched Edie from her Sunday school room with no explanation for her startled teacher. Dragging the child by the hand, she hurried down the hall to the two-year-olds' room, where Billy was happily playing with blocks.

His face brightened when he saw his mother. "Look, Mommy!" He pointed to his lopsided tower.

"It's nice, Billy, but we have to go now. We have to go home to Daddy."

Billy's face screwed up in confusion. "Daddy sick?"

"No, sweetheart," Kate said, struggling to keep her voice calm. "But we have to go, now!"

Sym and the other usher did the best they could to ward off the paparazzi as Kate hustled her children out to the van and strapped them hastily into their seats.

She slammed the side door and turned to open the driver's door. A camera flashed in her face. She jumped into the driver's seat and squealed out of the church parking lot, scattering reporters and photographers in front of her.

She thought maybe she'd clipped a couple of them with her fender. She smiled grimly.

~~~~~~~~

Skip's cell phone purred and danced around on his nightstand. Lying on his stomach, he reached out and groped around blindly until he located it. Dragging it toward his ear, he said, "Hello."

Nothing. He opened one eye and stared at it. Then realized he hadn't hit the button to actually answer it. He caught the call just before it went to voicemail.

"Skip." Rose's voice had an unusual urgency.

"Wha?" he answered groggily, managing to pull himself into a sitting position on the side of the bed.

"Skip, are you there?"

"Yeah, Rose. What's up?" He rubbed his hand over his stubbled face, trying to rub away the sleepiness. Glancing at the clock, he was surprised to see it was ten-thirty. He could have sworn he'd set the alarm before passing out last night.

"Skip, are you sitting down?"

"Yeah," he said, as he stood up and pulled on the jeans he'd left lying in a heap on the floor. Struggling to zip them one-handed, he headed for the kitchen and coffee.

"You know we have that media monitoring service, watches for any references to us or the agency. They fax me copies of anything in the print media," Rose was saying in his ear, as he rummaged in a cabinet for a filter and coffee beans.

"I stopped by the office this morning to pick something up. They'd faxed an article to us yesterday afternoon. Are you listening, Skip?"

"Yeah, I'm just making coffee."

"Skip, stop making coffee and sit down," his partner ordered.

Jolted by her tone, he sat in a kitchen chair.

"Some entertainment rag," she said. "Big picture, front page, above the fold."

Skip was distracted by the sound of screeching tires and then raised voices outside. He got up and walked to the window.

The meaning of the scene outside registered in his brain at the same moment as Rose's next words did. "You hauling Cherise toward the car, caption under it: 'Cherise's New Hunka Burnin' Love.'"

The man who'd calmly disarmed a would-be rapist the night before now lost it. He threw open the kitchen window and bellowed, "Get the hell away from my family!"

"Shit," Rose said. "Be there in five minutes, or less."

CHAPTER EIGHT

Skip was pacing back and forth in the living room. Through the big picture window, he could see the reporters trampling his lawn and hurling yelled questions toward the house.

The crowd shifted as Rose and Mac elbowed their way through it. They turned and faced the reporters. Rose shouted something but Skip couldn't make out the words.

Rose and Mac moved slowly forward and the reporters fell back to the sidewalk.

This time Skip made out her words as Rose pointed to the edge of the cement strip running along the street. "Any of you assholes put one pinky across that line, and I will gleefully pound you into dog meat."

She and Mac pivoted with military precision and marched up to the porch.

Skip opened the front door to let them in.

Once inside, Rose pulled a clump of papers out of her back pocket. She handed the top one to him.

It was the front-page picture from a national tabloid. He was escorting Cherise through the crowd at Merriweather after the concert, except the crowd and other guards had been cropped away, making it look like they were a romantic couple.

He stared at it for a moment, his insides in turmoil. Then he crumpled it into a ball and threw it across the room.

"Where's Kate?" Mac growled.

"Upstairs with the kids." Skip went back to pacing the room. "The assholes actually went into the vestibule of the church. She had to grab the kids out of their Sunday school rooms and drag them through that gauntlet to the van."

"Did you call Rob? Maybe he can do something," Rose said.

Skip shook his head, then said, "Yeah, call him."

Rose glanced at Mac and he pulled out his cell.

Skip could hear Rose suck in air, bracing herself. Then she handed him the rest of the papers.

"Follow up stories from inside. One speculating about you and her. Another announcing she and Johnny have broken up and he's turned to his old girlfriend for solace. Apparently they called her publicist for confirmation, and he figured this was a good time to spring that little goodie on the world."

"Great!" Skip threw up his hands, papers scattering everywhere. "That just lends credence to the bullshit about me and her." His stomach churned. He ground his teeth.

"Rob's on his way," Mac said. "He'll park 'round the block. Come to the back door." Peering up the stairs, he continued, without his usual growl, "How ya doin', sweet pea?"

Kate reached the bottom before she answered. "The kids are playing in Edie's room. She promised to watch her brother for a little while." Her voice was flat, emotionless. "I called Maria, to warn her. She's on her way home."

"Did you tell her to come around back?" Rose asked.

Kate nodded.

Skip was at Kate's side in two long strides. He took both her hands in his. "Are you okay, darlin'?"

Kate looked up at him. "No."

"I'll get this straightened out. I promise. I'll call Cherise. Have her hold a news conference. Explain that I'm her bodyguard."

The desperate tone sounded like somebody else's voice. Rose was staring at him.

He pulled out his cell phone and started punching numbers.

Rose stepped up beside him and gently took the phone out of his hand. "Let's think this through, Skip. Cherise doesn't want it known she's being stalked."

"And she's not likely to be willing to complicate her own life to save us from all this," Kate added, again in that flat voice.

Skip scrubbed his hand over his unshaven face, then ran long fingers through his hair, trying to get his bearings. He'd woken from a dead sleep to find himself thrust into this nightmare. Maybe he was still asleep and this was all a bad dream.

Someone knocked on the back door. Rose went to answer it.

Liz's booming voice, so out of sync with her petite body, came from the laundry room. "Rob's a little big to be skulking in the bushes but we managed to get around the horde out front."

They came into the living room. Rob made a beeline for Kate and put his arm around her shoulders. She turned into the hug, visibly struggling not to cry.

Liz joined them, wrapping her arms around Kate.

For the first time in five years, Skip found himself resenting the Franklins. He started pacing again.

"Everybody, sit." Rose gestured toward the kitchen.

They all sat down at the big oak table.

"Skip, this is *not* your fault." Rose's brown eyes bore into his, then she turned to Kate. "We'll get it straightened out. Rob, can we get a restraining order?"

"Yeah, but that'll only keep them out at the street, which is public property. Can't make 'em leave."

"How about a no-closer-than-fifty-feet order?" Liz suggested. "So Kate and the kids don't have to shove through them every time they leave the house."

"I can try," Rob said. "But the courts don't usually grant that for keeping the media at bay."

Kate shook her head. In a grim voice, she said, "We've got the old garage out back. We'll keep the van in there. Take the kids in and out through the back door."

Skip nodded mutely, his throat too clogged to speak.

A knock came again from the back of the house. Rose and Mac exchanged a look and he got up to let Maria in.

"Get out of my way, you blood-sucking heathen," a voice boomed from the front yard.

Kate's mouth actually quirked up at the corners. "I believe our priest has arrived to perform an exorcism." She went to the front door

"I tried to call," Elaine Johnson was saying as they rounded the corner into the kitchen.

"We've got the phone off the hook," Kate said.

"That's what I figured."

Liz got up to make coffee, waving the priest into her seat.

"So what's this about?" Elaine asked as she sat down.

Skip and Kate looked at each other. "Until further notice, this is confidential, Elaine," Kate said. "It's about one of Skip's cases. He's been providing bodyguard and investigating services to a celebrity who's being stalked."

Rose had retrieved the balled up picture from the floor. She smoothed it out on the table and turned it so the priest could see it.

"Crap," Elaine said when she read the caption, then crossed herself.

"Yeah," Kate said.

Elaine turned to Skip. Again, brown eyes bore into his. "Skip Canfield, you are not responsible for the insanity of others. Stop blaming yourself for this mess and engage your brain."

Kate let out a short chuckle. "You are a breath of fresh air, Elaine."

Skip shook his head. "More like a bucket of cold water. Thanks for coming, Elaine."

Then he turned to his wife. Struggling to keep his voice steady, he said, "I'm sorry my work has brought this into our lives."

She took his hand and gave him a small smile. "I know. And Elaine's right. We're not responsible for other people's craziness."

"So the question is, what are we going to do?" Liz's tone was matter-of-fact as she passed out cups of coffee. "I'm Liz Franklin, by the way, and this is my husband, Rob. Friends of the family."

"Rose Hernandez." Rose pointed her thumb at Mac, who had come back into the room and was now standing behind her chair. "Mac Reilly. Also friends, and I'm Skip's partner. Mac works for us."

"Maria's upstairs with the kids, sweet pea," Mac said to Kate.

"To answer Liz's question," Rose began. "Rob gets the restraining order, and I think we will be assigning a couple of our biggest and ugliest guys to enforce it."

Skip's insides were settling down. "Ben's with Kate," he said emphatically. "Mac with Maria and the kids, whenever they leave the house."

"You're pulling Ben off of Cherise?" Kate said.

"You bet. She's getting second string from now on. Our best are with my family. Especially with the kids, we've got to have somebody we can trust. We haven't screened these new hires for abuse."

"Good point," Rose said. "I'll have Dolph run more thorough background checks on them tomorrow."

"Cherise may not step up to the plate, but can we call a news conference?" Liz asked. "Something to the effect that Skip was just providing bodyguard services during the Merriweather concert. You don't have to say anything about the stalking."

"I can do that, as the family lawyer. And if they won't back off, we might want to threaten them with a libel and/or defamation of character suit," Rob said. "On the grounds that they're damaging your reputation which will impact on your professional standing and ability to make a living."

"Cherise may try to accuse you of conflict of interest," Kate said.

"She never hired him. I did," Skip said. "Then billed her for legal services."

~~~~

Elaine had noted the frequent use of *we* by her parishioners' friends. They were in good hands, earthly hands that is. She already knew they were in God's hands. "Anything I can do, besides pray, let me know." She pushed up out of her chair.

"That may be the most helpful thing of all," Kate said.

"Elaine, with your permission," Skip said, "there will be a half dozen or so burly guys surrounding the church grounds next Sunday. I don't want this to disrupt the congregation's worship again."

Elaine thought for a moment. "Thanks for the offer. I'll check with Sym Peters and have him call you if he feels that's necessary. But keep in mind, all power and protection ultimately comes from the Lord."

Skip lifted an arm and flexed his bicep. "I'm reminded of that every day, Reverend."

Elaine shook her head, confused.

"We've never told you the story?" Kate said, "about the scrawny sixteen-year-old named Skippy, who got the crap beaten out of him by bullies, until he was blessed with a late growth spurt."

The priest suppressed a smile. "Ah, that explains a lot." She headed for the door, Kate following to see her out.

Kate gave her a big hug. "Thank you for being so understanding and supportive."

Elaine put her hands on the other woman's shoulders. "Honey, I'd love you and that man in there even if I wasn't a Christian woman. You're good people. Now you know where to find me if you need to talk." She gave Kate another hug and left.

On Monday, things went from bad to worse. Rose checked the fax machine first thing. It was spewing out paper. As she sorted through the sheets, her mood darkened.

The caption under the picture of Kate, head down and walking away from the altar, read, *Betrayed Wife Prays for Guidance*. The second picture–Kate standing in the church aisle, a deer-in-the-headlights look on her face–had no caption.

Rose groaned at the sight of the third one. Kate was standing beside the family van, her expression both angry and confused, the kids' heads silhouetted inside. Under that one was *Can She Forgive Him?* and the lead-in to the story.

Kate Huntington-Canfield, the wife of Cherise Martin's latest lover, was visibly shocked and distressed when she attended church Sunday to seek solace and guidance. She was not willing to confirm yet whether she would be divorcing her husband. Despite being a devout woman, she will no doubt find it hard to forgive his sins... The article went on to describe the supposed recent break-up of Cherise and Johnny Troop.

"She ain't devout enough, asshole," Rose muttered under her breath, "that she's not gonna want to kill you with her bare hands when she sees this."

She intercepted her partner as he came out of the elevator.

"It took me a half hour out of my way to dodge the damn paparazzi," he said, his expression indicating that he was already in a foul mood.

Rose waited until he settled into his desk chair. Then she pulled the clump of papers out from behind her back. "Promise me you'll stay calm."

He gave her a hard look. "I do not make promises I'm not sure I can keep." He held out his hand.

Skip looked at the pictures, read the caption under the first one, didn't bother to turn the page to read the rest of the story. He grabbed his phone and punched a number. "Forget the press conference, Rob. They'll just twist whatever you say. There's another article, about Kate. Rose'll send it to you. Go for the threat of a lawsuit, and if they don't take the threat seriously, file it! I'm going to talk to Cherise."

Skip was out of his chair before he had finished hanging up the phone. Rose followed him down the hall to the elevator, jogging to keep up with his long strides.

His jaw was tight, his fists clenched. Not good signs. She'd seen this normally laid-back man blow before, when something was threatening his family.

"I'm going with you," she said.

"Suit yourself." Bypassing the elevator, he took the fire stairs three at a time.

Rose, preferring that all of her bones remain intact, did not follow suit. Once outside the fire door, she broke into a run. Skip was already two thirds of the way to his truck.

"Maybe I should drive." She inserted herself between the big man and the driver's door.

He shook his head. "It'll help me calm down."

Skip drove with studied control out I-70 to Howard County.

At the farm, in response to his pounding, one of the new hires called through the door, "Who's there?"

"Your bosses," Skip growled.

Inside, their client rushed toward him.

Skip held up both hands in front of him. "Don't touch me, Cherise," he said through clenched teeth.

She stopped two feet away. "Where's Ben?" she hissed at them in a low voice. "Why did you send this guy here?"

"Ben's protecting my wife and children from the paparazzi," Skip said, his voice cold. "I'm sure your publicist has sent you the article from Saturday. There's a new one today." He gestured to Rose.

Silently, she handed Cherise the pictures and article.

While the woman perused them, Skip continued, "Rob Franklin is threatening the paper with a defamation of character suit."

"That won't work," Cherise said absently, still reading. "The courts consider public figures fair game."

"I am *not* a public figure, Cherise. *You* may be, but I'm not, and my wife and kids certainly aren't."

"A judge may see it otherwise if you're perceived to be my boyfriend." Cherise walked across the room and sat down on one of the white sofas.

Skip swivelled in her direction. "But that's the whole point, isn't it? I am *not* your boyfriend. I am your bodyguard. And if it comes down to a lawsuit, you are going to testify to that fact."

"I'll have to check with my agent and lawyers on that. They may not feel it's in the best interests of my image to get involved."

Skip crossed the huge living room in two strides. He towered over the woman.

Rose was debating whether she should intervene.

"You're already *involved*," Skip said. "My family has been sucked into this because of you. You *will* testify if we need you to."

Cherise looked up at him, fire in her eyes. "Well now, you can't make me do that, now can you?"

"Oh, but I can. Rob Franklin will subpoena you and have you declared a hostile witness. And if you don't say, unequivocally, in court that you and I are *not* lovers, Rob will tear you apart. I've seen him in action, Cherise. He's the best. By the time he's done with you, you'll be telling the court you regularly have affairs with Martians and other extra-terrestrials."

Cherise's face was a neutral mask. Then an almost evil smile spread across it. "Well, then I'll just have to sue your good friend for conflict of interest."

"You never hired him. He's on retainer with Canfield and Hernandez. And you, Cherise, are no longer one of our clients. Find yourself another security firm. I'm not even willing to recommend somebody. I don't want to be responsible for having one of my colleagues' lives poisoned by an association with you."

Skip turned and headed for the door, but Cherise got there first. "No, Skip, please. I'm sorry I spoke rashly. Please don't abandon me!" She reached out to him.

He stepped back. "I told you not to touch me."

"Okay, okay." She held up her hands in surrender. "I'll testify if you need me to, but I'm telling you, a defamation suit is not the way to go. It just keeps the story alive for months on end in the media."

"So how about this, Cherise. You hold a news conference and tell the media it's all a misunderstanding. I was your bodyguard for that one concert, just to get you in and out of there without being overwhelmed by your fans. No mention of the stalker."

"I'm willing to do that, but my life is not completely my own, you know. I'll have to run it past my agent and publicist first. Make sure they're okay with that spin."

"You do that, Cherise, but hear this. If they don't like that *spin*, they'll like it even less when I go public and tell them what's really going on."

Cherise's eyes narrowed. "You do that, Skip Canfield, and I'll see that you're ruined."

Rose decided it was time to step in. "Just talk to your people and do the news conference, Cherise. It's not a big deal to explain that you hired a bodyguard for one night."

~~~~~~~~~

Cherise's 'people' did not like the idea of a news conference.

"Jim thinks it's time to change your image," Jannie said to her client over the phone. "You've outgrown the wholesome girl next door, so we'll go with you being a bit of a wild child, just don't carry things too far."

Actually the publicist had said, "We can't rein her in anymore, Jannie, so we might as well go with it. Let Johnny be the wholesome one, the good influence on her. I'm sending out a release that she and Troop are still good friends, and will continue to perform together."

"Skip's threatening to not handle my security anymore." There was panic in Cherise's voice. "And the stalker's still out there. His lawyer's looking into a defamation of character suit."

"Against you?"

"No, against the press, but he said he'd force me to testify that we're not lovers."

"Stall him, sweetie. I'll check with our lawyer and get back to you. No news conference until I do." Jannie hung up the phone, swore under her breath, and then picked up the receiver again.

But she didn't call her lawyer. Instead she buzzed her assistant to research who was the best security company in New York, and to find out how much they would charge to send a team to Maryland.

If she could get this Skip dude out of the picture, the whole story would die a natural death, with no need for news conferences or defamation suits.

CHAPTER NINE

By Wednesday morning, Cherise still had not set up a news conference. She kept telling Skip her life was not her own, that her 'people' had to look at it from all angles first to consider how it would impact her image.

"But I'll insist, Skip," she'd promised.

The paparazzi were leaving the kids alone. Harassing small children didn't play well with the general public, especially the star-struck women who were the main readers of the entertainment tabloids. Still, Mac was going with them and Maria whenever they left the house. He thought of Edie and Billy as his niece and nephew.

The press was keeping their distance from Kate as well, after Ben Johnson had picked one of the slimy bastards up by his shirt front. Lifting him completely off his feet, Ben had informed the reporter that he was Mrs. Huntington-Canfield's personal fifty-foot restraining order.

Unfortunately the paparazzi were not leaving Skip alone. He had to shake a tail every time he went anywhere. And the phones at Canfield and Hernandez were ringing non-stop. He'd hired a young woman from a temp agency to answer them. She was instructed to answer "no comment" and hang up on reporters.

That was only eliminating about half the calls, however. Some of the bastards were sneaky enough to pretend to be potential clients, giving the temporary receptionist some bogus reason why they wanted to hire the firm. Skip couldn't afford to refuse to take those calls, just in case it was a new client.

Their reputation would be damaged if potential clients couldn't get through, and they needed the income. Although Mac was refusing to take payment for guarding the kids, insisting they were family, they still had to pay Ben, and the four men stationed around his house to keep the paparazzi from sneaking up to the windows.

Skip had tried to pay for the guards out of his own pocket, but Rose wasn't hearing it, insisting they were necessary because of an agency case. He was seriously considering adding them to Cherise's bill.

The phone on Skip's desk rang, again. Picking it up, he barked, "Canfield."

"Well, good mornin' to you too, son."

"Sorry, Dolph. The paparazzi have been calling all morning."

"Got some good news, my boy. Talked to Robinson over in Howard County. They got the lab report back. Heart is canine. And there are prints, from several different people, all over that knife handle."

A long pause. "Are you waiting for a drum roll or what?" Skip growled.

A chuckle, then Dolph said, "Got a match on two sets of them. Lansing, and also Cherise."

Skip processed that for a moment. "What the hell does that mean?"

"Knife had to come from either Lansing's place, and Cherise touched it at some point when she was over there. Or it came from Cherise's house."

"What kind of knife was it?" Skip asked.

"Steak knife, expensive, sterling silver, slightly curved handle. Hopefully we can find a set somewhere that's missing one of its buddies. Robinson's coordinating with the City police to get a search warrant for Lansing's place. You wanna go check out Cherise's kitchen?"

"On my way." Skip's voice was downright cheerful.

If they could get this damned case solved, he and his family could go back to their blissful lives of anonymity.

"Thought that news would perk you up, son. Talk to you later."

Inside Cherise's front door, Skip held his hands out in front of him as she came to greet him, but she didn't try to hug him this time.

"To what do I owe this honor?" she said, a touch of ice in her voice.

"I have some news. But first I need to see your kitchen, and talk to your housekeeper."

"Ooohh, you're a man of mystery now," she said sarcastically. "How delightful."

Skip was tempted to tell her to cut the crap, but decided to let it go. At least she wasn't jumping on him.

He headed for the kitchen. She trailed behind him. "Where do you keep steak knives?" he asked over his shoulder.

"I have no clue." She punched a button on the intercom on the kitchen wall. "Bonnie, can you come to the kitchen, please?"

"Yes, ma'am. Be right there," came the disembodied answer.

Skip was already impatiently rummaging through kitchen drawers when Bonnie, a stout, middle-aged woman, came through the door.

"Where are the steak knives kept?" Cherise asked her.

"Hutch in the dining room." Bonnie led the way. In the dining room, the housekeeper moved to an elegant mahogany chest of drawers, with a set of shelves on top. She opened a drawer.

"Wait, Bonnie," Skip said.

She stopped and took a step backward.

Taking out his handkerchief, Skip lifted the leather box in the drawer by its corner and walked over to put it on the banquet-sized dining table. "Bonnie, get me a table knife, please."

The housekeeper quickly complied. Skip used the knife to flip the small latch on the box and lift the lid. Inside were eleven sharp knives, sterling silver, slightly curved handles, and one empty slot.

Skip's face broke into a huge grin. "I need something to put this whole case in, something that won't disturb any prints."

"I'll find something." Bonnie disappeared into the kitchen.

"What does this mean?" Cherise said.

"This means," Skip gestured for her to take a seat further down the table from the leather knife case, "that we have a solid case against your ex-boyfriend, Timothy Lansing."

"Tim?"

"Yup. He sent the bracelet. We can get the sales record from Tiffany's. He wiped everything real good, including the shiny wrapping paper, but he forgot about the scotch tape. His fat ole index fingerprint was on the sticky side." Skip tilted his head toward the leather case. "Knife in the bouquet of flowers matches those. His prints are on it, along with yours."

"How'd you get my fingerprints?" Cherise's voice was sharp, her face unhappy.

"Dolph probably pocketed something you'd touched. Focus on the important stuff here, Cherise. The case is solved. Lansing is your stalker."

Bonnie came back into the room, holding up two gallon-sized baggies. "Slide one on each end, put the whole thing in this." She waved a plastic grocery bag in her other plump hand.

"That'll work nicely," Skip said. "I'll get it in a minute. Sit down please, Bonnie." The woman pulled out a chair two down from her boss and carefully lowered herself into it.

"When was the last time those knives were used?" Skip asked.

"Oh, gosh," Bonnie said, "must have been last August, when we had a big cookout."

"Was that before you and Lansing broke up?" Skip asked Cherise.

"Actually *when* we broke up. We had a fight after the guests left. I don't even remember what it was about, but we'd been fighting a lot lately and I'd had enough. Told him to get out and not come back."

Skip turned back to the housekeeper. "Were all the knives there when you cleaned up afterwards?"

Bonnie thought for a moment. "Some of them were still on the buffet. Hadn't been used. I put them back in the case myself, but we had extra help on that night. I think one of those gals cleaned the used ones and put them away. I seem to recall that I've been into that knife case since then, though. I can't put my finger on when it was." She drummed plump fingertips against her lips. "Wait. It was when Mr. Thompson was here, couple of months ago. I served pork chops 'cause I remembered they were his favorite."

"Thompson?" Skip said. "He's another ex, isn't he?"

"Yeah," Cherise said. "He showed up one afternoon. Gotten himself kicked out of his penthouse in New York for wild partying. Wanted to stay here for a while, but I only let him stay one night, in the guest room."

"Gotta be some extraordinarily wild parties to get evicted in New York, I would think," Skip said.

"Yeah, Kirk's as wild as they come. That's why we broke up. He was getting more and more into drugs, and that is *not* my scene."

"Were there any knives missing when you opened the case then?" Skip asked Bonnie.

She thought for a moment. "I couldn't say for sure, Mr. Canfield," she finally answered. "Normally I'd notice, but I was in a hurry to set the table that night. Changing the menu at the last minute had thrown me off schedule. I might not have noticed if there was an empty slot when I took two out to put on the table."

"Were there two on the table when you cleared it?"

"I don't rightly recall. It was late. I think I left the silverware out on the counter to be polished the next day."

"How about when you put the knives away? Were they all there?"

"I don't remember putting them away. Was that a Thursday, Ms. Martin? The day after Mr. Thompson was here?"

Cherise thought for a moment. "I believe it was."

"That's the day I have a girl come in to help with the weekly cleaning. I might very well have had Jane polish the silver and put it away."

"So Jane comes tomorrow? Ask her for me, please, Bonnie."

"Okay, but she's a little dim. She might not remember."

Skip turned to Cherise. "Did Thompson leave without a fuss the next day?"

"More or less. He tried to manipulate me into letting him stay longer, but he left eventually, when I kept saying no. I never did let him stay here more than a night at a time. Last thing I need is to have this place raided by the police, because he's brought drugs onto the property."

"Thanks for your help, Bonnie," Skip said. He waited until the housekeeper had left the room. "So either Thompson or Lansing could have taken the knife, but since we know Lansing sent the bracelet, my vote is with him. It's time to press charges, Cherise."

She started to interrupt him but he put up his hand. "Hear me out. I know you're worried about copycats, but the crazies can get plenty of ideas just from watching TV. And if we get his sorry ass thrown in jail, that may be a deterrent for anyone else who might otherwise decide to get cute with you. These jerks will know you don't mess around. You get somebody to chase them down and lock them up."

"Okay, that makes sense, Skip. But I've got to run it past my agent first."

"You do that. Call her right now. While I bag up the knife case."

By the time Skip had finished wrestling the case into the bags without getting his own prints on it, Cherise had her agent on the phone in the living room.

When Skip came into the room, Cherise was pacing back and forth. "Jannie, it's the only way to get him to stop. I can't go on like this!"

Skip made a gimme gesture with his fingers. Cherise ignored him. "What about the saying, all publicity is good publicity?" she said into the phone.

"Okay, you talk to Jim about it, but then get right back to me."

"Give me the phone, Cherise," Skip said, in a tone that implied he would take it from her if she didn't comply.

"Hang on for a minute, Jannie." She put the phone against her chest to cover the mouthpiece. "Why do you want to talk to her?"

Skip just held out his hand and took a step toward her. She hesitated, then handed him the phone.

"Ms. Welsh, this is Skip Canfield. As Ms. Martin's security advisor, I'm strongly advising her to press charges against this guy. The only way to stop these bozos is to come down on them and come down hard, to discourage copycats."

The agent started in about needing to preserve Cherise's image.

"Ma'am," Skip interrupted, "I understand the concept of image management. And normally I'm a patient man. But in this case, my family is being hounded by the press, and I do not take kindly to people messing with my family."

"I'm not sure you do understand," the woman said crisply. "It may not be in Cherise's best interests to go public with–"

"Ms. Welsh," he interrupted again. "*You* need to understand this. If Cherise does not press charges, *I* will go public with the whole sorry mess. Because this will explain why I've been in Cherise's company recently."

"So that's your real reason for insisting she press charges."

"No, ma'am, that's not my only reason, although it's a damn fine one in my opinion. However, I also believe it's the best course of action for Cherise. We lock this guy up and we can all get on with our lives."

"I'll have to consult with her publicist, and our lawyers. I'll get back to—"

Skip gritted his teeth. "No, I'm *not* waiting while you talk to everybody under the sun about it. I've already waited two days for a press conference that never happened. I want the paparazzi off my front lawn. This afternoon!"

He thrust the phone at Cherise. "Tell her you're pressing charges or I schedule my own press conference."

"Jannie, he means it, and there's nothing we can do to stop him from going public. So we might as well do it on our terms. I'm pressing charges."

Cherise disconnected. "You see what I've got to deal with, Skip. These people try to run my life."

He took a deep breath, then blew it out. "Thank you, Cherise."

"You're welcome. Now how about keeping me company over lunch? And then you can walk me through the process of pressing charges."

He took another deep breath to calm himself, then nodded. He'd won that round so it was time to be gracious, even though he felt anything but.

They sat at the big dining room table and Bonnie served them a salad.

Skip was figuring he'd need to stop and get a burger on his way back to Towson—this rabbit food wasn't nearly enough—when Bonnie brought in a steaming bowl and set it in front of him.

"Lamb stew from last week, Mr. Canfield. There was one portion left in the freezer." She placed a plate of apple slices in front of Cherise.

"Thanks, Bonnie. It smells wonderful." The savory stew went a long way toward restoring his good mood.

While he ate, Cherise nibbled on her apple and expertly guided the conversation from one small-talk topic to another.

"Being from Texas," she said, "I'll bet you know how to ride a horse."

"You'd lose that bet. I don't ride, but my daughter's going to start taking lessons. She's totally horse crazy."

Cherise made a small moue with her mouth. "What do you do with your kids anyway? Children are such strange little creatures."

"Not really. They're just uninhibited, and very exuberant. And they're little sponges. They soak up new information and experiences. It's fun to watch."

Cherise shrugged. "Well, I can understand, I guess, wanting to pass on your genes through your progeny."

"I could care less about that." Skip wasn't about to tell her that one of his children wasn't even his biological offspring. And he had no desire to continue this topic of conversation.

He put down his spoon and said, "Let's go over what you need to do to press charges against Lansing."

The paparazzi weren't anywhere near Skip's front lawn that afternoon, since no one was home.

Instead a few of the more persistent ones had followed Kate and Ben first to her office that morning, and then at lunchtime to Mac's Place. Ben noted their presence but opted to ignore them as long as they kept their distance.

Two of the fools had the audacity to put their faces up to the big plate glass window in the front of the restaurant. Rob and Kate, seated in a booth along the back wall, didn't notice.

But Ben, from his position at the bar, did. He paused in the process of taking a bite of his sandwich, and glared at them.

They scurried away.

Diners came and went, barely registering on Ben's radar as he divided his attention between Kate's booth and the front window. Several of the paparazzi were hovering on the sidewalk, but best he could tell no one was trying to take pictures.

A tall, thin man with dark hair, a bit of gray sprinkled in it, came through the door and took a booth near the front. After ordering some food, he headed for the back hall behind the dining area, where the restrooms were located.

He walked past Kate's booth, just as Rob gave her hand a reassuring pat.

CHAPTER TEN

A little before eleven on Thursday morning, Skip's phone rang on his desk. He tried not to growl when he answered it.

"Mr. Canfield, it's Bonnie Samuels, Ms. Martin's housekeeper."

"Good morning, Bonnie."

"Good morning, sir. I asked Jane about the knives and she has no clue what I'm talking about."

Skip sighed. It would have been nice to narrow down which of Cherise's exes had taken the knife. "Well, thanks for asking her, Bonnie."

"Have a good day, sir."

"You, t..." He trailed off as Rose entered his office, her face grim, again with sheets of paper under her arm. Skip hung up the phone, his teeth clenched.

"Skip..." Rose faltered. After a beat, she handed him the papers.

The top one was a picture of Kate and Rob sitting in a booth at Mac's Place. It looked as if they were holding hands. The caption read *Wife Having Pay-back Affair with Her Lawyer?*

The second page was a picture of Rob and Kate hugging next to Kate's Prius, Ben standing nearby. Skip didn't bother to read the article under it.

"What the fuck!" he roared, shoving his chair back. Jumping to his feet, he turned and punched the wall behind his desk, leaving a sizeable dent in the drywall.

Rose winced, but he didn't feel the pain, thanks to the adrenaline coursing through his system. His eyes skittered around the room, looking for another outlet for his rage. He picked up his coffee cup and hauled back to throw it.

"Stop, Skip!" Rose yelled, as footsteps pounded down the hall toward the office. Mac and Dolph collided in the doorway, then froze, temporarily immobilized by the sight of their boss on a rampage.

The shock on their faces finally stopped him. He carefully put the mug back down on his desk, then sank into his chair. Chest heaving with emotion, he covered his face with his big hands. A strangled noise escaped from his throat.

"You know it's not true," Rose said.

He nodded his head, his face still covered by his hands. Swallowing hard to quell the nausea churning in his stomach, he tried to think. It was a futile effort.

A rustling noise, then his office door closing. The chair next to his desk scraped.

A moment later, Mac's roar came from down the hall. Rose had apparently filled him in on the content of the pictures and article.

More rustling. "Son of a bitch," Dolph muttered.

Skip looked up.

The older man turned over the last page of the article and dropped the papers on the desk. In a conversational tone, he said, "I vote we find this reporter, strap him to a chair, and pull his fingernails out, one at a time."

Skip let out a bark of harsh laughter. "Where's his paper's office?"

"I was jokin', son."

"I know, Dolph, but thanks for the great mental image."

"What are you going to do?"

"First, I'm going to call my wife. No check that. I can't tell her this and upset her when she has clients to deal with. I'll call Ben and fill him in. *Then* I'm going to call Cherise."

"Why don't you let me call the client, son? You're still a bit riled up. You might want to catch up with Rob. See what he thinks we should do?"

Skip nodded.

As Dolph opened the office door, Mac pushed past him, Rose tugging on his arm to try to slow him down. "That son of a bitch! How dare he take pictures of *my* friends in *my* restaurant. Where's the article? I wanna know that guy's name. I'm gonna tear him a new one."

"Calm down, Mac. Dolph and I already indulged in that fantasy," Skip said. "But violence isn't the answer, as tempting as it is. It would just pour fuel on the fire."

"Not to mention the little matter of jail time for assault and battery," Rose pointed out, as Skip dialed Ben and filled him in.

"I'll take care of her. Sorry I let you down, man," Ben said.

"Not your fault. Just try to keep them away from her until I can talk to her."

Hanging up the phone, Skip said to Mac, "Where are Maria and the kids?"

"Maria and Billy are home. Edie's at her preschool. I was goin' over later with Maria to pick her up."

"Go pick Edie up now and stay at the house with them. I wouldn't put it past these bozos to try to pump the kids for info about their Uncle Rob."

Mac hesitated.

"I know you want to be doing something more... combative," Skip said. "But you're the only one I trust with my kids." He figured Mac wouldn't argue with that. "I'll call the school and tell them you're coming. Code word's 'Daddy's little girl.' Or should I say code phrase."

Mac looked confused.

"Abuse prevention," Rose said. "Had to take a training when I was a cop. Teach the kid to never go with anybody but their parents, even if they know the person, unless the person gives them the code word or phrase."

Mac nodded and left.

Rose sank into Skip's visitor chair while he called Edie's school. Then he dialed Rob's office number.

He had trouble getting through. Apparently the paparazzi had already descended on the law firm and the receptionist had been given strict instructions. "Mr. Franklin is not available, sir. Mr. Bennett's office is taking his calls temporarily."

"But... Damn, she's already transferring me to Rob's partner," Skip told Rose.

A strange woman picked up. "Could I speak to Mr. Franklin's assistant, Fran, please?" Skip asked her.

"I am screening all of Mr. Franklin's calls, sir. May I ask which of his cases this is in reference to?"

"None, I'm a friend. This is a personal call."

"I'm afraid I cannot put through any personal calls at this time, sir."

"Look, I understand why you're screening calls, but I'm the reason those reporters are chasing after him. I really need to talk to him."

"I'm sorry, sir."

"Damn, she hung up."

Rose handed Skip her cell phone. "It's Rob," she said. "Apparently he tried to call your cell earlier. Went to voicemail."

No doubt that had been the call that had caused his pocket to vibrate while he was ranting at the bastard who had photographed his wife and their friend. He gave his partner a chagrined look as he took the phone.

"What the hell's going on, Skip? Why are these assholes out in the parking lot, yelling nonsense at my window? I gather it's something about Cherise."

"I take it you didn't see the article then."

"I don't usually read tabloids over breakfast. Tell me you're not about to tell me what you're about to tell me."

"Yup, they're suggesting Kate's having a pay-back affair with you. Got two pictures at Mac's Place yesterday." Skip heard a loud thud.

"Was that your head or your fist?"

"Neither. My coffee mug. I think I cracked it. Definitely dented the desk."

"Is that the best you can do?" Skip gave a humorless laugh. "I've got a hole in my office wall."

"What do you want to do, my friend?" Rob asked.

"People keep asking me that. What the hell can I do? I feel so damn helpless, Rob. This is America. Why can't we make these guys leave us alone?"

"Because it is America. Freedom of the press, a freedom which I sometimes feel is overrated."

"Should we go ahead with the lawsuit? Cherise has pointed out that such suits just drag out the drama."

"She's probably right. They milk the story for all it's worth, make a couple of million off it. Then settle with us for less than half that and print a small retraction on the bottom of page three."

"Shit."

"Let me try to scare them off. I'll tell them I'm going after thirty million, ten for each of us. Damage to our professional reputations, interference with our ability to earn a living, emotional pain and suffering, punitive damages, the whole nine yards."

"We likely to get that much?"

"Hell, no. But they may not be willing to take the risk. They're used to going after celebrities, for whom the courts have little sympathy. The precedent is that public figures should expect such things as part of the package. When a politician or celebrity is libeled, they have to prove malicious intent, that the other party knew it was untrue and printed it anyway. That's damn hard to prove. But we're not public figures. I'll tell the papers I'll be asking for a jury trial, have twelve good men and women imagine themselves in our shoes, just doing their jobs, and suddenly lies about them are being printed in the press."

"Might work."

"I'm not suggesting we take it to trial. It would be more trauma than it's worth. But it's a damn good threat."

"Threaten away, my friend."

"Uh, Skip, I'm thinking we should postpone Liz's party, until the dust settles."

"Damn! I'd forgotten about that. Kate will be disappointed. She's been looking forward to it."

"Don't know how we'd pull it off now, with the paparazzi chasing all of us. Don't want it to turn into a nightmare."

"Hang on, I have an idea. Let me consult with my partner." Skip looked at Rose, still sitting across the desk from him. "You okay with providing security for free for Liz's party Saturday?"

Rose nodded. "We're not giving these bastards the satisfaction of screwing that up. Put some guys around the perimeter of the property so nobody's taking pics from the bushes. Don't know how we'd explain all that security to Liz though. Might give the surprise away."

Skip conveyed Rose's plan and her concern to Rob, then said, "Maybe we should move the party inside."

"The RSVPs have already hit thirty-five. Don't think we can cram that many people into your living room. And I'm helping to pay for the guards. As for explaining them to Liz, I'll just point out that *Skippy*'s a little paranoid right now." There was a chuckle in his voice.

"Very funny," Skip said. "Just because you're paranoid and all that."

"Yeah, they really are out to get you right now. Stay cool, buddy."

"I'll try."

Skip's attempt to keep his cool was short-lived. Within minutes he was yelling curses at the walls again. He did manage to resist the temptation to punch holes in them this time.

Dolph had informed him that Cherise's agent had called the Baltimore City Chief of Police, requesting they keep the arrest of Timothy Lansing hush-hush. And Cherise was now refusing to buck her agent and publicist by publicly setting the record straight.

"Okay, they had their chance," Skip said when he had calmed down. "Rose, go tell the clowns out front there will be a press conference at two o'clock, location to be announced. I'll call Rob and see if he wants to do it there or does he want to lead his contingent of assholes to us. Either way, tell them this will be like the President's press room. They raise their hands. I will answer all of their questions, but the first one who calls out will be tossed out of the building on his or her ear."

Rose nodded and left his office.

CHAPTER ELEVEN

Skip went home after the press conference. He was wiped out. No point in even trying to work. And he dared not touch base with Cherise. He was afraid of what he might say to her.

She had been all sweetness and light yesterday over lunch, asking him about his youth, growing up in Texas. She had promised at least three times that she would cooperate with him to get the paparazzi to back off. Although she seemed clueless about why he cared so much about his family. She'd acted like children were a species from another planet.

Out of habit, Skip looked in his rearview mirror. Then he reminded himself there would be no more press following him around. The press conference had gone very well, even though it had taken almost two hours.

Rob had opted to come to Canfield and Hernandez. He'd driven there slowly so none of the reporters following him would get lost.

They'd stuffed everyone into the agency's conference room. The six musclemen Rose could stir up on short notice had stationed themselves strategically along the walls.

Rose had then introduced herself and informed them of the ground rules. Anybody broke the rules they would be escorted from the premises. The guys along the walls all crossed their meaty arms in unison.

Skip chuckled to himself. He could've sworn he'd heard an audible gulp or two at that moment.

After he had succinctly described his role as investigator and bodyguard for Ms. Martin, he told them the stalker had been identified and would be prosecuted to the full extent of the law. He informed them that he was not at liberty to divulge the culprit's name and that Ms. Martin would not be available for the foreseeable future for comment. He had then answered the same question, asked a dozen different ways, over and over again. No, he and Ms. Martin were not and had never been lovers. He was happily married as was his friend and lawyer Rob Franklin. The two families had been friends for years.

Then Rob had made his announcement. Any paper that continued to falsely malign Mr. Canfield, himself or any member of either of their families would be facing a thirty million dollar lawsuit for libel and defamation of character. "These are not public figures you are going after, ladies and gentlemen," Rob had concluded. "They are private citizens who value their privacy and are just doing their jobs. If your papers hesitate to take us seriously on this, you might point out that a jury of our peers is going to be much more sympathetic toward us than toward a tabloid that knowingly tells lies to make a buck."

Several grumbles of protest had started to rise from the crowded room. They had been silenced when the men around the perimeter had *uncrossed* their arms in unison.

Skip grinned to himself and whistled tunelessly under his breath as he turned onto his street. Not a reporter in sight. And Kate's Prius was parked in front of the house. She was home early as well.

Excellent!

His jubilation was short-lived.

The temperature in the house was below freezing. When his wife walked past him, trailing a chilly draft behind her, he took her by the arm. "What's the matter?" he asked quietly so the children, who were playing on the living room floor, wouldn't hear him.

"We will talk later," she said, her expression and tone carefully neutral. She tugged her arm loose from his grip.

"Fine," he said, a touch of anger creeping into his voice. "I'm taking a nap." He marched toward the bedroom, some of the rage he'd felt earlier stirring in his chest.

He'd spent the whole damn day getting the paparazzi off their backs, and this was the thanks he got.

But he couldn't sleep. He tossed and turned on top of the comforter until the king-sized bed looked like a giant rat's nest. Then he got up and paced the floor. He didn't dare go back out into the living room, for fear they would fight in front of the kids–something they had sworn they would never do.

Finally he smelled dinner cooking. He ventured out of the bedroom, yawning and pretending he had indeed napped. The children were already seated at the kitchen table. As he sat down in his place, Maria brought the last of the food to the table and Edie said the blessing.

The adults said very little except in response to the children's chatter. Both Skip and Kate picked at their food. When the meal was finally over, Maria, sensing something was wrong, started clearing the table, a chore Kate and Skip usually did together as they chatted about their day and the children played in the living room.

Not sure what else to do, Skip said to his daughter, "Come on, Pumkin. Let's draw horses while Mommy gives Billy his bath." Edie dutifully followed her father into the living room, the expression on her little face worried.

Thirty minutes later, Skip and Kate exchanged children in silence. Skip gave in to Billy's demands for a second story. He didn't have the energy to resist, and he wasn't in any hurry to go back downstairs.

Finally he got the boy settled and headed toward his daughter's room. Kate came out of Edie's door. "I did her story," she whispered, her mouth a tight thin line. "Just kiss her goodnight and come downstairs."

Skip did as he was told, planting a light kiss on the little girl's warm smooth forehead.

She looked up at him, her eyelids drooping. "Goodnight, Daddy," she mumbled.

"Night, Pumkin," Skip whispered. Then he squared his shoulders and went downstairs.

Kate was in the kitchen, a steaming cup of tea in front of her. She was stirring it vigorously but making no attempt to drink it.

He sat down across from her. "What is it? What's wrong?"

She looked at him in silence for a beat, then said, "My one o'clock appointment was with Cherise."

"Aw shit!"

"Yeah, aw shit. Thank you so much for letting me hear about what was on the front page of that filthy rag from her," Kate hissed. "Apparently Dolph had a lovely little chat with her about the story, but you couldn't be bothered to call me."

"I didn't call you because–"

She cut him off. "I could just barely get through the session. She's either so self-centered she didn't even notice I was upset, or she was politely ignoring the fact that I was trying not to burst into tears. I have no clue what she said or what I said back. I couldn't concentrate–"

"But that's why I didn't call you–"

Kate talked over him. "I thought I'd pulled myself together enough to deal with my next client, but apparently I didn't look all that together. When I went out to the waiting room, she asked, in the kindest voice, if I was taking care of myself, what with all the stress from the divorce. The *divorce*. Skip, my clients think I'm getting a *divorce!*" Her voice went up an octave on that final word.

"Sh, sh," Skip said, making a keep-your-voice-down gesture with his hands. "Take a deep breath, Kate, so we can talk about this calmly."

She threw her hands into the air. "Calmly? I may never be able to talk calmly again. I don't even remember what calm feels like anymore." Her voice started going up in volume again. Suddenly clamping her mouth shut, she got up to leave the room.

Skip jumped up. "Kate, don't walk..." But she was already gone. "Don't walk away from me, please," he whispered, his eyes stinging. They fought sometimes, although not often, but they had never walked away from each other before.

He followed her into the living room. But before he could tell her he had fixed it, she was hissing at him again. "Damn it. I can't have this, Skip. This crap has invaded every part of our lives, and now it's interfering with my ability to do my job."

He tried to tell her about the press conference but she interrupted again. He decided he would just have to wait for her to run out of steam. He stopped trying to talk, which seemed to make her more furious.

"Damn it, Skip, say something!" she yelled.

His patience snapped. "I've been trying to say something for the last half hour," he yelled back. "You won't let me talk!"

Wailing, coming from Billy's room. They both froze.

"Now see what you've done," Kate hissed as she dashed for the stairs.

"As I recall, you're the one who started this fight," he defended himself, following her to the foot of the steps.

Edie was standing at the top of the stairs, her eyes big as saucers. Kate had stopped beside her.

Skip's chest ached at the sight of the little girl. "I'll get her," he said quietly, taking the steps three at a time. "You take care of Billy."

With her back still toward him, Kate walked to Billy's door and went in.

Skip scooped his daughter up in his arms. "It's okay, Pumkin, everything's okay."

Maria was headed down the steep steps from the third floor. Skip quietly said in Spanish the equivalent of "We broke it, we'll fix it."

Maria gave him a solemn look. "*Si, Señor* Skip, you need fix it." She hadn't added *señor* in front of his name in three years, not since his wedding day when he had become family.

"I already fixed it, but she won't let me tell her that," he said through gritted teeth. Edie started crying in his tense arms.

Skip took a deep breath, then turned and carried his daughter down the stairs. He cuddled her on his lap on the sofa. "It's okay, Pumkin," he kept saying, until her sniffles subsided.

"Why's Mommy so *mad* at you, Daddy?" the little girl said, her voice plaintive.

"It's a long story, Pumkin. One you needn't worry your curly little head about. But it's all going to be okay. Mommies and Daddies fight sometimes. It's part of being a family. You know, like you and Billy fight sometimes 'cause you get on each other's nerves. But you still love each other. Mommy and Daddy still love each other and we still love you. We just get on each other's nerves sometimes, that's all."

Edie leaned back in his arms and looked up at him. "Is this about the bad men with the cameras, Daddy?"

"Yes, sweetheart, that's what Mommy's upset about. But it's going to be okay now. The bad men won't be coming around anymore. Daddy took care of it this afternoon."

"You did!" Edie said, awe in her voice. "Did you shoot 'em all with your gun?"

Skip suppressed a chuckle. "No, sweetie, I don't shoot people unless I absolutely have to. But I got rid of the men. I told them all the truth so they would go away."

"What's *truth*, Daddy?"

"When you say what really is, like when you spill something and you admit it, instead of pretending Billy did it."

"What were the bad men pretending, Daddy?"

"That's a long, long story, Pumkin. I'll tell you some other time 'cause it's way past your bedtime now." He gathered his daughter into his arms and stood up.

Nuzzling the little girl's neck until she giggled, he walked toward the stairs.

And almost collided with his wife, who was standing at the bottom of them. "You fixed it?" Kate asked in a small voice.

"Yes, darlin', I fixed it. I'll be right back."

When Skip returned to the living room, Kate was sitting on the sofa, her face wet with tears. "Oh, Skip, I am so sorry. I can't believe I yelled at you like that."

He sat down beside her and put an arm around her shoulders. "I was finding it a bit hard to believe there for a while myself."

"Can you ever forgive me?" she asked, looking down at her lap.

His anger at her had already melted away, replaced by the nagging guilt that his client had brought all this down on them in the first place. "Now that depends," he said in a teasing tone, "on what you're planning to do tonight to make it up to me."

She lifted her head and gave him a tentative smile. "I could probably come up with a few things that might make you like me again."

"Well then, yes, you're forgiven." He was tempted to kiss her. But he wasn't sure he could stop with just a kiss and he wanted to tell her how he'd fixed it, before he took her to bed.

"Is Cherise going to be pissed when she hears about the press conference?" Kate asked when he had finished the story.

"Frankly, I don't give a damn if she is. She had her chance to control the spin, as she put it, and she didn't. I told her and her agent what I was going to do, if they didn't come clean with the press. They had fair warning."

"Are you done with her case then?"

"Not completely yet. I need to hang in a little bit here until this guy is prosecuted, then I'm going to ask Rose if she's willing to take over the case. I can't be seen anywhere near Cherise now. If she's not willing to deal with Rose, then she can find herself another security company. I think you need to stop seeing her though. I don't want this case affecting our family anymore."

Kate thought for a moment. "I agree, not just for that reason. I know most of this is not her fault *per se,* but there's no way I can be objective or have any kind of clinical detachment with her anymore."

"You give me a colleague's name and I'll give it to her. I got you into this and I'm getting you out of it."

"No, I have to tell her myself that I can't work with her anymore and why. It's unethical to just abandon a client without some kind of closure."

"But she can't come to see you now," Skip said. "If the media got wind of it, they'd assume she was there for some kind of showdown, not for therapy, and the whole mess would be stirred up again."

"An excellent point, and probably the one that will convince Cherise this is in her own best interests. But I still have to call her."

Skip didn't say anything. He put a finger under her chin and tilted her head up to kiss her. When they came up for air, he stood and pulled her to her feet. Then he wrapped his arms around her and kissed her again.

When she broke away, gasping, he started steering her toward the bedroom. They both froze when they heard the soft purr of Skip's phone vibrating in his pocket.

Filled with dread, he pulled out the phone and read the caller ID. He swore under his breath, then he turned the phone off and put it back in his pocket. Pulling his wife up against him, he said, "Now where was I?"

He nuzzled her neck, finding that sweet spot where shoulder begins to curve upward into neck. He kissed her there. The mother, unlike her daughter, did not giggle. The mother swayed against him as she sucked in her breath and her knees gave out on her.

'How is it you can still turn my joints to jelly, Mr. Canfield?' she whispered.

"Darlin', I plan to be turnin' your joints to jelly when we're eighty-nine." He was about to pick her up in his arms and carry her to bed when the house phone rang.

Kate broke away and dashed into the kitchen to pick it up before it rang a second time and woke the children.

Jaw tight and fists clenched, Skip followed her. If Cherise was calling on his home phone, he would kill her with his bare hands.

"It's Rose." Kate handed him the phone.

He listened with a growing sense of dread, then said, "I'll be there as quick as I can."

Dropping the phone on the counter, he grabbed both of Kate's hands in his. "Please don't be mad, darlin'. I gotta go out there. There's a bad situation brewing and our men are at risk."

He let go of her and headed for the study and his gun cabinet, explaining as he went. "Half an hour ago, a bunch of guys showed up, saying they were from some security service up in New York. Her agent sent them down. Our men wouldn't let them on the property, which these guys did not take well. Head guy insisted on talking to Cherise. She sent one of our men out instead to tell them to get lost. They didn't take that well either. The message they sent back was that they had their orders and our men had an hour to clear out. Cherise was trying to call me while our man in charge was calling Rose. She told him to sit tight until we get there."

Kate was staring at him, incredulous. "Where do these guys think they are, some third world country?"

Skip shook his head as he headed toward the front door. "A lot of private security guys are ex-cops. Unfortunately, a few of them are the ones who like to throw their weight around. That's what attracts them to that job, when they leave the force."

"Dear God! Be careful, Skip."

He turned at the door and took her hands. "I will be, darlin'. I'm calling the Howard County police when I'm within shouting distance. But I want to get there first, so I can intercept the officers and tell them our side of the story. People tend to believe what they hear first."

"True."

Skip pecked her on the lips, then took off out the door.

At the top of Cherise's driveway, Rose's car was parked on the shoulder across the road and a hulk of a guy was banging on the window, shouting for her to move on.

Skip pulled in behind her and flicked on his high beams as the guy turned toward him. Skip lowered his window a few inches.

"I suggest you back away from my partner's car, sir, before she feels the need to shoot you in self defense. The Howard County police are on the way."

The guy squinted into the light and started moving in Skip's direction. His hand was on his holster which did not bode well for civil discourse. Skip raised his window, leaving only a crack at the top. He picked up the gun that was lying on the passenger seat.

"You make a move to pull your weapon, mister, and it'll be the last move you make," Skip growled, poking the .38's barrel out through the crack, pointed at the middle of the guy's chest.

The man had the good sense to freeze, just as another guy jogged up carrying a Maglite. The asshole shown the light in Skip's face.

"Turn that light off, or my finger might just slip on this trigger," Skip called out.

"Turn the light off, George," the guy beside the car said, his voice ending on a squeak.

"The man said to turn the light off," Mac's growl came out of the darkness. The light went out.

Skip blinked a couple times, then made out a shadow next to George. Mac's gun was jammed into the guy's side.

"I'm thinking George and Squeaky Voice need to put their hands on their heads, just so there's no misunderstanding, that might lead to an unfortunate consequence," Rose said conversationally as she stepped into the light from Skip's headlights. Her snub nose .32 was in her hand. Both men complied with the suggestion.

Skip heard a siren in the distance and breathed a tentative sigh of relief. He opened his door into Squeaky's gut and climbed out of his truck. Flipping the flap on the man's holster open, he lifted the gun from it with two fingers and tossed it inside his own truck. "You got Georgie's gun, Mac?"

"Yup."

"Okay, George, spread eagle on the hood," Skip ordered. "You, Squeaky, you do the same against the side of the truck. Pat 'em down, Mac."

While Mac did so, removing a second gun from George's ankle holster, Skip pointed out the obvious. "*We* are the security people the owner of this property hired. We have a legal right to be here. *You* do not."

"Are you Skip Canfield?" George asked.

Skip didn't say anything. He wasn't in the mood to get in a pissing match with these guys.

"If you are, my orders were to inform you that your services are no longer needed."

"Yeah, well, I don't take orders from you, or Ms. Walsh."

The siren was getting louder. "Gentlemen," Skip said, "you will stand politely between my colleagues over there, hands on your heads. Either of you twitches and you'll be on the ground eating dirt before you can spit."

Skip turned to Mac and Rose. "Holster your guns. Keep your hands where the cops can see 'em, but keep your eyes peeled for any more members of this travelin' road show."

"My men are well trained," George growled. "They'll hold their positions until ordered to do otherwise."

Skip nodded at the man as swirling lights came around the curve a mile down the road, siren blaring. "Let me do the talking, guys," he said to Mac and Rose. "Hopefully I can avoid letting on who Carol Ann Morris really is."

"Is there any point at which *I* get to boss *you* around," Rose said. Her tone was teasing but her eyes were scanning the front of Cherise's property.

"Now I thought you'd already acknowledged I was the sweet talkin' one amongst us," Skip drawled good-naturedly, as he watched the police cruiser pull onto the shoulder behind his truck.

"If it'll make ya feel better, Honey Bun, I'll let you boss *me* 'round," Mac said, a chuckle in his voice. "You can even handcuff me."

Rose shot Mac a quick glare.

Skip snickered without taking his eyes off the shadowy figures of the two police officers who were climbing out of the cruiser. "He calls you *Honey Bun*?"

"Aw, shut up, partner, and go sweet talk the cops."

~~~~~~~~~

It was midnight by the time Skip got home, but Kate was waiting up for him. Between guilt and worry, there was no way she was going to sleep anyway.

She rushed to greet him at the door when she heard his key in the lock.

He gathered her up in an exuberant hug. "Shootout at the OK Corral diverted. And I shamefully cowered in my truck until Mac and Rose had the bad guys subdued."

"As if that would have stopped a bullet," she said, her face pressed against his chest.

He held her away from him. "Remember when I had that truck special ordered? I had steel plates put in the doors, and the glass is bulletproof. Rose's car's the same way. How many times do I have to tell you? I *am* careful."

Relief washed through her, along with more guilt that she hadn't trusted him when he said he was being careful. She led him toward the kitchen. "Are you hungry?"

He stopped and looked down at her, an eyebrow cocked in the air. "I thought I just told you I'm careful. That means I do not eat anything you cook," he teased.

"Okay, smart ass, I was going to make you a sandwich."

"Sandwich would be good since I don't recall eating a whole lot of dinner. I was waiting for the other shoe to drop."

Her gut twisted. "I'm so sorry, Skip," she pushed past her clogged throat. "I don't know what got into me."

"Stop apologizing, darlin'. This is about the strangest situation we've ever been in. Not as scary as some of the stuff we've dealt with but pretty damn stressful." He pulled her into a quick hug, then held her away from him again to smile down at her. "Now get me some grub, woman."

She made him a sandwich while he locked up his gun.

He was almost finished gobbling it down when Kate sat down on his knee and snuggled her head against his shoulder. "I love you," she breathed into his ear.

Maria found a quarter of a turkey sandwich on the kitchen table the next morning.

CHAPTER TWELVE

Dolph was sitting in Skip's office the next morning, shooting the breeze. "Rose tells me Cherise was hopping mad that you didn't come inside to comfort her last night, after the cops left."

Skip was sucking down his third cup of coffee, trying to get awake enough to get some paperwork done.

"I had better things to do than listen to her hysterics." He flashed Dolph a grin. "Kate and I had a fight and we were right in the middle of the makin' up part when the damn phone rang."

Dolph grinned back at him. "You got a good woman there, son, and don't you ever forget it."

"Don't worry. Cherise may have her fantasies but they are just that. I'm a one-woman man and I have me my wo... Aw, shit!"

Rose was standing in his open doorway, her expression grim, sheets of paper under her arm.

Skip heaved a weary sigh. "Give 'em to me." He held out his hand.

There was only one picture, of him standing in the packed conference room, talking. The caption read *Boyfriend or Bodyguard? He Claims the Latter*. Not great but not all that bad either. Skip started reading the attached article.

"Why such a grim face, Rose?" he asked, as he continued reading. Then he got to the last paragraph.

Jim Bolton, Ms. Martin's publicist, when asked to comment, said, "The man does seem to be protesting a bit too much, isn't he?"

Skip chest tightened. He banged his fist down on the desk, then tossed the pages in Dolph's direction. "Cut to the last line. In one sentence, that man undid everything we accomplished yesterday."

"And no grounds for defamation. They only reported what you said and then what Bolton said," Rose pointed out.

Dolph skimmed the end of the article. "Why'd the hell he do that?"

Rose shrugged. "Probably to keep the story going. What's the saying in showbiz, 'There's no such thing as bad publicity.'"

"That's it! I am done with that woman." Skip grabbed up his phone and started to punch in Cherise's number.

"Wait, Skip," Rose said. "Let's think this through. Threatening to quit is the only leverage we have with her. Once we've done it, she'll be pissed and who knows what she'll tell the press."

"She's got an excellent point, son."

Rose's logic penetrated the red haze in Skip's brain. He hung up the phone without hitting the last number. "So what do you recommend?"

She tilted her head to one side. "I'm inclined to say, sit tight and let the whole thing die down. Bolton didn't completely undo what the press conference accomplished. And the rags seem to be taking the lawsuit threat at least somewhat seriously, 'cause there's no additional speculation. Anything we try to do at this point may just stir things up more."

"I'm inclined to agree with her," Dolph said.

Skip threw his hands in the air. "Okay, I'm out-voted. And you're probably right. Goes against the grain but we sit tight. We're going to need guards for tomorrow after all, for Liz's party... Damn, I better call Kate. She sees the paparazzi outside again and I haven't warned her, I'll be in the doghouse for a year."

"You don't own a dog," Rose pointed out.

"She'll get one, just so she can make me sleep with it," Skip replied as he reached for his phone.

It rang under his hand. He picked it up. "Canfield." He listened for a couple minutes. "I think that was the right thing to do, Cherise," he said, grinning at Rose and Dolph. "Yeah, they'd forgotten who was the boss."

After another few seconds, he said, "Thanks for the invite, Cherise, but I need to steer clear of the farm for a while. I don't want the paparazzi to follow me out there." A pause while Skip listened. "Okay. I'll call later to check on you."

He hung up and said, "Hot damn! She fired her agent and Bolton."

He quickly dialed his wife's office number, and, of course, got voicemail. She would be in session at ten-fifteen. "Hey, darlin'," he drawled cheerfully into the phone. "I got a bad news, good news thing goin' here. Call me when you get a break, and in the meantime, stay inside."

As he hung up, he asked Rose, "Where are Mac and Ben? They available to ward off the paparazzi again?"

"Mac was going by the restaurant this morning to check on his new manager. I'll send him over to the house from there," Rose said. "Ben's back out at Cherise's. You want me to pull him off of her again?"

"No, let's keep the lady happy for now. I think I'll go pick up my wife myself this afternoon. Any press hanging around can watch me give her a big fat kiss right in the middle of the parking lot."

"Okay, let me call Mac and then I need you guys to help me with something important," Rose said.

"What's that?" her partner asked.

"You need to help me figure out what the hell to get Liz for her birthday."

Dolph jumped up. "That's what wives are for. I'm outta here."

"That's what I need," Rose said. "A wife to take care of the girlie stuff."

Skip snorted. "Somehow I don't see Mac going along with that role."

"Not in this lifetime," Rose agreed, and went off to call her honey bun with his new assignment.

~~~~~~~~~

At lunchtime, Kate was intrigued by Skip's message. But before she could call him back, her office phone rang.

It was Cherise. She filled Kate in on the morning's events and apologized that her publicist had stirred the pot again. "I think I'd better not come to see you on Monday," she said. "Just in case the paparazzi are watching your office."

It was just the opening Kate needed. "I've been thinking it may not be a good idea for us to continue working together, for that and other reasons. In order for a therapist to do a good job, you can't be too involved in the client's life. Otherwise, you lose your objectivity and you can't provide good guidance anymore."

After a pregnant pause, Cherise said, "So you're bailing on me." There was an edge to her voice.

Kate gritted her teeth. Not the reaction she had hoped for. Client abandonment was grounds for a malpractice suit and she knew it was a hot button for Cherise, considering her history with her father. "I don't want to, but Skip is very concerned about the possible repercussions should any of these jerks see you coming into my building. At best they'll assume you're here for some kind of confrontation, which will stir everything up again, and at worst, they'll track you back to the farm. Skip is really worried about that, and so am I. We do not want your sanctuary to be discovered."

A pause, then a sigh. "I guess you're right."

"Let me give some thought to who would be the best person for you to work with, and I'll call you later with a referral, okay?"

"Yeah, that'll be fine." Another sigh. "Why is life so complicated sometimes?"

Kate was suddenly struck by how young and alone this woman was. Her voice gentle, she said, "That's a very good question, for which I have no good answer. There are just times when reality sucks, but Rob Franklin gave me some great advice one time. Whenever life is rough, he tells himself, 'A few months from now, this will all just be a bad memory.' I've started doing that myself, when life get complicated. It does help to put things in perspective."

A low chuckle. "Only a lawyer would come up with a way to turn 'this too shall pass' into a complex sentence."

Kate smiled. "Yeah, he can be wordy sometimes. You take care, Cherise. I'll get that name to you by this evening."

Kate sighed as she hung up the phone. She had expected to feel elated to be rid of this client, but all she felt was sad. Cherise was truly a poor little rich girl. The only people she could trust were the private investigator she'd hired and the therapist she'd seen less than a half dozen times. And both of them couldn't wait to get away from her.

~~~~~~~

At one o'clock the next day, six burly guys, plus Mac, were scattered around Skip and Kate's property. Only a few paparazzi were hanging out on the front sidewalk, but Skip wasn't taking any chances.

The preparations for Liz's party went fairly smoothly, despite it being an armed camp. The Franklin daughters arrived at one-thirty to help Kate decorate. Maria was busy cooking in the kitchen. Skip was charged with watching the kids. The guests were due at four and Rob and Liz at five.

At two-thirty, Skip heard a beeping noise from out front. He looked out the front window and saw a U.S. post office jeep. Apparently, the mail carrier was unwilling to run the gauntlet to get to the mailbox on the front porch.

The paparazzi had swelled to a small crowd of nine. Word must have gone out on their slimy little grapevine that something was happening at the Canfields' house.

Skip told Edie to watch her brother for a minute while he jogged out to the street to get the mail. He ignored the questions yelled in his direction, but gave a jaunty wave to the female reporter who'd snapped a shot of him kissing Kate the day before in front of her office building.

Inside he was chased out of the kitchen where they usually sorted the mail. He took it into the study instead, checking on the kids playing in the living room on the way through.

He stared at the envelope for a few seconds, perplexed. Then he went to the back door and called to Kate. "Come look at something, please."

In the study, he handed her the envelope, addressed to her with Rob's return address.

"What in the world?" Kate said. "He never mails me stuff. He calls. Maybe it's something to do with the party." She opened it. Inside was a sheet of paper with one paragraph typed on it.

She read it, then handed it to Skip, her expression a mixture of anxiety and confusion. He skimmed it quickly, then went back to the top and read it again more slowly.

Sweetheart, I can't wait until next Wednesday to see you again. Can you get away to meet me before then? I've taken the liberty of reserving our usual room at the Towson Hilton, for four on Monday. Hope you can make it. We can tell them we had an 'emergency meeting.' LOL. Love, Rob.

"This is crazy. Who the hell could have sent that?" Kate said.

"You sure Rob didn't? Maybe as a joke."

"Hell, no. Rob would *never* joke about having a usual room at the Hilton. He gets far more upset than I do when people assume we're lovers. He's just old-fashioned enough to feel like he should defend the lady's honor, mine and/or Liz's. Besides, he's a technophobe. Fran handles his e-mails for him at work. He doesn't have a personal account. I'll bet he has no clue what LOL even means."

"Might be one of the paparazzi trying to stir things up," Skip speculated, ignoring the queasy feeling in the pit of his stomach.

"That's got to be it." Kate's face relaxed a little. "It can't be anybody who knows us very well."

"I don't know. They got the *sweetheart* right. That's what he calls you. And they know you usually meet on Wednesdays," Skip said.

"Any of these clowns would know that from watching us. And the one who took the picture in Mac's Place last week could have overheard him calling me *sweetheart*."

"Do you want to call him, or wait until they get here?" Skip asked.

"Neither one," Kate said. "I don't want to ruin the party for him or Liz. We keep this to ourselves for now. I'll call him tomorrow and tell him about it."

"Okay, I guess." But he wasn't totally convinced that was the best course of action.

"Damn it!" Kate's eyes pooled with angry tears. "Who's doing this to us? Why can't they leave us alone?"

Skip hesitated. Then he tossed the letter in the direction of his desk and gathered her into his arms. "Don't let this ruin the party for you, 'cause then the bastard's won."

Kate leaned back in the circle of his arms, swiping at her cheeks with the back of her hand. "I love you, Skip Canfield. How many men would automatically assume this was a hoax?" She smiled up at him.

He smiled back at her, trying to hide the guilt. Because for a few awful seconds, he had thought the letter *was* from Rob.

But he knew it wasn't. In addition to all the reasons Kate had given, Rob was not stupid. He wouldn't send a letter to his lover's house where her husband might intercept it.

~~~~~~~~~

Rob and Liz arrived at Kate's house exactly at five. Rob was praying the reporters wouldn't call out some question that would reveal the fact that thirty-eight people were huddled in silence in the backyard.

Once one of the guards had gotten the two of them safely to the porch, Rob wrapped his arms around his petite wife and lifted her off her feet as he gave her an exuberant kiss. Putting her down, he called out to the reporters, "This is my wife, ladies and gentlemen."

He hustled Liz through the front door Mac was holding open. Maria, on cue, sang out from the kitchen, "Dey out back." Rob moved through the laundry room to the back door, then waited for his wife to catch up before he swung it open with a flourish. Liz stepped out into the backyard.

~~~~

The paparazzi could hear the shouts of "Surprise!" from the front sidewalk. Most of them left, convinced the Canfields and Franklins were indeed just good friends. The three who remained—one, a tall, thin fellow with a bit of gray in his dark hair, and the others, a female reporter and her photographer—didn't really care.

CHAPTER THIRTEEN

Sunday morning, nobody in the Canfield residence went to church or Sunday school, not even Maria. Kate e-mailed Elaine to say they would be back the following week. *God willing*, she wrote, *the ground will have opened up and swallowed all the paparazzi by then.*

At one o'clock, the rector e-mailed back simply *LOL*.

Kate and Skip decided to go to the Franklins rather than just call. Kate called Liz's cell, knowing Rob would pick up on her tension and demand to know what was going on. "Hey Liz," she said, in a breezy voice. "We were going to go for a Sunday drive. Mind if we drop by?"

A beat of silence. "This got anything to do with why Rob's been acting strange all morning?"

Kate sighed. "Probably."

"Come on over."

Kate disconnected and nodded to her husband. "Road trip," he yelled. The kids came running.

~~~~

This was Maria's day off, but Skip pointed out that it might not be a good idea for her to stay home by herself with some of the paparazzi still lurking in the neighborhood. He was concerned for her sake, but also worried about how the press would twist something she might say in all innocence.

He kept the latter thought to himself.

Maria opted to go with them. At the Franklins, she and Samantha herded the children into the family room, while the other adults gathered around the kitchen table. Liz passed out mugs of coffee and put a plate of homemade cookies in the middle of the table.

"Maybe we're overreacting," Kate said, "but we got a strange letter in yesterday's mail."

"So did I," Rob said before she could go on.

"Shit," Skip said, then shot Liz an apologetic look.

"Yeah," Rob agreed with the sentiment. "Sweetheart, yada, yada, meet me at the Hilton, four o'clock, Monday."

"He showed me the letter while you were *en route*," Liz said.

"Where is it?" Skip asked.

"I've been hanging around you too long." Rob handed him the letter and envelope encased in a large baggie. "My first thought was fingerprints."

Skip held the letter up in front of his face, partly to hide his embarrassment from the others. He'd been shaken enough the day before that he hadn't thought about prints until after he and Kate had handled the letter. "No prints on ours," he said.

Except mine and Kate's.

"The wording's essentially the same on both." He felt the heat recede from his cheeks and lowered the baggie-encased letter. "I'm going to have Rose and Dolph strategically located in the Hilton's lobby tomorrow at four. See who shows up."

"The *sweetheart* was just a lucky guess then," Kate said. "Whoever sent the letters doesn't know that I don't call Rob that."

Skip nodded. She often called Rob *dear*, but *sweetheart* was reserved for him.

He ground his teeth. "Who the hell's doing this? Sorry, Liz."

"Curse all you want," she said. "It helps me vent vicariously."

Rob chuckled and took a cookie to nibble on. No one else seemed to have much appetite, not even for Liz's gourmet treats.

After a long pause, Kate said, "I hate this! And I hate that we've dragged you two into it."

"I am so sorry I brought this down on us," Skip added fervently.

"Stop it, damn it!" Liz smacked the table with her open hand, rattling the cookie plate. "Both of you."

They all jumped a little, then stared at Liz. She never cussed.

"It's nobody's fault," she added, in a no-nonsense voice. "Nobody asked for this. And somehow, someway, we're gonna figure out who's doing it and make them leave us alone."

~~~~~~~~~

Monday morning was relatively uneventful. That is if one ignored the fact that Mac and Ben were once again shielding the kids and Kate from the paparazzi.

Cherise was not happy about Ben being pulled from duty at the farm. She'd figured out that his replacement, Mark, was the second string quarterback. He did his job well, but his social skills were lacking. His conversation consisted of, "Yes, ma'am," "No, ma'am," and grunts.

At lunchtime, Skip had his gym bag in hand when a woman appeared in his office doorway, blocking his exit. It took him a second to recognize her. Her blonde hair was up in a tight bun, a big hat and enormous sunglasses completing her disguise. Said disguise would have been more effective if she hadn't been wearing a snug sundress that was bound to attract the attention of every male she encountered.

"Come on in, Cherise. What brings you here?" He prayed that Mark had brought her in the back door of the building and that no one had seen her entering the offices of Canfield and Hernandez.

"I'm going crazy, cooped up at the farm. I thought I'd take you to lunch."

"Cherise, we can't be seen in public," he pointed out patiently. "I can order sandwiches, if you like."

"I guess, but I don't understand why we can't go out. I'm *in cognito.*"

"Well, you may be able to disguise your appearance but I'm a little big to hide behind a hat and sunglasses. One look at me, and the paparazzi will figure out who you are as well."

"Sandwiches it is then." She whipped off the sunglasses and smiled up at him.

Skip turned back to his desk to call the deli down the street.

"You don't have a girl to do that for you?" Cherise asked.

Skip marveled at this woman's lack of political correctness. "We hire clerical help as needed. Most of the time, it's not needed."

Except when celebrity clients bring the paparazzi down on us.

After ordering a turkey and Swiss for himself and a veggie wrap for Cherise, he led her down the hall to the conference room. He waited until she had taken a seat, then went around the table and sat across from her.

They made small talk until Mark stuck his head in the door to announce their food had arrived. Cherise protested that it was her treat when Skip handed Mark the money to pay the delivery boy.

Skip smiled to soften his words. "Don't worry, it'll be on my next expense report." He had no intentions of pretending this was a social lunch.

"So, besides the desire for an excursion, what brings you to our humble offices?" He asked as he unwrapped his sandwich.

"Well, since the mountain wouldn't come to me." She gave him a coy look. "I figured I'd have to come to the mountain. I wanted to negotiate the terms for you to become my permanent security chief."

Skip chose his words carefully. "My partner and I may be able to continue to provide security services for you, once the stalker situation is completely resolved. Lansing refused to confess to all of the notes and other incidents, by the way. He's only admitted to sending the bracelet, and his fingerprints weren't on the outside of the knife case. He's out on bail but *our* lawyer has obtained a restraining order against him. If he comes within a hundred feet of you or the farm, he'll be arrested again, and the judge is likely to rescind bail at that point."

Rather than pleased, Cherise looked annoyed. "Well, thank you for that update. But I'm not talking about retaining your agency, Skip. I want to hire you directly, as my security chief."

"Again, I appreciate the offer but I like being self-employed. Rose and I have a thriving enterprise going here."

"But what if this bad publicity undermines that? The agency may not continue to thrive then," Cherise pointed out.

Skip shook his head as he took a bite of his sandwich. After swallowing, he said, "Nobody's pulled their business yet. As a matter of fact, we got three new clients last week." Apparently there was some truth to the concept that even bad publicity could be good. "Our clients don't give a rat's ass about what's in the tabloids. They just care whether or not we can get the job done."

"But what if some clients weren't happy with the job you did?" Cherise said, her tone a bit too innocent. "The agency might start to lose business then."

Skip had been about to take another bite of his sandwich. He put it down instead. "That sounded a little bit like a threat, Cherise, and you ought to know by now I don't take threats lightly."

"Oh, no, no, that's not what I meant at all," she backpedaled. "I'm just making the point that self-employment is not very secure, whereas I can offer long-term job security."

"Until I piss you off and you fire me." Cherise started to protest but Skip held up his hand. "Like you just did your agent and publicist, because you didn't like that they were trying to control your life. So why are you trying to control me?"

"I'm not. I'm just... I'm trying to offer you job security and more money and you call that control?" she said, sounding offended, but Skip figured it was part of her act. "I will pay you four times what you currently make. I want you for my security chief. You're the only person I trust to keep me safe."

"Don't bother to keep upping the salary. I'm married to a moderately wealthy woman so I have the luxury of saying there isn't enough money in the world to entice me to give up my independence."

"Oh, well that explains her attraction."

Skip's jaw tightened. He narrowed his eyes at her. "Did I just hear you malign my wife, Cherise?"

"I'm sorry. I didn't mean that the way it sounded. Kate's very nice and she's a reasonably attractive woman. But I had been kind of wondering why you were with her, since she's really not in your league."

"And what league would that be? The gorgeous but shallow league?" He kept his voice deceptively calm.

"Let's change the subject. I don't know how we got off on that path anyway."

"Excellent idea. Let's get back to the subject of why I'm not interested in your job offer." He let some of his anger creep into his voice. "Being self-employed gives me the option of setting limits on what I will do for and what I will tolerate *from* my clients. So here's a limit, Cherise. Don't ever say anything about my wife again, even if you mean it to be the nicest compliment imaginable. That topic of conversation is completely off limits or Canfield and Hernandez will no longer be interested in retaining you as a client."

After a beat, Cherise stood up. "I've lost my appetite," she said haughtily.

"Well, I'm sorry to hear that. Hope you're not comin' down with something," Skip rose to his feet. "Have a nice day, Cherise."

Chin in the air, she pivoted and walked out of the room in a huff. He followed her out and watched as she walked down the hall, swishing her attractive little butt at him. No doubt to remind him of what he was missing by not traveling in his appropriate league.

Skip didn't know whether to laugh at her or find something to throw at her head. He opted for going into his office and retrieving his gym bag. He now needed a workout, for multiple reasons.

~~~~~~~~~

By three-thirty, Dolph and Rose had strategically placed themselves on either end of the Hilton's lobby. They were looking for anyone who was hanging around, like they were, and seemed to be waiting for others to show up.

By four-thirty, all the traffic through the lobby had kept moving. People arrived, checked in, got on the elevator. People came off the elevator, and headed for the doors, a few stopping briefly at the desk for some reason. But nobody appeared more than once.

At five, Rose strolled past the chair where Dolph was reading one of the free newspapers provided by the hotel for its patrons. She tripped over his outstretched feet.

"Oh, sorry, mister."

"No problem, ma'am."

Rose kept going.

Dolph got the message. Rose was tired of waiting. He stood up and stretched, dropped the paper on the table next to his chair, and strolled nonchalantly over to the front desk. "You got a reservation for Robert Franklin?" he asked the young African-American desk clerk.

She clicked keys on her computer. "Sure do, sir." She flashed him a bright smile. "How would you like to pay for that, Mr. Franklin?"

"I'm not Franklin," Dolph said, showing her his private investigator's license.

"Oh, dear." Her expression became worried. "I'm not supposed to give out information regarding our guests."

"You aren't. You're giving out information regarding a reservation. Does your computer tell you who made the reservation?"

"No, sir. But I would assume it was Mr. Franklin."

"Yes, that would be the assumption, of course. Was it guaranteed with a credit card, by any chance?"

She glanced at her screen, then caught herself before she spoke. "I can't tell you that, sir."

"Okay, let me ask you this. If no one shows up to check in under that reservation by a certain hour, will it automatically be cancelled?"

She hesitated a moment. Dolph considered slipping her some money but decided that would probably offend her. She seemed quite earnest.

"Yes, sir. The computer will automatically delete the reservation at six o'clock."

Dolph resisted the urge to curse. "Thank you," he glanced at her name badge, "Natalie. You have a charming manner and a beautiful smile. You will go far in this field."

He reached over and hit the delete key on her keyboard.

Her smile shifted to a look of horror.

"Mr. Franklin asked me to cancel his reservation," Dolph said, as he turned to leave.

~~~~~~~~

Tuesday morning, Rose appeared in Skip's office doorway, papers under her arm. Skip sighed and mimicked banging his head against the desktop.

"Different rag than the others. Fly-by-night, comes out once a week," Rose said, flopping into his visitor's chair and tossing the papers on the desk. "Rehashing all the garbage by quoting the first story. So they can say they're not defaming you, just reporting what the other paper said. Doubt that'll work though. Have to ask Rob."

Skip was looking at the two pictures, side by side, at the top of the first page–one of him and Kate kissing in front of her office building and the other of Rob and Liz on his front porch. The caption slashed across the page was *Pulling the Wool Over Their Spouses' Eyes?* Next to the article immediately below those pictures was the one of Skip escorting Cherise through the crowd at Merriweather, cropped to make it look like a man holding his girlfriend by the arm.

He didn't bother to read the article, but he did zero in on the byline. It was a woman. He could guess which one.

Skip tossed the pages back to Rose. "Fax them to Fran while I call Rob," was all he said.

Rob concurred with Rose's assessment. Posing statements as questions and saying they were just quoting another paper would be a poor defense.

"File the lawsuit," Skip said.

"Are you sure you want to do that?" Rob asked.

"No, but do it anyway. I've gotta let these jackasses know they can't mess with my friends and family without suffering some consequences."

CHAPTER FOURTEEN

More bad news arrived on Wednesday morning in the biweekly sack of fan mail, forwarded from Cherise's Los Angeles condo. In it was a shoe box-sized package, wrapped in brown paper, no return address. It smelled of decaying meat.

Sarah had dropped it back into the sack without opening it and called Skip.

Skip dispatched Dolph to go out to the farm and check it out.

He called in an hour later. "Dog's head, looks like a golden retriever. Guy keeps this up we'll have the whole dog eventually. Note in a baggie, I guess to keep the blood off it. Says, 'This is what will happen to anyone who gets between us.'"

"Any prints?" Skip asked.

"Dozens outside, probably postal workers. None inside. And more bad news, son. Date and time on the little strip of postage is the morning Lansing was in jail waiting for his bail hearing."

Skip grabbed his hair and yanked. "Where was it mailed from?"

"New York City."

"Oh, ho. Now that's interesting. Ask Cherise where in New York Kirk Thompson's former penthouse is. Then check to see if it's the same zip code."

"We need to tell Howard County about this," Dolph pointed out. "Kind of blows holes in their case against Lansing."

"Yeah, tell them Cherise will be dropping all the charges except those related to the bracelet."

"Might want to drop that one, as well. Without the pattern of harassment, that's just a sick joke. She might come across as petty for pursuing it. She drops that one too and then he wouldn't have much grounds for accusing her of false arrest, since he'd already admitted to sending the bracelet."

"Let me check with Rob on that," Skip said. "Hopefully we can keep the restraining order in place, so he doesn't get any more cute ideas."

"You think this Thompson guy's the stalker?" Dolph asked.

"Might be. Get me that penthouse address, and ask her if she has any current contact info for him."

"Will do. Then I'll take the package and note to Robinson. Fido's head can be reunited with his heart in the Howard County evidence freezer."

"Robinson isn't going to be happy you didn't call him to come out there."

"Cherise freaked out when I suggested calling the police," Dolph said. "She's paranoid someone will spill the beans to the press about the location of the farm."

"She's got a point. Too many people find out about it, it's gonna leak out eventually."

Rose walked into Skip's office as he was hanging up the phone. She raised an eyebrow at his grim expression.

"What? No tabloid article to top off my morning?" he said.

"Not today. Maybe the assholes are finally losing interest."

Skip filled her in on the dog's head and all its implications.

"Thompson looks like a good suspect," Rose said. "Mild to moderate set-back in my book. Why are you looking so unhappy, partner?"

"Because I was hoping to get shuck of this woman soon. But we can't abandon her as a client while she's still being stalked. Word gets out we did that and our reputation wouldn't be worth shit. And she'll make sure that the word gets out. She as much as threatened just that on Monday."

"You want me to take over the case?" Rose said, her tone conveying her reluctance.

Skip's chest warmed. He smiled at his partner. "No, but thanks for offering. I already told her I can't come out to the farm because I might lead the press to her, and Mark now has orders not to bring her here. I can just deal with her over the phone, and send you or Dolph out there as needed, if that's okay?"

"Sure, partner. Anything you need me to do at the moment?"

"Dolph's getting that address in New York. How would you feel about a road trip? I'm not real comfortable leaving Kate and the kids right now, with the paparazzi still hanging around."

"Think I'll need my jammies?"

"Wouldn't hurt, in case you need to stay over."

"Okay, I'm going to check to see if Thompson's got a record. Then I'll head home and pack. Have Dolph call me when he has the info."

~~~~

Thompson didn't have a record *per se* but he had been arrested twice in New York for drunk and disorderly and possession of small amounts of drugs. The charges were later dropped and his prints weren't in the national database.

Rose figured he probably had connections. She called Robinson in Howard County to suggest he request Thompson's fingerprints from NYPD and check them against those on the knife from the gory bouquet.

She stuck her head in her partner's door. He was on the phone.

"Hold on, Rob," Skip said.

Rose gave him a quick update before heading home to collect her jammies.

~~~~~~~~

Kate and Rob had decided to have their weekly lunch in the Franklins' kitchen since being seen in public together was probably not a good idea at the moment.

Worry tightened Rob's stomach when he answered his door. Kate looked like hell. Her fair skin was way too pale, and she had dark circles under her eyes, which were the gray they became when she was worried or stressed.

"Sorry I'm a little late. Ben circled the block around my office building several times to make sure we weren't being followed before heading here. So what's on the menu?"

Rob led the way to the kitchen, saying over his shoulder, "Liz made us some chicken salad this morning, before she left for work."

"Yum. I love her chicken salad."

"Sit down. I'll make the sandwiches. You look exhausted."

"That's because I am. Haven't been sleeping well. All this stuff with Cherise and the press." She settled into a chair at the kitchen table. "We think we've got the situation resolved and then something else happens. Skip and I had a major fight last week. Worst one we've ever had. Woke up the kids, scared them to death."

"What was the fight about?" Rob asked as he put a plate in front of her. He walked to the fridge for a pitcher of iced tea.

"The article about you and me. I found out about it from Cherise, when she came in for a session that afternoon. Totally threw me. I was so pissed at him that he didn't call and tell me. He'd already had that press conference with you, but I wouldn't stop yelling long enough for him to tell me that. I felt so bad when I found out he really had tried to fix the mess." Kate took a small bite of her sandwich, then shook her head. "The mess just won't stay fixed."

Rob brought over the glasses of iced tea, then took his seat at the table. He patted her hand, decided that was insufficient and leaned over to peck her on the cheek, before picking up his sandwich. They ate in silence for a couple minutes.

He took a sip of his tea. "Now they're back to square one, almost, although it sounds like they've got a good suspect for the stalker."

Kate looked at him in confusion. "What are you talking about?"

"Uh, there was a new development this morning." He'd only gotten halfway through telling her about the macabre package and the implications of the date it was mailed when Kate jumped up and started pacing around the kitchen.

"Damn it to hell. He did it again. Something happens that affects me and he doesn't even pick up the phone."

"Kate, calm down. He's had a busy morning, and how does this affect you anyway?"

She dropped back into her chair. "Because... this case keeps affecting our family. He gets yanked away from home at all hours. The paparazzi are hounding us. We thought the case was almost wrapped up. He was just waiting for Lansing's conviction, then he was going to turn the routine security at Cherise's farm over to Rose."

"So the only way this affects you is because the case is still alive," Rob said. "Not exactly in the same category as our supposed affair making the front page."

"Oh, stop being the logical lawyer when I'm trying to–"

"Be illogical?"

Kate glared at him.

He held up his hands. "Hey, I'm just trying to look out for my buddy here, when the man's not around to stand up for himself."

"I thought you were *my* friend."

"I am, but us men have to stick together when our women start getting irrational on us." Unfortunately, Kate was too worked up to hear his teasing tone.

"Irrational?" She started to rise from her chair again.

Rob put a big hand on each shoulder and gently nudged her back down. "Calm down, sweetheart. The man is just doing his job, trying his damnedest to make this case go away. You really expect him to stop every ten minutes and call you with an update?"

Kate deflated. "No, you're right. I am being irrational. But that's the problem, this whole situation is making me crazy."

Rob nudged her plate. She picked up her sandwich and took another bite.

"You know what you guys need?" he said. "A vacation, just the two of you, when the dust finally settles from this damned case. Liz and I will help Maria with the kids."

"Wow! What a great idea. I've always wanted to go on a cruise. That would be ideal. Get him out in the middle of the ocean where the damn cell phones won't work."

She glanced at the calendar hanging on the kitchen wall next to the fridge. "And I know just the occasion, coming up in a few weeks."

Rob's brow furrowed. "That may be a little soon. Case might not be resolved by then."

"True, but I can buy the tickets, for September maybe, and give them to him next month."

"What's the special occasion? I thought his birthday was in the spring," Rob said.

"It is. July twenty-first is the anniversary of our first kiss."

"You remember the exact date of your first kiss?" After two and a half decades of marriage, Rob wasn't sure what season it had been when he and Liz started dating, much less the date of their first kiss.

"It kind of stood out, since I wouldn't let him touch me again for five months, while I was still grieving for Eddie."

He chuckled. "Yeah, I can see where only one kiss per five months might help one remember the date."

"So where should we go?"

"Don't want to be in the Caribbean in September. Height of hurricane season," he pointed out.

Kate spent the rest of the next half hour happily bouncing ideas off of him about where and when she and Skip should take their cruise.

"Hmm..." She tapped her lips with her fingers. "I've gotta stop at the grocery store on the way home tonight. I think I'll swing by the travel agency next door and get some brochures."

~~~~~~~~~

"Kate's not home yet?" Skip asked Maria as he walked into the kitchen.

"No. She say she run errands on way home today."

"Where'd the flowers come from?" There were a dozen red roses in a vase in the middle of the kitchen table.

Maria turned from the sink. "You no send?"

"No." He plucked the card from its holder. It was blank. "What the hell?"

"Skip, little pitchers have de big ears." Maria tilted her head toward Billy playing on the kitchen floor.

"Whada hell," Billy dutifully mimicked.

"Billy, that's a big person word. It's not appropriate for a child to say," Skip admonished gently.

The boy gave him an annoyed look, then went back to stacking his blocks in a wobbly tower.

"How did these get here?" Skip asked Maria.

"Man come to door, wit' de letters on hiz hat, FDT."

FTD. So they were from a legitimate florist. He looked down at the card again.

Well, duh.

There was the florist's name, address and telephone number in small print across the bottom. He picked up the phone and dialed the number.

The lady who answered reluctantly described the gentleman who had ordered the roses to be delivered to 2610 Linden Lane. "Big guy, dark hair, some gray in it."

"How did he pay?"

"Cash."

That was no help. He thanked her and hung up.

Skip sat down at the table and rubbed his hand over his face. What did this mean? Niggling doubts gnawed at his stomach.

He thought about calling Kate, but decided to touch base with Ben first.

"She's been running all over town, but I think this is the last stop." Ben had an indulgent chuckle in his voice. "We're in the grocery store. Hey, I got some good news for you. No sign of any paparazzi today, and I triple-checked before taking her over to Rob's for lunch."

"Rob's office?"

"No. His house."

"Did you go inside with her?"

"No. I stayed out front, just in case some asshole showed up with a camera."

"What's your ETA?"

"Soon, I think. She's barreling down the aisle ahead of me, heading for the cashiers." Ben was chuckling again as he disconnected.

Skip stared at the roses. "What time did these come?" he asked Maria.

She paused in her dinner preparations. "Bout tree o'clock," she said after a moment of thought.

Three. Right timing for a thank you gift after a noon rendezvous. Stop off at the florist's on the way back to the office.

What the hell was he thinking? Kate wouldn't cheat on him. His heart ached in his chest at the mere possibility.

Obviously someone was trying to get him to consider that possibility. The question was who, and why?

He went into the study. He wanted to examine the wording again on that bogus love letter, see if it would give him any clues as to who might have sent it.

The letter wasn't on his desk.

Skip looked on Kate's desk, the book shelves, the top of the file cabinet. The letter was gone.

Now, what the hell does that mean? Did she throw it away?

He shook his head in confusion, trying to ignore the brick of dread now lying in his gut.

Once the kids are in bed, we'll have to try to figure out what all this means.

Skip sat down at his desk and booted up the family computer to check their e-mail. He logged onto KateNSkip2007 at yahoo.com. Hmm, still no reply from his college friend. They'd been back and forth trying to set up a time to get together while Dave would be in D.C. next month on business.

Maybe his last message hadn't gotten through. He went into Sent Mail to find it and forward it again. Scrolling down the list of messages, he suddenly stopped, his heart gone cold in his chest.

There was a message sent to MrLawyer123 at gmail—subject line: *Hey Lover*.

He clicked on the message.

Hi, I miss you so much. Can't wait until tomorrow. Love, Kate.

Skip checked the date. It had been sent yesterday at five-fifteen. He hadn't gotten home until almost six.

He sat back in his chair, unable for a moment to even process what this could mean. This couldn't be what it looked like. It just couldn't. For one thing, Kate wouldn't be so stupid as to leave the message in the Sent Mail list. But maybe she'd just forgotten to go back in and delete it.

What am I thinking? Kate's not cheating on me.

He printed out the message, then folded the sheet of paper and put it in his pocket. He couldn't think straight. "Damn it, you're an investigator," he muttered to himself.

What was the best way to investigate this?

After another moment of hesitation, he clicked on Compose Mail and typed: *Dear heart, I had a wonderful time today. And Skip doesn't suspect a thing. All my love, Kate.* After adding the MrLawyer123 address, he moved the cursor to the Send button.

His finger hovered for a few seconds before clicking the mouse key.

He rose and went into the kitchen. "Go ahead and feed the children," he told Maria. "When Kate comes home, she and I need to talk about something." He carried the vase of roses into their bedroom and put it on her dresser.

By the time he returned to the study, there was a new message in the e-mail inbox from MrLawyer123. It just said *Same goes for me. I'll call you tomorrow. Rob.* The text of Skip's outgoing message had been deleted from the reply. This message, by itself, looked totally innocent.

So then why would Rob be so indiscreet as to send flowers?

He printed out the message he had sent and the reply. Those sheets joined the first one in his pocket.

How the hell was he going to approach all this with Kate?

CHAPTER FIFTEEN

Skip met Kate as she came through the front door, arms full of groceries. She smiled at him. "Here, before I drop something." She thrust a bag at him.

Without speaking, he followed her to her car.

Ben was lifting a bag from the trunk.

Skip took it from him. "Thanks, Ben. You can go home now."

Ben nodded and sketched a wave at Kate.

Skip helped her bring in the rest of the groceries. Sitting the last of the bags on the counter, he said, "Maria will put the stuff away. She's gonna feed the kids. We need to talk." He headed down the hall.

"What's going on?" Kate asked, her voice anxious. She followed him to the bedroom.

He closed the door behind her. Jaw clenched, he silently pointed to the roses.

"Oh, sweetheart, they're lovely." Her face lit up. "You scoundrel. You had me going there. I thought you were pissed at me for something."

"They're not from me," he said in a low, even voice, handing her the small white card.

She examined the blank sides. "What the hell?"

"Funny, those were my exact words," he said, his voice grim.

"What the devil does this mean?" Confusion and worry were etched on Kate's face.

Skip gave a small shake of his head as his only answer. After a beat, he asked, "Have you seen the letter? It's missing."

"What letter?"

"The letter. It was on my desk, now it's gone. Do you know where it is?"

"I have no clue what you're talking about."

"The love note from... that came on Saturday?"

Kate stared at him for several beats. "I haven't seen that letter since Saturday afternoon. I have no idea where it might be."

She seemed genuinely confused and Skip could tell she was starting to get pissed at his interrogation. He ran his fingers through his hair, stared at the ceiling for a moment and blew out his breath.

He took the papers out of his pocket and handed them to her one at a time, waiting for her to read each one. When she'd finished the last one, she looked up at him. "Where did these come from?"

"First one was in our Sent Mail box, sent out yesterday afternoon. Second one I sent to that address, to see what would happen. Third one was the reply that came back within minutes." He kept his voice as neutral as he could get it, waiting for her reaction.

Kate sat down on the side of the bed and read the three messages again. "This is totally insane," she finally said. "How did this first one get into our e-mail account?"

"Good question." This time, he wasn't able to keep all of the anger out of his voice.

"You don't honestly think that Rob and I are having an affair?" Her tone was incredulous.

"I don't honestly know what to think. On the one hand, the roses are pretty darn indiscreet, and Rob's not a stupid man. But as you say, how'd that message get into our e-mail outbox?"

"What the hell are you talking about, Skip? Rob wouldn't send me flowers."

"I called the florist shop. Guy who ordered them matches Rob's description." Skip jammed his hands in his pockets and stared at the ceiling again for a moment, desperately seeking some logical explanation that didn't include his wife being unfaithful.

"I don't know. Maybe Rob's playing some kind of game," he finally said. "He's fifty-one, after all. He could be having some kind of crisis. Maybe his feelings toward you have changed?"

Kate just stared at him. She opened her mouth and closed it again.

After several seconds, he added, "Kate, I'm an investigator. I've been trained to keep my mind open to all possibilities."

She stood up. Her eyes narrowed, she planted her hands on her hips. "Damn it, Skip, it sounds like your mind's so frickin' open, your brain has fallen out. We are not having an affair."

He made a calm-down gesture with his hands. "Keep your voice down. The kids'll hear you. I'm not saying you're having an affair. I'm suggesting the possibility that something is going on with Rob."

"Skip, *I* happen to be a *trained* therapist. If there's one thing I'm good at, it's picking up on people's feelings. I would know if something was going on with Rob. He and I are as close as two people can be."

Her last words stung. "Closer than you and me?" he blurted out.

The hands on her hips were now fisted. Not a good sign. Through gritted teeth, she said, "Are we talking about how close we are right now, or how close we normally are?"

"Kate, please... I'm just trying to figure out what all this means." He waved his arm in the direction of the roses.

"I have no clue what all this means, other than someone's trying to stir things up."

"That's what I'm afraid Rob might be trying to do." He started talking fast to get the words out before she could interrupt. "Maybe his feelings for you have changed and he's trying to break us up."

"You are truly out of your mind, Skip Canfield!" Her voice rose in anger. "For the last time, Rob did not send those flowers."

"Then who the hell did?" he snapped. "And keep your damned voice down."

Kate marched over to her dresser and swept the vase off onto the floor with her forearm. She stomped the flowers into the soggy carpet. "I. Do. Not. Know. Who. Sent. These." She turned and glared at him. "But it sure as hell wasn't Rob. And there's no way he had anything to do with those e-mails. He can just barely operate a cell phone."

He'd never seen her quite this furious, at least not at him. He knew he should stop, declare that he trusted her. There had to be some logical explanation for all this.

But the irrational fear twisting in his gut took over his brain. "Ben said you went to Rob's house today."

She stared at him again, not responding to the implied question. Instead she walked to the end of her dresser, where she had dropped her purse. She pulled a colorful brochure out of it, turned toward him and slowly, methodically, tore it into tiny little pieces.

Skip thought he might throw up. He had no idea what that brochure was, but he had a real bad feeling she was wishing it was their marriage license.

"We went to his house to eat *lunch*, Skip." Sadness now mixed with the anger in her voice as she looked down at the mess at her feet. "Since we can't go out in public right now. We ate the chicken salad Liz, his *trusting* wife, had made for us."

She looked across the room at him, her voice now flat, defeated. "And we talked, about you. He defended you, called you his buddy. Told me I should get off your back, that you were trying your damnedest to make this case go away." She sank down in the middle of the mutilated flowers and the confetti. Crossing her arms on her knees, she buried her face.

Talons of fear ripped at his heart. What had he done?

He crossed the room and sat on the wet carpet. He tried to gather her onto his lap. She tensed and resisted. He wrapped his arms around her anyway and pulled her against him. "Please forgive me, Kate." He choked on the lump in his throat, swallowed hard to dislodge it. "I don't know what got into me. I'm sorry. I love you! Please..." He trailed off.

She sat rigid as the seconds ticked by. He lowered his face into her dark curls and tried not to cry. The flowery scent of her shampoo almost defeated him.

Finally she turned sideways in his arms and rested her cheek against his chest. Her arms slid under his to wrap around his broad back.

Silently, they held each other.

Skip's racing heart slowed some, but his chest still ached with the hurt he'd caused her, and from fear that he'd done irreparable harm.

"I'll make this stop," he whispered. "I'll make it go away."

"How?" she asked, in that same defeated voice. "What can you do, Skip? We don't even know who's doing this."

He didn't know how to answer her. What *could* he do?

He could tell Cherise he quit, and then watch the agency he and Rose had built up be destroyed by the bad press the woman would make sure they received. And that wouldn't necessarily stop whoever was trying to convince him that Kate and Rob were having an affair.

Who could be doing that? Most likely one of the damned reporters, stirring the pot. So what could he do? Go to the offices of each of the tabloids that had run stories about them, find the reporters and pound them into the dirt.

It would be very satisfying for a few minutes, but he'd end up in jail for assault, with no PI license when he got out.

A timid knock on the door, about three feet from the ground.

Skip gently disentangled himself from Kate and stood to go to the door.

Edie's eyes were wide, her face solemn. "Maria said not to 'sturb you, Daddy, but I wanted to show you my picture."

She handed him a sheet of paper, purple crayon scribbles on one side that vaguely resembled a four-legged animal. Typed words were on the other side, a few smudges of fingerprint dust along the edges.

Edie looked up into his face and added anxiously, "I din't have no more paper. It was on the floor in the study."

Skip turned away from his daughter so she wouldn't see his expression. Kate was behind him.

She nudged him aside and crouched down in front of the little girl. "It's okay, sweetie," she said gently. "It's a lovely picture. May we keep it?"

A beat of silence. Despite the chaos of emotions inside of him, Skip had the presence of mind not to turn around. The little girl would think he was upset with her.

"Tell you what," Kate said, "we're going to skip baths tonight. Can you take your brother upstairs and help him get into his PJ's?"

"Maria already took him up."

"Okay, then you go get into your pajamas and Daddy or I will be up in a few minutes for story time, okay?"

Rustling as Kate hugged their daughter.

A half-stifled sob escaped Skip's throat. He staggered toward the bed.

"Go on up, sweetie," his wife said behind him. "I'll be along in a minute."

~~~~

Kate turned her daughter around and gently pushed her toward the stairs. Then she stood and closed the door. She took a deep breath and blew it out.

Skip was sitting on the edge of the bed, his face in his hands.

She sat down beside him, wrapped her arms around his shoulders. "It's okay, sweetheart," she said softly.

He shook his head, without looking up. "No, it's not okay," he choked out. "The missing note was what started to tip me over the edge. I thought you or Rob had taken it, destroyed it."

He turned toward her, grabbing for her hands. "How could I think that? How could I not trust you?"

"Because you're human, and whoever is doing this is *trying* to make you not trust me." She stared into her husband's red-rimmed eyes. "Honestly, Skip, if I'd found an e-mail like that, and then had gotten a reply to one I sent out, I probably would have doubted *you*. The other stuff, the letter and the roses, no, they wouldn't have done it, but the e-mails. That's pretty damning evidence somebody's planted."

"How did they do that, get that e-mail into our sent mail?"

"I don't know, but I'll bet Liz can figure it out," Kate said.

"Dear God, please don't tell them I got jealous, that I thought, even for a minute, you and Rob could be having an affair."

"Of course not. I tell Rob a lot, almost everything that's going on with me. But there are some things that are just between you and me, and this is certainly one of them."

He stared into her eyes, his jaw tight. "I'm sorry, Kate," he said again in a choked voice.

"It's okay." She wrapped her arms around him. "I love you." Laying her cheek against his chest, she looked down at his hands, clenched in fists on his thighs.

She felt him kiss the top of her head, then he whispered, "I love you, too."

There was an undercurrent of anxiety in his voice. Not sure what it was about, she straightened up to look at him. "Skip, I would never, ever have an affair, and especially not with Rob. Can you imagine sleeping with your sister?"

"No. Ick." He shuddered slightly.

"Exactly. I love Rob dearly. Almost as much as I love you, but in a very different way. Having sex... No, I can't even say *that* out loud. Sleeping with Rob would be like sleeping with one of my brothers." She shuddered this time. "Not gonna happen."

His lips twitched–she was pretty sure he was trying to smile–but his mouth twisted into a half grimace instead. "You'd better go do story time before the kids come looking for us."

She kissed him on the cheek, then stood up. "You just sit here and rest up, Mr. Canfield, 'cause you owe me some *really* good make-up sex tonight."

This time his grin materialized, although it was a bit lopsided.

"Hold that thought," she said and headed for the door.

She told the children Daddy wasn't feeling well this evening and had asked her to kiss them goodnight for him. After their stories, she hugged each child a little longer than usual, praying that God would help her family get through this mess soon.

Billy had squirmed after a few seconds, but Edie clung to her mother. "Is Daddy gonna be okay, Mommy?" she asked in a small voice.

"Yes, Precious. He's gonna be fine." Kate stroked the dark curls off the little girl's forehead. Then she kissed that forehead and said, in a deep voice, "Goodnight, Pumkin."

Edie's normal cheerful smile replaced the solemn look that the child had been wearing all too often lately.

Kate breathed an internal sigh of relief.

When she returned to the master bedroom, Skip was pacing back and forth next to his side of the bed, fists clenched, his face grim. She knew he was desperately trying to figure out how to stop this craziness that had invaded their lives. She felt her own surge of anger at the paparazzi who seemed to think she and her family were fair game.

Unable to think of anything to say to calm him down, she went into the bathroom to wash her face and brush her teeth.

When she came out, Skip had kicked off his shoes and was stretched out on top of the comforter, still fully clothed, his eyes staring sightlessly at the ceiling.

She walked around the bed to his side and sat down on the edge. He looked up at her and gave her a small smile, but behind the love in his eyes was sadness, and something else.

It took her a moment to recognize it. Worry. He was afraid he'd stepped over a line, broken trust with her in a way they wouldn't be able to repair.

She picked up one of his hands and stroked the back of it. She had discovered that big men's hands were not all the same. Rob's were thick meaty paws that enveloped her own when he took one of them to reassure or comfort her. Skip's were long and surprisingly slender.

Usually she let those agile hands make sweet love to her. Tonight she reversed roles. She straddled his hips and pinned his hands with her own on either side of his head. Leaning down, she kissed him feather-light on his lips, then slowly deepened the kiss.

After several moments, she reluctantly came up for air. Letting go of his hands, she began to undress him, trailing tiny kisses down his chest as she unbuttoned and pushed aside his shirt. He closed his eyes and moaned.

Once he tried to pull her down and roll her over. She resisted.

She stood up just long enough to shed her own slacks, then pinned him beneath her again as she shrugged out of the rest of her clothes. Then she continued the slow delicious torture as she relieved him of his jeans.

~~~~

The tangle of emotions was driven out of his mind by his body's response to her feather-light touches. Her kisses trailed fire over his skin. He couldn't think, couldn't feel anything but an all-consuming love for this woman.

Their eyes locked on each other's.

He gasped as she slowly guided him into her.

He wrapped his arms around her. This time she allowed him to pull her down against his chest. He buried his face in her hair, breathed in the scent of her.

For a long time there was only the slow movement, the exquisite sensations, the sense of melting together. She moaned and quivered in his arms, tightening around him.

He held her closer, moving faster, his back arching of its own volition. She shuddered above him, around him.

A burst of sensation so sweet it bordered on unbearable surged through him. She shuddered again, more vehemently. He heard the sound he loved most escape her throat, a cross between a moan and a sigh.

If only he could hold onto this moment forever.

They lay still for a long time, her chest heaving against his.

Holding her tight–not wanting to lose the connection–he rolled them over. He lifted his weight off of her, locked his elbows and gazed down into her eyes. They were a smoky indigo from passion.

"Promise me," he whispered, "that you'll never leave me."

"I already did." Her voice was gentle. She ran her fingers through his hair. "Til death do us part, remember? I'll never leave you." She pulled his head down to touch her lips to his.

When they surfaced from the kiss, Kate looked up at him with drowsy eyes. "We really should get some sleep."

He kissed her forehead, then rolled onto his side and snuggled her up against him. She threw an arm across his chest.

He gently stroked that arm until her breathing slowed.

I'll never leave you.

He knew she meant those words. She would never, of her own will, leave him.

A shiver of premonition raised the hairs on his neck.

There are other ways to lose her.

CHAPTER SIXTEEN

Kate got up before dawn so they could call the Franklins. Liz and Rob were early risers. She knew it would be best to call well before seven-thirty, the time when they started getting ready for work.

She put a cup of coffee on Skip's nightstand and nudged him. He groaned.

She picked up the receiver for the bedroom phone and tried to put it in his limp hand. "We're gonna have a conference call, sweetheart."

He opened one eye and looked up at her, standing next to the bed in her bathrobe. "What time is it?" he mumbled.

"Not quite six-thirty."

"Is the sun up?"

"Just barely."

She knew the moment when the memory of the previous evening came flooding back. His eyes filled with pain. "Kate, I–"

"Shh." She put her fingertips against his lips. "It's okay."

He grabbed her arm and pulled her down on top of him, fiercely sought her mouth. Pushing aside her robe, his hands were hot against bare skin.

She broke the kiss. "Sweetheart, please," she gasped. "We need to call Rob and Liz before it gets too late."

He let her go reluctantly. She stood up. To be on the safe side, she took a step back from the bed as she rearranged her robe. "It really is okay. We're okay."

He swung his legs out of bed, sitting up. She took his hand, gave it a squeeze, then put the phone receiver in it.

"I'll be on the kitchen extension," she said.

~~~~

The phone beeped in Skip's ear as Kate punched in the Franklins' number on the portable in the kitchen.

Liz's voice boomed. "Hey, Kate, what are you up to this early in the morning?"

"We had a development here last night," Kate said.

"You want to talk to Rob?"

"Yes, but you stay on the line too, Liz. Skip's on the bedroom phone."

The clatter of Rob picking up an extension.

As Kate succinctly told them about the flowers and the e-mails, Skip felt his face flush. Guilt weighed down his limbs. He almost missed Liz's response.

"It's not that hard to get into people's e-mail accounts," the computer whiz was saying. "It's Hacking 101. Once in, it's a piece of cake to send a bogus outgoing e-mail."

"But I can't understand how whoever is doing this could be monitoring the account so closely," Kate said. "They wouldn't know when the sent message would be discovered. How could they reply so quickly when Skip sent the test message?"

Liz snorted. "If they've got a smart phone they can stay logged into their e-mail. They'd hear a beep whenever a new message came in. Day or night, they could respond within seconds."

Skip spoke for the first time. "Crap, I should've figured that out." His voice was gravelly.

"Good morning, Mr. Canfield," Liz said in a teasing tone.

"Humph."

"Obviously Skip is not a morning person," Rob commented good-naturedly.

"This is not morning. This is the middle of the freakin' night." Skip's tone was grumpy, but he was secretly glad to be joking with the Franklins.

"So the question is who is doing this and why?" Liz brought them back to task.

There was silence on the line as they all thought about that. "The most obvious answer," Rob finally said, "is that one of the paparazzi is trying to keep the story alive. But these seem like extreme measures. The first letters maybe, to try to get Kate and me to show up at that hotel, but this is a bit much, even for them."

"I don't know," Kate said. "A reporter might not send the roses themselves but an editor might suggest it and foot the bill, hoping to get something juicy out of it. These are not mainstream journalists. They play fast and loose with the rules. But the e-mails seem kind of over the top."

"Maybe the editor suggested the roses," Liz said, "and an overzealous reporter thought of the e-mails, figuring the two together would be sure to do the trick."

And they almost did.

Ignoring the heat creeping up his cheeks, Skip cleared his throat. "It kind of feels like two different people. The roses are way too obvious. The e-mail much more subtle. It, by itself, would have actually been more convincing."

"Maybe the roses were designed to make you go looking for evidence in our e-mail?" Kate suggested.

"Could be," Liz said.

"Okay, so the paparazzi might be behind this, but it's a bit of a stretch just to stir up a story," Rob said. "Anybody else come to mind?"

Silence again. The name that popped into Skip's head made his body tense. "Jim Bolton," he ground out through gritted teeth.

"Who's that?" Liz asked.

"Cherise's publicist. The man has the ethics of a toad." Hot anger surged through him, tightening his chest, his fists, his jaw. He preferred it to the guilt. "Bolton's had no problem so far with hanging me and my family out in the wind, if it means publicity for Cherise."

"I thought she fired him," Kate said.

"She said she did, but now I'm wondering if she just told me that to appease me."

"Could it be her?" Kate asked.

Skip considered that possibility. "Maybe," he finally said. "But it doesn't feel like her style. She's so convinced she's hot stuff, if she really wanted me, she'd assume she could win me away from you."

"She's come on to you?" Rob asked.

"Yeah, but it has a force-of-habit feel to it. She flirts a little, and she gets pretty clingy when she's scared. I don't think she's turning on her full charm, though. I can usually tell when a woman's seriously interested in me. But there is something else going on. She's been trying to get me to sign on as her employee, to be her full-time security chief."

"As in, ditch the agency?" Kate asked, surprise in her voice.

"Yeah, and she's been kind of manipulative about it."

"I can't imagine how putting a wedge between you and Kate would help that cause," Rob said.

"I can't either, but she's got this thing about I'm the only one she feels safe with."

"I can't see a connection there either," Liz said.

"And she's not all that subtle," Skip added. "She believes she can get anything she wants with either money or her womanly charms."

He thought he detected a soft snort of agreement from Kate.

"So we've got the paparazzi, or maybe Jim Bolton," Rob said. "Anybody else come to mind?"

"You got any enemies, hon," Liz said in a teasing tone, "who might want to commit murder by proxy by getting Skip to come after you?"

Rob chuckled. "That would be a pretty convoluted way to get to me."

Skip's mind jumped back to Bolton. His hand clenched around the phone receiver. "I think I'll be giving ole Jimbo a call."

"*I'll* call him," Rob said. "He may be more willing to talk to me and if it does sound like he's the culprit, I can threaten the appropriate legal actions if he doesn't cease and desist."

When Skip didn't answer, Kate said, "Let him do it, sweetheart. You're too close to it."

"Can you get his number from Cherise?" Rob asked.

"No," Liz jumped in. "Might not be a good idea to bring her into this. I'll find his number for you. He's probably got a website."

"Thanks, guys, for doing this," Skip said, with heartfelt sincerity.

"No, thanks necessary. That's what friends are for," Liz said.

"And besides, Skip, this affects me too," Rob said, an edge to his voice. "I don't like it one bit that someone is using my friendship with your wife to try to come between you two."

Shame heated his cheeks again. He was very glad Rob couldn't see his face.

~~~~~~~~~

A week went by with no further excitement, but Skip couldn't relax. Had the paparazzi lost interest that readily?

Rob had reported back that after leaving several messages, the last of which was a bit menacing, he'd managed to get Jim Bolton on the phone. The man had acknowledged he was Cherise Martin's publicist and had reacted with confusion when Rob mentioned Cherise had said she'd fired him.

As Skip had suspected, she'd lied about that.

Bolton had denied to Rob that he'd had anything to do with the letters, flowers or e-mails. Nonetheless, Rob ended the conversation with the threat that any further misrepresentation of Mr. Canfield's role in Ms. Martin's life would result in legal consequences.

The operatives of Canfield and Hernandez strongly suspected Kirk Thompson was Cherise's stalker, but they couldn't prove it. There had been a match between his prints and some of those on the knife from the bouquet, but the presence of other people's prints, including Lansing's and Cherise's own, weakened the value of that evidence. Any halfway decent defense attorney could make the case that the knife had been handled on several occasions, hadn't been used and had been put back away without being washed.

Rose had discovered Thompson was still hanging around his old neighborhood in New York, sponging off friends and acquaintances for a few nights' lodging at a time. But she hadn't been able to catch up with him.

She'd found posters, attached to lamp posts and in store windows in the area, offering a reward for a lost golden retriever. "I opted not to call the number on them," she'd told Skip. "Better to be left wondering than to know the gruesome fate their Fido met."

Cherise hadn't received any more gory packages or anonymous notes. Perhaps Thompson had assumed Skip's comments–that the stalker had been identified and would be prosecuted–were aimed at him. So the dog head, mailed the morning of the day they had held the press conference, had been his last missive.

Hoping they had indeed scared Thompson off for good, Skip decided it was time to officially hand over the Martin account to Rose. He drove out to Howard County–taking the precaution to check for tails before leaving Towson–to inform Cherise that his partner would be handling her security needs from now on.

Cherise greeted him with pleasure, until he told her his reason for coming. For ten minutes, she alternated between clinging and ranting–he was the only one she could trust, how could he abandon her like this. He finally got her calmed down enough to listen to reason.

"Cherise, the tabloids have moved on to fresher prey, but if we're seen together in public again, they'll be right back on our scent. And the risk is too great that they will eventually follow me here. This farm, your sanctuary, is too damned important to risk that. I cannot be directly involved with your account on a regular basis. But it is *Canfield* and Hernandez. I'm not moving to Mars. I'll be around if needed."

On the drive out, Skip had decided not to mention the repercussions to his family should the rumors that he was Cherise's lover resurface. She wouldn't give a damn about that.

But he'd vowed to himself that his daughter would never again have that solemn, wide-eyed look on her face. Nor did he ever want to be responsible for that defeated tone in Kate's voice ever again.

"Rose handles the assignment of personnel anyway. It just makes sense that she handle your routine security needs."

"She's not going to make a pass at me, is she?" Cherise said.

"Say what?" Skip stared at her for several seconds. "Rose is not a lesbian, Cherise."

"Are you sure? She's so manly."

Skip's jaw tightened, but he reined in his temper. "Rose is tough. That's why she's my partner. But the ex-Green Beret, the *male* ex-Green Beret she's been living with for the past three years is even tougher." He opted not to point out that she'd met Mac Reilly, that Rose's tough-guy domestic partner was none other than the scraggly looking dude who'd been amongst her bodyguards the night of the concert.

Cherise just made a little moue with her mouth. "You'll get involved again, if something else happens?"

"Correct," Skip said, trying to muster a genuine-looking smile. He stood up.

Cherise jumped up and threw her arms around him. "I'm going to miss you." He put his hands on her shoulders and gently held her away from him.

"I'm not going anywhere. Rose and I confer on cases every day. I'll be monitoring how things are going."

He tried not to let the relief show in his face when Sarah entered the room. "I was just telling Cherise," he said to the PA, "that Rose will be handling the routine security now that the stalker has apparently been scared off."

"Yes, that's such a relief. No more doggie parts in the mail sack." Sarah shuddered.

Skip let go of Cherise's shoulders and backed toward the door. The PA maneuvered herself between him and her boss, so he could make his escape.

~~~~~~~~~

Another week of tranquility went by, punctuated only by the normal dramas of two-year-old temper tantrums, a three a.m. emergency call from one of Kate's clients and the news that Mark had gotten a better job offer.

Since there'd been no paparazzi in two weeks, Rose had reassigned Ben as Cherise's main bodyguard.

At the dinner table on Thursday, Skip pulled out his vibrating cell phone, scowled at the caller ID, then put the phone back in his pocket. "So how was your day, Pumkin?" he asked Edie as he picked up his fork.

Halfway through her description of her first riding lesson, Skip's pocket vibrated again. He ignored it.

Two minutes later the house phone rang. Kate went to the counter to retrieve the portable and handed it to Skip without answering it.

"Sorry, Edie. Daddy's gotta take this," he said to his daughter, then barked into the phone, "Canfield."

"She got another letter," Rose said without preamble.

Skip caught himself just in time. He'd almost said a big-person word in front of the little people. "It's Rose," he told Kate, and got up to walk into the living room.

Once there he asked, "What's it say?"

"Says, 'Nobody's ever going to love you the way I do. What do I have to do to get you to give me a chance?' Came in the fan mail, postmarked in L.A."

"Hmm, different tone than the recent ones, more like the earlier notes."

"Yeah. Maybe Thompson got scared off from making threats, but he can't resist sending her love notes."

"What's he doing in L.A.?" Skip wondered.

"Mooching off more of his druggie buddies maybe, or he got someone to re-post it," Rose replied. "Ben said the stationary's not the fancy stuff, like the other notes. Just plain paper."

"He may have run out of the fancy stuff."

"Cherise is demanding you come to the farm, but I'm recommending against it."

"How hysterical is she?"

"On a scale of one to ten about a six point five."

"You willing to go out there?"

"I'm in my car, already on my way. It is my case now," Rose said. "One of us needs to go to New York to try again to track down Thompson. I was gonna tell her you were so concerned that you headed right up there tonight, while I came out to get the note and make sure the guards were on their toes."

"I've got a meeting in the morning with a potential new client," Skip said.

"I wasn't suggesting you actually go to New York. I'll do that tomorrow."

"You're going to lie to the client?" Skip asked, somewhat surprised. Rose was normally a bit of a stickler about honesty, although she had come to understand the necessity of an occasional white lie in the performance of a PI's duties.

"To this client, yeah. We don't need the paparazzi stirred up again. I've got a general idea of where to start looking for Thompson, but once I find him, you may need to come up to talk to him. You're a bit more intimidating than I am."

"Only when people don't know you well, Rosie," Skip said, with a chuckle.

"Good thing you're twenty miles away, *Skippy*."

"I shouldn't be giving you a hard time when you're doing me a favor. Thanks for catching this hot potato, Rose. I'll get the next one."

"Not if Cherise is the one tossin' it. She's my hot potato now," Rose said.

"Uh, watch what you say around her. She thinks you're gay."

"Say what?"

"Yeah, that was my reaction, but don't take it personally. She believes in all the politically incorrect stereotypes."

"Grrr. Do I have your permission, partner, to fire this client if she pushes the wrong buttons?" Rose asked.

"We can't do that. She'd badmouth us to the press and destroy everything we've worked for."

"I'm willing to risk it if you are. I've found work before, I can find it again."

Skip only hesitated a second. "Yeah, if you get to the point where you can't stand her anymore, feel free to politely tell her to stick her security contract where the sun don't shine."

Rose chuckled and disconnected.

Skip felt a weight lift he hadn't even realized he'd been carrying. No more letting a client, even a famous and powerful one, call the shots.

There was a relaxed smile on his face as he returned to the kitchen to finish having dinner with his family.

~~~~~~~~

At a little past noon the next day, Skip's office phone rang. When he answered, Cherise purred in his ear, "Back so soon from New York?"

"Uh, yeah, got a lead on Thompson. Rose is following it up," he quickly improvised. "I had to come back for a meeting."

"Must be a very important meeting if it took precedence over finding the man who's stalking me." Her tone wasn't so sweet now.

"Rose is perfectly capable of following leads, and you're not our only client."

"I need to talk to you."

"So talk."

"It's not something I want to get into over the phone. I've had a couple insights about Kirk, why he might be doing this. And there's something else I need to tell you, but I'm just not comfortable talking about it on the phone."

"It's a bad idea for me to come out there. If some diligent reporter is still lurking in the wings, he or she might follow me to the farm. And I'm not willing to put my family through all that crap with the paparazzi again."

"Then I'll come to you."

"Worse idea," Skip said.

"I trust you are good enough at your job to shake anybody trying to follow you." There was a touch of acid in Cherise's voice. "When will your meeting be over?"

"Not until four, at the earliest," he lied.

"I'll expect you at five then." She disconnected.

Damn, he'd painted himself into a corner. Now he was going to be late for dinner with the kids, his favorite part of the day.

Well, until bedtime that is. He grinned to himself.

Okay, he wasn't letting Cherise control him anymore, so what to do? Wait half an hour and then call her and say the client had cancelled the meeting.

If she had something valuable to tell him about Thompson it would be worth the trip to Howard County. The sooner they put a stop to the stalking, the sooner they could dump her as a client. He'd decided to tell Cherise that Canfield and Hernandez would not be able to handle her routine security needs once the stalker was stopped. But he hadn't thought of a good reason to give her, so that was a discussion for another day.

Today he would find out what she had to say and pass it on to Rose, who was hot on the trail of Kirk Thompson up in New York.

Skip was zipping along I-70 when his cell phone rang. It was Rose. "Hang on a sec," he said, then punched a button on his dashboard. Hot damn, he loved this new truck with all its little doodads, including a wireless hands-free network linked in with his cell.

"What's up, partner?"

"Thompson's in Maryland," Rose said. "Baltimore City to be exact."

"Oh yeah?"

"Yup. Located the last buddy he mooched off of up here. Said Kirk was headed for another mutual friend's place down there. Got an address and phone number for the friend. Address sounds familiar." She rattled it off.

"That's Lansing's building," Skip said. "Now ain't that interesting?"

"Is it a ritzy place?"

"Yeah, one of the most expensive in the Inner Harbor area."

"Then it may be a coincidence. His family's got money. He travels in a pretty upper crust crowd."

"As Dolph would say, I'm allergic to coincidences. If Thompson's got bucks, why's he mooching off of friends?" Skip said.

"Had money. Apparently his family got fed up with him and cut him loose. Buddy up here says he's pretty far gone on the drugs. Brain's turnin' to mush."

"Okay, I'm on my way to the farm. Cherise insisted she needed to talk to me about something. Call my cell back after we hang up and leave me the apartment and phone number on voicemail. I'll go pay good ole Kirk a little visit this afternoon."

After a pause, Rose said, "You think that's a good idea, going out there?"

"Like I said, she insisted. I checked for tails. Hey Rose, let me clarify something. You're okay with it if *I* tell her to shove it?"

"More than okay."

"Good, then I'm making a New Year's resolution, six months early. Clients either accept our services on our terms or they make other arrangements."

"Amen to that, partner. Take Dolph or Mac with you to see Thompson. Drugs can make people crazy strong sometimes."

CHAPTER SEVENTEEN

Skip decided on a tactic as he swung into Cherise's driveway. At the door, he didn't give her time to try to hug him. He strode past her, headed for the horseshoe group of white sofas. "We need to make this quick, Cherise," he said over his shoulder. "That hot lead on Thompson just got hotter. I need to follow up on it."

"I thought Rose was doing that."

"She was, but she's in New York and she just found out that he's down here, in Baltimore."

Cherise paled.

"Yeah, a little too close for comfort," Skip said. "I have a current address for him, but he hasn't been staying put for long."

He sat down and was relieved when Cherise sat across from him, not beside him. She was wearing a revealing halter top and shorts, but she crossed her bare legs demurely.

"I've been thinking about that last time Kirk was here. I think he was trying to get back together with me, not just looking for a place to hang his hat. And that would have been just a couple weeks before the notes started."

"I'd kind of figured that out already." He tried to keep his voice patient.

"Of course, but there's more. Kirk was a real charmer when we first met, lavished me with gifts, acted like he'd do anything to please me, but after a while he started to change. Got more demanding and controlling, and he had a temper. He'd get pissed off over little stuff, and say mean things, turn everything around so it was my fault. Around that time I realized that his drug use was more than recreational, like he'd claimed, and I broke it off with him."

"Did he ever get physically violent?"

"No, but he was starting to scare me with his temper. And the way he could twist things, he was almost delusional at times, especially when he was high. I think he's quite capable of doing all this sick stuff."

"But this latest note's tone is a lot different than the other stuff?"

She shook her head. "He's just changed tactics. He'd do that, whenever I'd get pissed and start thinking about breaking up with him, he'd backpedal and get all sweet again." She uncrossed her legs and leaned forward, her elbows on her knees. "The other thing I wanted to discuss, Skip, was whether I should put up a fence around the property."

He was trying to ignore the fact that he now had a good view of her cleavage. "It's what, fifteen acres? That's a lot of fencing, and fences don't keep out determined people. It might just give you a false sense of security. A couple of big dogs would be a better investment."

"I hate dogs." Cherise shuddered. "I guess you'd say I'm down-right phobic of them. That's another reason why I think Kirk's the stalker. It's something we had in common, although he's not afraid of them like I am. He just doesn't like them, or most animals for that matter. He'd know that was a good way to get to me. If I'd been the one to open that box, and seen that dog's head looking up at me, I'd have probably passed out cold."

"How many of your other ex-lovers would also know that?"

She bristled and sat up straight. "I don't have *that* many ex-lovers. You make it sound like I change men along with my underwear."

Skip struggled to keep his expression neutral. That wasn't too far from his actual thoughts on the matter.

"To answer your question, Kirk was the only one I ever admitted that to. I fancied myself in love with him until he started to change."

Skip nodded, glancing at his watch.

"I know this is supposed to be a verboten subject," Cherise quickly went on. "But I wanted to apologize again for my totally unintentional slur against Kate. I know I've flirted with you. It's just second nature for me to do so with a handsome man. But I hope you didn't think I was coming on to you. Number one, I like Kate, and number two, I don't date married men. Way, way too messy."

When he didn't say anything, she added, "By the way, thank her for me, for the referral. The new therapist is working out fine."

"Will do. Is that all, Cherise? 'Cause I really need to get going. I don't want this guy to slip through our fingers." Skip pushed himself to a stand.

A quick flash of something crossed her face. Anger? But then she smiled, also standing up. "Yes, that's all. Give my best to Kate."

~~~~~~~~~~

Kirk's new roommate turned out to be a woman, which was a little awkward considering the reason for their visit. She invited them to have a seat and offered refreshments, assuming they were also friends of her friend.

"Iced tea would be great," Dolph quickly said. "I'll help you carry things in." He jumped up and followed the young woman out of the room. "Walkies," he said to Skip under his breath as he moved past him.

Skip suppressed a grin. He studied Thompson, slouched down in an overstuffed armchair. The guy couldn't be much more than thirty but he looked at least a decade older. There were signs he'd once been handsome, but his face was gaunt now, his eyes not quite focused and his shoulder-length dark hair was frizzy and tangled. His gray tee-shirt and torn jeans were loose on a tall but too-thin frame.

"Hey Kirk, did you know your old neighbor's golden retriever's missing?"

Sure enough, the asshole's dark eyes widened and his mouth fell open for a second. Then he tried to cover his reaction with a nonchalant gesture, pushing hair out of his face with an unsteady hand.

"Okay, so we know you sent the dog parts," Skip said conversationally. "And I gotta give you credit for having the good sense to stop after Lansing was arrested. But then you had to go and get stupid on us and start up again."

The man did a good job of faking confusion. "Start up? I don't know what you mean."

"Oh, I think you do. And I'll be able to prove it once the lab gets finished lifting prints off the latest note. They can do wonders these days, even with paper."

"I..." Thompson stopped, narrowing his eyes, as his damaged brain cells tried to function. "Uh, I'd assume a stalker would use gloves."

"A smart one would, but I'm not so sure you're all that smart. You really should have stopped with the dog."

"I..." Thompson caught himself again.

Skip resisted the temptation to shake his head in disgust. This guy's brain really was mush. "Baltimore City requested your prints from New York. They got a match with some from the knife." Skip was hoping he'd let something slip about the gory bouquet, which they'd managed to keep out of the news.

Thompson's eyes skittered around the room. After too long a pause, he said, "What knife?"

"You'd better stop now," Skip said, in a nonchalant voice. He stood and stretched a bit to emphasize his height and muscular chest. He leaned over toward Thompson and was gratified to see a flicker of fear in the guy's eyes. "Cause I know where to find you. And scampering off to somebody else's house won't do you much good. I found you once, I'll find you again."

The young woman, Nancy Knight, carried a tray with glasses, sugar bowl and a dish of lemon slices into the room. Dolph had a half empty glass of iced tea in one hand and the pitcher in the other. Nancy looked a bit surprised to see Skip standing.

"I'm sorry, ma'am," he drawled, laying on the Texas. "I just now remembered another engagement. That tea sure does look temptin' though. Mind if I have me a quick half a glass?" He nabbed a glass off the tray and held it out toward Dolph, who dutifully filled it half full.

"Sugar or lemon, Mr. Canfield?"

"Neither, thanks. This'll do just fine." Skip was only taking the tea to be polite. He didn't want to linger long enough to doctor it to taste. Keeping an eye on Thompson in his peripheral vision, he chugged down the tea and smacked his lips. As he handed the empty glass to the young woman, he noted that she looked a lot like

Cherise–long blonde hair, baby blue eyes, slender figure and fair skin.

"That sure hit the spot. Sorry we have to run off. Nice chattin' with ya, Kirk." Skip turned his back to Nancy Knight and towered over Thompson, still slouched in his chair trying to look unfazed. "Behave yerself now, boy, ya hear. An' take good care of this little lady."

While they waited for the elevator out in the well-appointed hallway, Dolph whispered, "Wish I could turn on fake accents like that."

Skip looked at him and drawled, "That ain't no fake, I'll have ya know." Then in his normal voice, he said, "You didn't know I'm from Texas? Thought I'd told you that somewhere along the way. I've been in Maryland long enough now I talk funny like you Northerners, but I like to revisit my roots, now an' agin."

"When you want to charm a lady," Dolph observed as they entered the empty elevator.

"Does come in handy that way. You get anything useful out of her in the kitchen?"

"Not really, but the stars in her eyes say she's in love, poor kid."

"Probably thinks she can save him if she just loves him enough. You notice how much she resembles Cherise?"

"Yup, but her personality's completely different. She seemed kind of sweet. Hope the bastard doesn't break her heart."

"He probably will. Kate said that anyone who would kill animals to get Cherise's attention might very well be a psychopath. He's our stalker, or at least he was, up through the dog's head. Not so sure about this last note." Skip filled Dolph in on his conversation with Thompson.

"You threw a little fear into him, huh?"

"As best I could. Thug isn't my favorite role. Time will tell now, I guess. If she gets more notes, then either Thompson doesn't scare all that easy..."

"Or we've got a copycat," Dolph said.

Skip cringed. "Please don't say that out loud again, or I might be tempted to shoot myself."

~~~~~~~~

When Kate left her office that afternoon, she was exhausted. It had been an intense day. She'd finally had to hospitalize Carol Foster, which meant she'd been on the phone every minute between clients, calling Carol's husband to get him to watch his wife until arrangements could be made, then checking the two closest hospitals before she found an available bed, and coordinating with the psychiatrist who would do the actual admission.

Lacking the energy to walk to the corner, Kate was debating whether or not to risk jaywalking through the rush-hour traffic to get to the parking lot where her car was parked. She heard someone calling her name. She turned to see a woman hurrying along the crowded sidewalk in her direction. She was wearing a low-cut sundress, stiletto-heeled sandals, and sunglasses, and holding a big floppy hat clamped to her head. It took Kate a moment to realize who it was.

She almost blurted out Cherise's name, but caught herself in time. What was the woman's real name? Oh, yeah, Carol, like her suicidal client.

"Hi, Carol."

"Hi, Kate. I'm so glad I ran into you," Cherise said breathlessly. "I wanted to talk to you."

After an awkward pause, as they were jostled by the people hurrying past them, Kate said, "I, uh, was just heading for my car." She gestured across the street and started moving toward the corner.

Cherise fell into step with her. "I wanted to tell you how sorry I am for all the stress you and your family went through because of the stupid press thinking Skip was my boyfriend. And then they were chasing after you and Rob Franklin. I'm kind of used to the fools, but that must have been horrible for you."

"Thank you for your concern," Kate said, "but you don't need to apologize. You didn't cause the problem. As you say, the press jumped to conclusions."

"Well, I'm glad you don't hold it against me."

Actually I do.

But even though Cherise wasn't her client anymore, Kate had felt compelled to be the good therapist and ease the woman's guilt.

They reached the corner. Kate stopped, waiting for the walk signal. She held out her hand to Cherise. "It was good seeing you."

Cherise smiled as she shook her hand. "Likewise. You take care—"

Suddenly Kate was flying out into the street, right into the path of a taxi speeding toward the intersection. Someone grabbed her arm, yanking her back. Scrambling to keep her feet under her, Kate tripped on the curb. She came down on the sidewalk, landing hard on her right side. Pain shot up her arm.

Kate looked up into two pairs of worried eyes, one set blue, the other brown. "Are you okay?" a man's voice asked.

"I don't know. I think so. What just happened?"

The owner of the brown eyes, an elderly gentleman with a thick thatch of white hair, helped her to her feet.

"People were pushing and shoving behind you," Cherise said. "I saw you starting to fall and this gentleman grabbed your arm."

The gentleman in question introduced himself. "Anthony Vinzant."

Kate extended her right hand, then winced as Mr. Vinzant shook it. "Kate Huntington," she managed to get out through gritted teeth. "Thank you, sir."

"Are you sure you're okay?" her rescuer asked.

Kate assessed the damage, as pedestrians surged around them. A few paused for a moment to stare, but most were too intent on getting home on a Friday evening to care about a woman dripping blood on the sidewalk.

Damn!

Her jacket sleeve was torn, and it was her favorite suit. She flexed her fingers, then carefully bent her arm at the elbow. "I don't think anything is broken."

"You're bleeding. We need to get you inside and clean that up." Cherise tried to herd her back toward her building.

Kate resisted. She just wanted to go home. "It's not a big deal, just a scrape."

"Well, if you're sure you're okay," Mr. Vinzant said.

Kate nodded, then thanked her rescuer again.

"Let me walk you to your car, at least," Cherise said.

There was no way Kate could graciously refuse. As the light changed, she and Cherise joined the pedestrians flowing across the street.

"Uh, Kate, the sidewalk *was* really crowded," Cherise said, once they'd stepped up on the opposite curb. "But it looked like a man standing behind you pushed you intentionally."

"What? Why would he do that?" Kate turned to the left, toward the parking lot where her car was parked.

"I don't know, and maybe I'm wrong. It did all happen pretty fast."

"What did the guy look like?" Kate asked.

"I only got a quick impression before he turned away, and then I was focused on you. He was on the tall side, thin. I think he was wearing a tee-shirt. I didn't see his face. Wait a minute." Cherise stopped suddenly in the middle of the sidewalk, causing a mini traffic jam. "That's odd. He had a knit cap over his hair, pulled almost down to his eyes."

"That is odd for this time of year," Kate said, moving forward again.

Cherise fell in step with her. "It was all so quick, more impressions than anything else. I might be completely wrong. Maybe the guy got jostled himself and bumped into you by accident. Never even realized he'd knocked you off the curb."

Kate stopped at the entrance to the parking lot. "Well, it was good seeing you today." She reached out her left hand to shake Cherise's. Her right arm was beginning to throb.

"You too. Take care." Cherise squeezed her hand, then turned and headed back up the block.

For the first time, it occurred to Kate to wonder where Ben was.

CHAPTER EIGHTEEN

Despite the delay, Kate still beat Skip home.

When he came in the door and saw her sitting on the sofa, her arm wrapped in gauze with an ice pack on her elbow, his face tensed. He moved quickly to her side. "What happened?"

"I got jostled in the crowd waiting to cross the street after work and fell on the sidewalk." She'd decided not to tell him how close she'd come to becoming a taxicab's hood ornament. And she'd dismissed Cherise's belief that the man behind her might have pushed her on purpose, coming to the conclusion that the young woman had a lively imagination.

"I just scraped my arm and banged up my elbow a bit. It's not as bad as it looks. The kids insisted on helping me bandage it. They got a little carried away."

Skip chuckled when he took a closer look at the gauze. "How many rolls did they use?"

"Two. They started fighting over the first one so I had to give each of them a roll. It's a little hard to play referee one-handed." She grimaced. "Uh, would you sit next to me at dinner tonight? Otherwise, they're going to insist on cutting my food for me and maybe even feeding me."

Skip laughed out loud as he wrapped his arms around her, bulky bandage, ice pack and all. He kissed her lightly, then he held her gently against him.

She rested her cheek on his shirtfront and sighed, letting the tensions of the long, crazy day drain away. The sound of children squabbling in the kitchen finally penetrated their little bubble.

Skip escorted her into the kitchen, then distracted Edie from tormenting her brother by recruiting her to help set the table. "So other than that, how was your day?" he asked Kate.

"Ugh, I don't even want to talk about it, I'm just glad it's over. Hey, you'll never guess who I ran into today. Your famous client."

"What the... H," Skip caught himself.

"Whada H," Billy sang out from where he was playing with his cars on the floor.

"Skip!" Maria scolded as she brought the last of the dishes of food over.

Skip looked chagrined.

Kate grinned. "Why is it they *always* repeat the words you *don't* want them to learn?"

Skip shook his head and grinned back at her. "So what was she doing there?"

"She said she just happened to be in the area. She was actually there when I fell. She and an elderly gentleman helped me up."

Skip started to take his seat, then veered over to sit in Edie's usual spot. "You sit in Daddy's chair tonight, Pumkin, so I can help Mommy, okay?"

"Okay, Daddy."

"I say blessing," Billy yelled.

"Not so loud, son, but okay, go ahead," Kate said.

"Godz great, Godz good, now I lay me down to sleep. Amen!"

"Wrong prayer, dummy," his sister informed him.

"Never mind, Edie, he's only two," Kate said.

"Two an' half," he insisted.

"I stand corrected."

"So where was Ben?" Skip asked, as he cut up her chicken breast for her.

Picking up her fork awkwardly in her left hand, Kate said, "I didn't see him around. I'm sure if he'd been with her, he would have come running when I fell."

Skip's jaw tense. "What's she doing going around town without him?"

"Maybe she's getting tired of constant company. Ben's a sweetheart but he was starting to get on my nerves a couple weeks ago."

Skip's phone beeped in his pocket. He pulled it out and looked at the screen. She heard his teeth grinding together.

He turned the phone so Kate could see the text message. It was from Rose.

Ben says client slipped leash this afternoon. Home safe now.

"I've had this happen a few times before," Skip said. "Why would someone pay for a bodyguard and then ditch them?"

Kate shrugged. "Everybody needs alone time but introverts need it more than most people. Being around others all the time drains them."

Skip gave her a funny look. "Cher...uh, Carol is an introvert?"

"Yes, I think she is, somewhat at least, but her profession forces her to be more outgoing. That's probably why she bought the farm and cherishes her privacy there so much. It's where she recharges her batteries."

Skip shook his head again, then changed the subject. "We think we know who's been sending the notes and packages. Another former boyfriend. We can't prove anything, although a good police interrogator could probably break him in about ten minutes. I threw a little fear of God into him this afternoon, hopefully, until we can talk to her about pressing charges."

"You didn't–" Kate stopped, not wanting to say "hit him" in front of the children.

"Oh no. I just stretched." Skip demonstrated by lifting his arms high above his head and arching his back until his muscular chest almost popped the buttons off his shirt. Kate snickered and the kids giggled.

Maria had no clue what they were talking about but she smiled at her happy little family.

"Then I said, in my best Texas drawl, 'Y'all be good now, boy, ya hear.' Not sure about the last note, but I'm pretty sure he's our culprit up through the dog."

"Dog?" Edie said. "Did somebody get a doggie?"

"No, it was just a stuffed one," Skip said.

"Time for a change of subject, I think," Kate said. "But I did want to mention that... the client was particularly nice today."

"Oh yeah?" Skip held up the bowl of wild rice. Kate nodded and he spooned a second helping onto her plate.

"Yeah, and I'm not sure what that means. I could have been too hasty with the narcissism label. Someone in her position, who's being catered to all the time, might naturally become more self-centered, and that would get worse under stress."

Skip nodded. "I met with her earlier today. She was much calmer, and saner, than I've seen her in a while. She even apologized for, uh, some things."

"What things?" Kate asked.

"Uh, later." His cheeks turned pink and he tilted his head in the direction of the kids. "I was thinking we should do something tomorrow as a family. Any ideas?"

"Has to be something I can do one-handed, or one-armed rather. This elbow's probably going to be pretty sore for a few days."

After some discussion, they settled on a drive out Cromwell Bridge Road to the park next to Loch Raven Reservoir.

"We can consider it a little celebration," Skip said. "I think this lousy case is finally coming to an end. But I need to talk to you some more about our suspect, once little ears are bedded down."

After dinner, Maria volunteered to supervise baths, something their mother usually did. Kate offered a feeble protest, since Maria was theoretically off duty. The nanny just arched an eyebrow in the direction of the bandaged arm and then shooed the children toward the stairs.

Once they were out of earshot, Skip said, "Remember you said this guy could be a full-blown psychopath?"

"Yes."

"Well, I'm trying to figure out if he is or not. Some of the things Cherise told me about him would fit. But he didn't really strike me that way when I was with him today. I've dealt with my share of psychopaths, back when I was a state trooper. They were a lot more ruthless and nasty than this guy seems to be."

As he cleared the table, Skip gave her a summary of what Rose had found out and his conversation with Cherise. Kate joined him at the sink and rinsed dishes one-handed, while he loaded the dishwasher and told her about the confrontation with Thompson.

"This guy may have been fairly bright once upon a time, but his brain isn't firing on all cylinders now," Skip concluded. "I find it hard to believe he's got it together enough to sneak onto the farm and kill the cat, or get into Cherise's dressing room with that bouquet."

"Three things to keep in mind," Kate said, as she handed him the last plate. "One, antisocial personality disorder, like all disorders, is on a continuum–that's the official diagnostic label for psychopaths, by the way–so he may be pathological enough to hurt animals but not be as blatantly aggressive as the guys you've encountered before."

Skip started the dishwasher and they went back over to sit at the table.

"Second, as I mentioned before, psychopaths can look quite normal. And third, his level of lucidity would vary, based on how many and which kinds of drugs he has in his system at any given time."

Skip grinned at her. "I love it when you talk psychobabble. It's so sexy."

She gave him a mock scowl, then returned his grin.

"I'm gonna add psychological consultations to Cherise's bill, by the way," Skip said. "So you think Thompson could have antisocial personality disorder?"

"If this is an official consultation, let me make sure of what I'm saying." Kate got up and went into the study to retrieve a thick, gray-covered volume from a shelf. Carrying it awkwardly to the table in one hand, she plopped it down and leafed through the pages.

"Here it is, 'Diagnostic criteria for Antisocial Personality Disorder.'" She ran her finger down the page, then waggled her hand in a maybe-maybe not gesture. "Based on what we know, he just barely meets three, maybe four, of the criteria, which is the minimum to justify the diagnosis. Impulsive and irresponsible, definitely. Irritable and aggressive, yeah, but we don't know if he's ever actually been violent. His twisting things around so they're always Cherise's fault might indicate a broader pattern of lack of remorse."

"So you don't think he's sick enough to be our stalker?"

"I didn't say that. If we assume he *is* the stalker, he fits the criteria better. Killing animals is definitely aggressive, and he's engaging in unlawful behavior, another criteria, by sending threatening notes and dog parts through the mail. But I'd have to know more about his history to tell you if he's full-blown antisocial. Did he torture animals as a child? Get into fights with little provocation? Lie and steal in his teens?

"What you *are* describing is something that's not in the diagnostic manual." She tapped the book in front of her. "An abusive personality. Starts out charming and sweet. Once the partner is hooked, he becomes controlling and angry. Blames the victim, et cetera."

"So, bottom line?" Skip asked.

"Someone who is abusive is capable of being your stalker. If your instincts are telling you that he was behind the bouquet and the dog head, I'd trust that. Also, his parents cutting off his money could have been a trigger, made him feel desperate. He's rejected by them and has no place to live. So he focuses on getting Cherise to let him move in. When she rejects him too, it sends him around the bend."

Skip processed all that for a moment. "What about the timing? It's been well over a year, closer to two years, since they broke up. Why's Thompson suddenly obsessed with her now?"

Kate shrugged, then winced when the gesture tugged at her sore elbow. "I'm just speculating, but it's possible that he normally does the dumping when he's tired of a relationship. Cherise may be the only woman who's ever broken up with him. He's managing to ignore that blow to his ego, until his parents cut off his funds and he gets tossed out of his apartment. Now his life is spinning out of control, and he twists it around to be Cherise's fault. His problems all started when she dumped him. I'm sure he's convinced he's in love with her, but it's really about control and possession. His women are his, until he doesn't want them anymore. So she's still his, and he's bound and determined to get her back under his control."

Skip nodded. "If we push her to press charges and the police can't get him to confess, we may not have enough evidence to get a conviction. What's his reaction likely to be then?"

Kate shook her head. "I'd be afraid to guess. It might scare him into backing off, or piss him off and he'll escalate."

"So maybe celebrating's a bit premature then, huh?" Skip said.

Kate patted his hand, lying on the table. He wrapped his long fingers around hers.

"Enough talk about psychopaths," he said, as he lifted her hand toward his mouth to kiss the palm. The action was aborted when they heard the children clattering down the stairs.

"You may have to behave yourself tonight, Mr. Canfield," Kate said, tapping her bandaged arm.

Skip pushed himself to a stand to go perform his storytelling and tuck-in duties. As he moved around her chair, he dropped a kiss on the top of her head. "I'll be extra gentle," he whispered.

~~~~~~~~~~

Skip called Rose first thing Saturday morning and gave her the gist of Kate's observations about their suspect.

"I'm thinking we need more evidence before she presses charges," Rose said when he'd repeated Kate's comment that Thompson could escalate. "Let me do some research. See if I can find a pattern of this kind of stuff in the past. Thompson grew up in Montgomery County. I've got a buddy from the force who transferred over there. He can at least confirm or deny if he has a juvie record. Then I'll see if any of his old neighbors or school friends are still around."

"Let me know if you need my help with anything," Skip said. "Kate had a rough week, so we're going on a family outing this afternoon to de-stress."

"I'll let you know if I dig up anything interesting," Rose said and disconnected.

The red minivan got somewhat better gas mileage than Skip's Expedition, so they used it for their outing. The weather was gorgeous, one of those rare summer days in Maryland when a cool front from the north pushed the temperature and humidity down to tolerable levels. They spent the afternoon hiking some of the paths around the reservoir, then stopped for homemade ice cream at a little country store on the way back, even though it would spoil the children's appetites for dinner.

By Sunday, Kate's scraped up arm had healed enough to take the bandage off but her elbow was still swollen and bruised. She decided against going to church since she didn't particularly want to recount her adventure to every well-meaning parishioner who would ask her how she'd come by her injury.

Skip dropped the kids off for Sunday school, and then came back home with a glint in his eye.

Forty-five minutes later, Kate left Skip sleeping in post-coital bliss and went to pick up the kids. Heading out of the church parking lot, she decided to swing by the pharmacy and pick up a prescription, something she should have done the day before. After utilizing Walgreen's drive-through window—such a convenience for parents of small children—she looped back around via Charles Street to head home.

As the van crested a hill and started down the long incline to the light at Towsontown Boulevard, Billy whined, "Mommy, I wanna go home."

Kate glanced up in the rearview mirror. "We're headed there now, son." It took a second for her brain to register that the light tap she'd just given the brakes had not slowed the van. Instead, it was picking up speed. Kate hit the brake pedal harder. It went to the floor.

Glancing quickly over her shoulder, Kate veered into the far right lane and prayed no one would pull over in front of her and the light would stay green. Her first prayer was answered.

The light turned yellow when she was still a hundred feet away. She remembered the emergency brake and crammed her left foot down on it. Nothing happened.

She lay on the horn, praying the drivers on Towsontown Boulevard would hear it and look her way, before they turned in front of her. She hit the intersection doing sixty.

"Mommy?" Edie's worried voice came from the backseat.

"Wheee," Billy squealed. He had no concept that one was not supposed to run red lights at sixty miles an hour.

A driver turning left onto Charles Street saw the van careening toward him. He swerved to miss her but the tail end of his car spun around into her path. Kate yanked her steering wheel to the right, almost losing control when two of the van's tires hit the gravel of the shoulder. She held her breath as she narrowly missed the man's back bumper.

Still wrestling with the steering wheel, she realized they were now going up a gradual incline. The van was slowing ever so slightly. She downshifted. With a jolt, they slowed a bit more.

Now some idiot was behind her, blowing his horn. Turning on her flashers, she pulled the rest of the way onto the shoulder, then downshifted again. Another jolt and the van slowed to twenty, then ten, as the upward incline became a bit steeper.

She shifted into neutral. At the exact moment the van came to a stop, she jammed the gearshift into park. The transmission banged in protest but it kept the van from rolling back down the hill.

Kate turned off the ignition and collapsed onto the steering wheel, trying not to pass out from hyperventilation.

"What happened, Mommy?" Edie asked in a small, scared voice.

"Do again, Mommy!" Billy yelled.

"I don't think so, son!"

CHAPTER NINETEEN

After arranging to have the disabled van towed to their mechanic's shop, Skip took his family to the Sunday evening church service in his truck. There was an extra degree of fervor in his and Kate's voices as they recited the prayers.

Afterwards they were among the stragglers greeting the rector at the back of the church. Kate gave Elaine Johnson a brief synopsis of her adventure earlier in the day.

"Oh, child," Elaine said, as she enveloped Kate in a hug.

"It fun. Do again!" Billy chirped.

Elaine and Kate broke the hug, both laughing.

"I guess it was, from the perspective of a two-year-old," Elaine said, ruffling Billy's hair.

"Two an' half," Billy said, crossing his chubby little arms.

Shortly after eleven on Monday, Skip's phone rang.

"Got a development out here," Ben said. "Another note in today's mail sack. This one says, 'I'm going to take care of those people who are keeping us apart. Then we'll be together forever, my love.'"

"Shit. When was it mailed?"

"Lemme see...Wednesday in L.A."

"I'll call you back in a minute." Skip had a bad feeling. He punched in the number of the auto shop.

"I was 'bout to call you, Mr. Canfield. I ain't never seen both the front and back brakes fail at the same time, not in twenty years of fixin' cars, so I looked the whole system over real good. There was almost no brake fluid in the reservoir, but none of the hoses was loose or cracked. Finally found a small hole poked in the side of the reservoir, near the bottom. Woulda leaked out slow, little faster in stop an' go traffic. And the emergency brake cable was disconnected. Coulda come loose on it's own but considerin' the hole in the reservoir, I'd say somebody tampered with it."

"You didn't fix anything yet, did you?"

"No, sir."

"Good. Don't touch anything else. I'll be there shortly. With the police."

Skip was out of his chair and striding down the hall to Rose's office. Her door was open. She was on her computer and Mac was sitting in her visitor's chair. Skip filled them in with two sentences. "Another note at Cherise's, threatening 'those people who are keeping us apart.' The van's brakes were sabotaged."

"I'm on the kids," Mac said, jumping up from his chair.

Skip turned to Rose. "Who we got to replace Ben out at Cherise's? I want him on Kate again."

"I'll go out for now. With the new note, she's not gonna be happy with second string."

"Who we got outside who can go in until you get there? I want Ben with Kate now!"

Rose brought up the duty roster on her screen. "Manuel Ortiz. He's been with us two years. He's solid."

Skip nodded. "Dolph around?"

Rose nodded, already punching Ben's number on her phone. "I'll have Ben at Kate's office within an hour."

Skip pulled out his cell as he headed for Dolph's cubicle. He got Kate's office voicemail. "Darlin', there's been a development. Kind of complicated. But there's a slight chance of some danger to you and the kids. Very minimal but to be on the safe side, Mac's with Maria and the kids, and Ben's on his way to your office. You know me." He faked a chuckle. "I'm Mr. Overly Cautious when it comes to my family." He disconnected and dialed her cell, also got voicemail there and left the same message.

He collected Dolph and headed for Jimmy's Auto Place. "Who do you know at the Baltimore County Police Department who will take this seriously?" he asked after filling Dolph in.

The older man scratched his head. "We call it in the normal route, they'll send uniforms."

"That's why I'm asking. Who do you know who will connect the dots without two hours of explanation?"

Dolph made a call while Skip drove. "Judith, sweetheart, I need a favor," he said into the phone.

At Jimmy's, Dolph's former partner, Detective Judith Anderson, connected the dots in less than five minutes. "Shit, what are you doin' to me here, Dolph? This is a jurisdictional nightmare. We got one vic in Howard County, another in Baltimore County and the perp's in the city."

"If he's even still there," Skip said. "He tends to be a moving target."

After a short squabble over whether or not the civilians would be included in the questioning of the suspect, it was agreed that Skip would lead the way in his truck, Judith following in her unmarked car. No sirens to spook the guy.

"I'll ride with Judith," Dolph said. "Give her some more background."

In the elegant hallway, Judith knocked on the door of apartment 310. After thirty seconds, she knocked again and leaned close to the door, listening for a response. She shook her head slightly, barely ruffling the cap of short dark hair surrounding her narrow face. "Hollow sound in there, bad feeling in here." She pointed toward her chest, that was covered by a crisp white cotton shirt, tucked into tailored black slacks.

She pushed aside the edge of the matching black jacket. Putting her hand on the butt of the gun holstered at her waist, she knocked again with her left hand. "Police. Open up," she called out.

A man came down the hall, a small, yappy dog tucked under one arm, leash dangling. As he slipped a key in the lock of the apartment next door, he called over to them, "They moved out yesterday, lock, stock and barrel. Shut up, Princess." The dog only paused for breath. "Actually the young woman was house-sitting for the tenants, so they didn't have a whole lot of stock and barrel to take. Hauled out of here with a couple of suitcases each."

"I don't suppose they mentioned where they were going?" Skip raised his voice over the noise of the dog as he walked toward the man. The dog shifted to a growl.

The man clamped a hand around the tiny muzzle. "Don't mind her, she's a legend in her own mind. But to answer your question, nope. Nancy mumbled a goodbye as they rushed past me. The guy just ducked his head and raced after her."

"Who are the regular tenants?" Judith asked from behind Skip, setting off a new round of yapping from Princess.

"Damn mutt," the man muttered, recapturing the dog's snout. "Sorry. It's the wife's dog. Bill and Jane Jessup live there. They're traveling in Europe this summer. I'm John Harper, by the way." The man disentangled his right arm from Princess.

Skip watched the dog warily as he shook the offered hand. He pointed to his companions. "Judith Anderson. Dolph Randolph."

Judith was scribbling names in her notepad.

"Did I hear you say police?" Harper asked.

"Baltimore County," she said, producing her detective's badge. "We just wanted to have a friendly chat with the gentleman. Anything else you can tell us about them?"

"Well, they had a rip-roaring argument the night before they left. Walls are thick here, but when people yell loud enough, you can still hear them."

"Could you make out any words?" Skip asked.

"Not a lot. Seemed to be fighting over whether or not to leave. Don't think she wanted to go. His words, the few I could make out, didn't make much sense, but he sounded kind of paranoid."

"Thanks for the information, sir." Judith handed Harper her card. "Please call me if they come back. I'd appreciate it if you wouldn't tell them we were here."

Once they were out on the hot sidewalk, she said, "Sounds like you scared this guy off. He may not be your saboteur."

Skip thought for a moment. "He still could've sent this last letter. We think Thompson's been sending them to friends or a mailing service and then they're re-mailed to Cherise's L.A. address. Twice a week her fan mail is forwarded here. All that takes a few days, so this latest note would've been sent last week, before we showed up on his doorstep. After our little visit he knew he'd better scram before it was delivered."

"Do you think he would've taken the time to come after you, Mr. Canfield? He doesn't sound like he has his act together all that well. Tracking you down and tampering with your brakes would take some clarity of thought, and at least a little bit of planning."

"Call me Skip, please, ma'am—"

"Not unless you cut the ma'am crap," Judith interrupted.

Skip grinned. "Well, Detective, I agree this guy's a brick or two short of a load since he's been frying his brain with drugs for years, but the fact he went after the van tells me it was a sloppy job. I'm not that hard to find. I'm thinking he was hanging around my house Saturday, looking for an opening to get to me. Maybe with no real plan in mind. He saw me at the wheel of the van taking my family for a drive, and assumed that's my regular vehicle. Messed with the brakes after dark, then went home to inform his honey they have to skedaddle."

"And he's got multiple reasons to want you out of the way," Judith said. "Thinks you're his lady love's new squeeze, knows you're her bodyguard which is keeping him from getting to her, and you now know who he is and have threatened him."

"I did no such thing. I just stood up." Skip straightened his spine and pushed out his chest.

Judith smiled up at him. "Like I said, you threatened him."

"Or we could have a copycat," Dolph threw in. "And our visit just plain spooked Thompson into running even though he didn't send the last two notes."

Skip mimicked pulling his gun and shooting himself in the head.

Dolph slapped him on the back. "Son, denial is not a river in Egypt."

~~~~~~~~

Wednesday evening, Rose went directly from the train station to Kate and Skip's house. She'd just spent two fruitless days in New York trying to get another lead on Kirk Thompson. Most of his friends seemed pretty fed up with his mooching. She'd passed out cards, asking them to call her if he contacted them.

When Maria let her in the front door, she found her honey bun rolling around on the floor with Billy and Edie. They seemed to be playing some game that involved mostly tickling and giggling. Rose hid a smile. Mac's normal curmudgeon personality seemed to melt away when he was around the kids.

Maria informed her in Spanish that Skip had just called. He would be home any minute. "You and Mac stay for dinner," she added in English, most likely for Mac's benefit.

Then she bustled off before Rose could respond. Not that she would have said no. Her cousin was a great cook and she was starving.

Once Skip had arrived and they'd all settled into their places, Edie said the blessing. During the chorus of amens, the three women crossed themselves.

For Rose, it was more habit than anything else. She hadn't been to church in years. As the others dug in, she paused to look around at the polyglot group at the big oak table–all of whom she considered to be family as surely as her biological parents and siblings were.

It was pure happenstance that she'd been assigned as Kate's police protection four and a half years ago, when Kate was being stalked by her first husband's killer. So much had changed in Rose's life as a result of that assignment.

The Lord does work in mysterious ways.

"Dolph got a progress report from his former partner this afternoon," Skip said between bites of Maria's chicken enchiladas. "She hasn't had any luck tracking down Thompson and his girlfriend, but she's got BOLOs out on them, and she's notified the L.A. and New York police to be on the lookout for them as well." He took a swig of iced tea. "This guy might not have the brain power he once had, but he's still smart enough to cover his tracks. Nancy Knight's cell phone account has been closed, and her parents have no idea where she is. They'd assumed she was still house-sitting for their friends."

"More like a no-progress report," Mac grumbled.

"The police lab find anything on the sabotaged car parts?" Rose asked, choosing her words with care in front of the children.

Skip shook his head. "They haven't gotten to them yet. A car being tampered with when there were no resulting injuries isn't considered a high priority."

Rose gave the others her succinct and discouraging report from the New York trip, then she turned to Kate. "I did find out some interesting things about Thompson's background though. He has a juvenile record in Montgomery County, sealed of course. Talked to a couple of his old neighbors over the weekend. General consensus, he was spoiled rotten and out of control, but nothing specific about, uh..." Taking in the avid look on Edie's face, Rose rephrased what she'd been about to say. "Nothing about animals or fights. He left for college in New York at eighteen. Dropped out after two years but stayed up there. Parents continued to foot the bills and bail him out of trouble, until a few months ago. Some of the gang he partied with admitted that he could turn mean when he was high. Located a couple of girlfriends up there. Reading between the lines of what they said and what they weren't saying, I think he could be a batterer."

"What's a baddader, Aunt Rose?" Edie asked.

Rose looked helplessly at the child's mother.

Kate's mouth quirked up on one end. "Someone who sells batteries for a living."

Rose heard a stifled snort coming from Mac's direction. She shot him a mock glare. He grinned back at her.

By unspoken agreement, they chatted about inconsequential things for the rest of the meal.

Afterward, Maria offered to give the kids their baths. She herded them out the door and up the stairs.

Skip got up to clear the table. When Kate lifted her arm to hand him her plate, Rose caught sight of scabs and the purple and yellow remnants of bruises on her arm. She raised an eyebrow. "What'd you do to yourself, Kate?"

"Oh, I got jostled on the sidewalk and fell down."

Rose switched eyebrows. "When did this happen?"

"Friday, as I was walking to my car after work."

"Who jostled you?"

Kate seemed to hesitate. "I don't know," she finally said, as Skip stacked the dishes in the sink and came back to the table. "I'd been talking to Cherise and we were about to part company, when somebody–"

Rose shook her head in confusion. "Wait a minute. What was Cherise doing there?"

"She and I ran into each other as I was walking out of my building. We talked for a few minutes and we were saying goodbye when it happened. I almost fell into the street. A man grabbed me and dragged me back onto the sidewalk. I tripped and landed on my arm. But then Cherise said she thought some guy who was standing behind me might have pushed me on purpose."

"Why didn't you tell me that before?" Skip's voice was sharp.

"Because I dismissed it as Cherise's imagination. She even said it was just an impression and she could be wrong. But in light of what's happened since..."

"She get a look at the guy?" Mac asked.

"Not much of one. He was tall and thin, wearing a tee shirt and a knit cap pulled down to his ears."

"In ninety degree weather?" Rose said.

"Yeah, we thought that was pretty odd."

Rose's brow furrowed. "Where was her guard?"

"That was the day you texted me that she'd slipped her leash," Skip said.

"Oh, yeah," Rose said. "Cherise insisted she needed some alone time. Took a drive by herself, after promising Ben she'd stay locked in the car."

Mac growled, "Instead she's runnin' around Towson."

"She tends to have too much confidence in her ability to disguise her appearance," Skip said.

"Well," Kate said, "I didn't recognize her at first–"

"Wait," Skip interrupted. "She said the guy she thought had pushed you was tall?"

"Yeah."

"The florist's description of the guy who sent the flowers a few weeks ago. It could be the same guy. She said either that he was a tall guy or a big guy, I can't remember which. I thought of a man my size or Rob's. A big guy in general. But she might have just meant he was tall."

"Don't make sense," Mac said. "If it's the paparazzi, the flowers to stir things up does. But not tryin' to push you into traffic, sweet pea."

"Unless this guy had been trying to get a picture of me and Cherise together and he accidentally bumped into me," Kate said.

"Could the guy have been Thompson?" Rose asked.

"Fits the description but Cherise would've recognized him," Skip said.

"Not necessarily," Kate said. "She never saw his face. Maybe that's why he had the hat on. Is his hair distinctive looking?"

"Yeah, dark, shoulder length and curly. I just thought of something else. That was Friday, the day Dolph and I talked to Thompson. Maybe he'd followed Cherise to your office at some point and had figured out that she was seeing you for therapy. He could perceive you as one of the people who's telling Cherise to stay away from him. So I confront him. He gets desperate and comes to Towson to make good on his threat to, quote, take care of those people who are keeping them apart. Tries to shove you into traffic, then sabotages the van to take me out."

"Tamperin' with the van coulda been aimed at either of you," Mac said. "An' it coulda been done Friday night. Leak was slow. Brakes wouldn't go out right away."

Kate blanched. "We were all in that van Saturday, on Cromwell Bridge Road."

Rose's stomach clenched. Cromwell Bridge Road was a hilly, winding road, cut into the side of a ridge with a sharp drop off on one side. If the brake fluid had leaked out faster...

She shook her head to rid it of what might have been. "So what we've got here is Dog Boy as our stalker," she summarized. "Maybe he shoved Kate off that curb, but someone, possibly him, tried to take either Kate or Skip or both out with the van brakes. Now he's in the wind. And some tall paparazzi dude is trying to stir up trouble between you two. And it's also possible he's the one who pushed Kate, trying to get a picture of her and Cherise."

Kate nodded. "He must not have succeeded, or the photo would've shown up in a tabloid by now."

"Ya know," Skip said, "it's almost anticlimactic to discover this bad guy we've been chasing is just a druggie with a burned-out brain."

Rose snorted. "Yeah, well, most bad guys are more lucky than smart, until they get caught."

Skip nodded.

"We shouldn't be underestimating him, though," Rose said.

"Yeah," Skip said. "As my daddy used to say, 'He's dumb like a fox.'"

Mac let out a low chuckle.

"Well, hopefully Detective Anderson will catch up with him soon," Kate said. "My brain's tired, guys. Let's call it a night. Rose, take your man home."

That sounded like a jimdandy idea to Rose.

"You be careful, sweet pea," Mac said to Kate as they left.

~~~~~~~~~

Rose was elbow deep in paperwork the next morning when her phone rang.

"Got another letter in the fan mail sack," Manny Ortiz informed her.

Rose swore under her breath. "What's it say exactly, Manny?"

She heard rustling. "It says, 'I can't believe you don't know who I am. That hurts. You're breaking my heart, my love.'"

"When was it mailed?"

"Monday, from L.A."

Rose had been jotting down the words. She crossed out *your* and re-wrote it correctly. "Wait," she said. "How's *you're* spelled?"

"Uh, y-o-u, apostrophe, r-e. Why do you ask?"

"'Cause a lot of times, people forget it's a contraction for *you are* and spell it like the possessive *your.*"

Especially if their brains are mush from drugs.

"So what's that mean?" Manny asked.

"What that means is this whole note doesn't sound like our prime suspect, which is not going to make Skip very happy. How's Cherise taking it?"

"Uh, she doesn't know yet. She's not here, went for a drive."

"Who's with her?" Now that Ben was once again guarding Kate, Manny was Cherise's personal guard. He was supposed to take her wherever she wanted to go.

"Nobody. She wouldn't let me go with her."

Rose ground her teeth. "Oh, goody, we have a prime suspect in the wind, a note that doesn't match the previous ones, and an uncooperative client. Excuse me, Manny, while I find a brick wall to bang my head against."

"Use Cherise's head. It's about that hard."

Rose chuckled. "Okay, send the note into the office with one of the outside guys."

"Will do." Manny disconnected.

Rose headed for Skip's office. She filled him in, then shook her head. "We can't be responsible for this woman's safety if she's gonna keep slipping the leash."

Skip pushed himself to a stand. "Come on, partner. It's time we had it out with Cherise, and with any kinda luck she'll get pissed off enough to fire us."

"I was lookin' for a job when I found this one," Rose muttered as she followed him out the door.

Three minutes after they'd left the offices of Canfield and Hernandez, the fax machine spit out two sheets of paper.

CHAPTER TWENTY

While Skip drove, his partner tried to call Cherise's cell phone.

"Went right to voicemail," Rose said as she disconnected. "Lady doesn't want to get found right now apparently. What happens if she's not home by the time we get there?"

Skip was praying she wasn't. "We leave her a polite note suggesting she retain another company to meet her security needs."

Rose grinned at him.

Cherise's car was in the driveway when they arrived, and Cherise herself opened her front door. A smile spread across her face when she saw Skip. "What a delightful surprise."

Before he could stop her, she had her arms almost all the way around his waist. He twisted away slightly before she could connect with his gun butt. "I wish you wouldn't do that, Cherise. It makes me nervous when people get too close to my gun. Can't we just air kiss like they do in Hollywood."

Cherise laughed and mimicked kissing him on each cheek. "Sorry, I keep forgetting that's where you carry your pistol."

Like hell you do.

Out loud he said, "We need to discuss a few things with you. Did Manny tell you about the latest note?"

"Yes, and it doesn't make any sense at all." Cherise led them over to the group of sofas. "If Kirk's the stalker, he knows we've identified him, so why would he say that I don't know who he is?"

"Couple other things don't add up," Rose said. "The tone of the recent notes is different. And this guy's never called you 'my love' until recently. Did Thompson call you that when you were together?"

Cherise shook her head.

Skip threw his hands up in the air. "Great! We've got a copycat."

"I think I want to put up that fence," Cherise said, with a quaver in her voice.

"Go ahead, but remember what I said. Don't let it give you a false sense of security. Fences can be climbed, cut or tunneled under."

Rose arched an eyebrow at him, as if to say, *As good an opening as we're gonna get.*

He nodded slightly.

"Actually, Cherise," Rose said, "Skip and I feel like we're not able to handle your security needs properly at this point. We're primarily a private investigating agency. The bodyguard service is just a sideline. Providing people, long-term, to patrol fences day and night is just not our thing. But we'd be happy to do some research and find a reputable firm to take over."

"I think that's what you need now, Cherise," Skip chimed in. "A company that can provide regular patrols around the property indefinitely, 'cause even if we figure out who this guy is, there may be other copycats. We can't go on like this. Our personnel are just stretched too thin now."

"So that's why you both came out today, to tell me in person that I'm not your client anymore," Cherise said, her face a neutral mask.

"I'm afraid so." Skip tried to make his voice sound regretful. "We didn't feel it was right to tell you over the phone."

Suddenly Cherise's face brightened. "Hey, I've got an idea. Why don't you vet a security firm for me to do the patrols here at the farm, but you all still provide my personal bodyguard and keep investigating who the stalker is? And you can consider the other firm a subcontractor. I'm fine with you adding a percentage for yourselves to what they bill you."

Skip and Rose looked at each other. They both gave the other a slight shake of their heads, but Cherise was looking at Rose. Her face tightened.

"Well, we have a couple of problems with that," Skip said. "Number one, we understand you've been refusing to take your bodyguard with you sometimes, when you've gone out recently."

"I'm sorry, Skip. I just started to feel like I couldn't hear myself think with somebody else around all the time."

He held up his hand. "I understand that feeling, but nonetheless, we can't be responsible for protecting you if you're not going to cooperate. And our second issue is that we really have almost nothing to go on now regarding who might be sending these notes. We're just plain out of leads."

"I may have an idea about that," Cherise said. "Something just occurred to me. But first can we agree that you'll stay my main security people and subcontract whatever services you're not directly equipped to handle?"

The partners looked at each other again. This time Rose spoke for both of them. "We will find another company and set it up for you, but not as our subcontractor. We'll try to shake loose some leads on these more recent notes, but once we've either caught the stalker or reach a total dead end, we're off the case."

"What about my personal bodyguard?" Cherise asked, a tremor in her voice. "I know your guys. I don't want a total stranger in my house again. It gets kind of creepy."

Skip looked at Rose. "It's your call, partner."

Rose thought for a moment. "We'll provide you with a personal bodyguard as long as we continue to investigate the notes, but once that's done, we're done completely. And if you ditch your bodyguard again, we're done completely. Including the investigating."

"I'll be good from now on." Cherise turned to Skip. "So since you came out here today you must feel that the threat of the paparazzi following you is gone. Does this mean you'll be my bodyguard again?"

"No, I have a business to run. I was only guarding you in public before, when the risk was the greatest, and we don't dare do that now. It'll stir up the paparazzi again."

"Oh, I think I've put that to rest permanently," Cherise said.

"What do you mean?"

"You'll see. It's a surprise."

Skip wasn't too sure he wanted any surprises from Cherise but he let it go. She was being remarkably calm and cooperative. He didn't want to tick her off at this point.

"So what was your idea about who might be sending the notes now?" Rose asked.

"Gee, I almost hate to say this, in case I'm wrong. But I'm wondering if these more recent notes are coming from Johnny."

"Your singing partner?" Skip asked. "I thought he was happily engaged to somebody?"

"He is, engaged anyway, but maybe not so happily anymore. When we were pretending to be a couple, we had to act like one in public. We hugged, danced close, even kissed sometimes. I'm wondering now if maybe he's carrying a secret torch for me."

"That would fit with this last note," Rose said. "He might be expecting you to figure out that he's in love with you. Does he call you 'my love'?"

"Not in private, but he did in public when we were pretending to date."

"Let's back up a note," Skip said. "Who would he consider to be the people who are keeping you apart? What's stopping him from breaking up with his fiancée and declaring his love for you?"

"I don't know, but anybody who sends anonymous notes as a way to court a woman is not totally rational, especially when he knows how much the other notes upset me."

"To answer your question, Skip," Rose said. "If Troop believed the media hype that you were Cherise's new boyfriend, he would see you as in the way."

Skip shook his head slightly at his partner. He didn't want to get into the sabotage of the van.

Rose nodded and stood up. "I'll keep you posted on the investigation," she said to Cherise. "Manny will be with you during the day, but I'm afraid you'll have to get used to a new guy on the night shift. He's been very carefully screened and he'll try to stay out of your hair."

"Isn't Ben available?"

"No, he's on another assignment." Rose's tone was crisp.

Cherise made a little moue with her mouth, then gave them a smile that didn't quite make it to her eyes. "Tell him I said hi. He's a nice guy."

Rose and Skip started for the door.

"Uh, Skip, could I speak to you privately please, for just a moment?" Cherise said.

Rose gave a little shake of her head, but Skip didn't see how he could politely refuse. "Sure. I'll be out in a minute, Rose." His eyes telegraphed, *Come rescue me if I'm not.*

Rose smirked a little, then walked out the door.

Cherise turned to Skip with fire in her eyes. "I can't believe you let your dyke partner talk you into abandoning me."

Skip stepped back, his hands flew up in front of him. He made himself take a deep breath. "Rose is not gay and she did not talk me into anything. We are equal business partners, but *I* am the one who has the final say in what cases we take, or keep, because I'm the more experienced investigator."

"So what were all the little head shakes and nods about?"

Skip had a short debate with himself. They had just negotiated themselves a gracious escape route out of this case. Logic said he should make nice-nice to preserve that. He shook his head. Screw logic. He was fed up with this woman.

"It's called nonverbal communication, Cherise, and we were both doing it. Now, unless you want to end your contract with us right now, I need to go."

"Oh, no, no. Skip, I'm sorry. I misunderstood."

He reached the door in two long strides. Cherise followed him out onto the porch. "Stop, Skip. Don't go away mad. I'm sorry I jumped to conclusions." She grabbed at his arm. "Kiss, kiss." She made air kisses in the general direction of his cheeks.

"Gotta go, Cherise. We'll let you know about the other firm as soon as we've got them vetted." Skip jogged down the sidewalk toward his truck where Rose was waiting for him.

Cherise waved at him from the porch, then suddenly she was bolting toward him as he started to climb into the truck.

"Wait, Skip!"

"What now?" Rose muttered from the passenger seat. Skip stopped, half in the vehicle, half out.

Cherise ran behind the truck and stooped down. She came up with two kittens in her hands. "Sorry, these little idiots haven't figured out yet that the middle of the driveway is not a good place to sun themselves." She smiled sweetly at him. "Talk to you soon." She turned and walked back to the house.

Skip ended up talking to her a lot sooner than he expected.

Back at the agency, he was barely settled into his desk chair when Rose appeared in his doorway. "What now?" he said, his voice sharper than he'd intended.

"Hey, don't shoot the messenger," Rose said.

"Sorry." He let out a resigned sigh and held out his hand. "Give 'em to me."

Same old picture of him and Cherise at Merriweather. "Aren't they getting tired of that one. Edges must be ragged by now."

The caption was *New Beau?* He read the first sentence of the article. *Cherise Martin's publicist confirmed today that the popular singer does indeed have a new boyfriend, although he would not say who the new beau was.*

"Damn it to hell!" Skip threw the pages across his desk. Rose nabbed them before they slithered off the other side. He put his elbows on the desk and buried his face in his hands. "Does it get any worse than the first sentence?"

"Not really. Just rehashes the original speculations, your press conference denial," Rose said, as she skimmed the article. "Oops, wait a minute. Not good."

"What is it?"

"At the end." She read out loud, "When Jim Bolton, Ms. Martin's publicist, was asked who the new boyfriend is, he said, 'Cherise has told you before that a girl doesn't kiss and tell.'"

"Shit, shit, shit!" Skip picked up his phone and punched in Cherise's number. Rose sat down in his visitor's chair.

As soon as Cherise answered, he said without preamble, "This is your little surprise? You announce to the press you've got a new boyfriend, then give them the coy little line, 'a girl doesn't kiss and tell'."

"What? What are you talking about, Skip?"

"Hot off the presses. 'Ms. Martin's publicist confirms she has a new beau.' Then three paragraphs rehashing the same old shit, next to the picture of us from Merriweather. Then Bolton quotes you with the 'a girl never tells' line. I thought you fired that ass anyway."

"I did, but then I had second thoughts. He is one of the best publicists out there."

"No he's not, Cherise. He's a fuckin' loose cannon!"

"Don't curse at me, Skip."

"I'll curse at you all I want, Cherise. You've fucked up my life, and my family's life. Again!"

"Skip, that's not what I told him to say. I told him to announce I had a new boyfriend and I gave him a fake name to give them."

"Then what's with the 'girl never tells' line. Did you say that?"

"Yeah, last year. When some reporter was trying to find out who I was dating. That's why I went along with the fake romance with Johnny, because it kept the paparazzi from trying to find out who I was really seeing."

"So technically you had told them that before, but you weren't saying it in this context, like he implied."

"I'm sorry. I'll fix this. I promise."

"That scares me, Cherise. 'Cause every time you try to fix it, it gets worse."

"I *will* fix it this time. First, I'm going to fire Jim Bolton. Then I'm going to ruin him by telling the press exactly what he did. That I told him one thing, in an effort to clear up a misunderstanding that was causing my bodyguard and his family distress, and he told the press something different and made the situation worse, just to get the publicity. The jerk will never work again."

Skip didn't say anything.

"Skip, this isn't my fault, but I will fix it."

"You do that, Cherise." He hung up and went back to holding his head in his hands. "How am I going to explain this to Kate?"

Rose was silent.

He looked up.

"Got no clue," she said.

~~~~~~~~

When Kate came out of her last session, Skip was sitting in her waiting room instead of Ben.

After the client was out the door, she came over to him and kissed his cheek. "Well, this is a pleasant surprise."

Skip didn't say anything.

Kate sat down next to him. "What's wrong, Skip? The kids! My God, are the kids okay?"

"Yeah, the kids are fine. Nobody's hurt or anything," he reassured her. "It's, uh, a bad development, but not that kind of thing."

"Then what is it, sweetheart?" she asked. She took his hand in both of hers.

"I... she..." He shook his head, not sure how to explain it succinctly, afraid of what her reaction would be.

Her eyes searched his face. Suddenly her breath caught in her throat. "You and her... You didn't sleep with her, did you?" she whispered.

Skip looked at her, dumbfounded. "Of course not." He almost blurted out, *How could you think such a thing?* But he'd forfeited the right to say those words to her.

He jumped up and started pacing. "Cherise tried to fix it with the press. She told Bolton to announce she had a new boyfriend and she gave him a fake name." The words tumbled out as he circled the room, clenching his fists. "But the asshole only told the press the first part, then when they asked who the guy was, he misquoted her. 'As Cherise has told you before, a girl doesn't kiss and tell.' So instead of putting to rest the rumor that she and I are lovers, he's resurrected it."

Kate sat back in her chair and put her head against the waiting room wall. "And I suppose this has already made it into print," she said, in that defeated voice he had never wanted to hear again.

He stopped and looked at her from across the room. The washed-out gray of her eyes made his chest ache. He just nodded mutely, not sure he could trust his voice at that moment. He crossed the space between them and sat down beside his wife. "Kate, I'm so sorry I brought this down on us."

"It's not your fault," she said, but her voice was still flat.

"Maybe not, but I should be able to fix it, and I can't. I feel so damned helpless." He pounded on his knees with clenched fists.

She grabbed one of those fists and held it between her own hands. "Sweetheart, this is one of those better or worse moments. *You* don't have to fix it. *We* will deal with it together."

Her words helped, but only a little.

"Rob had a suggestion a couple weeks ago," Kate said. "That we should go on a vacation once this case was resolved. I'm thinking we should do a modified version of that idea and go away for the weekend. Get out of town for a few days and hopefully the paparazzi will lose interest."

Skip nodded. "That's not a bad idea. You and the kids should go somewhere, tonight if you can afford to cancel your appointments for tomorrow."

"I have a client at eleven that I have to see. She's been suicidal lately and just got out of the hospital. I can cancel my afternoon clients though. They're all in pretty good shape at the moment. But I'm not going anywhere without you. I'm not sure you realize how much all this is stressing you out. You're just focused on protecting us."

"I'm okay." He stared into space, his mind frantically searching for a way to fix the problem.

Kate reached up and turned his face toward her. She smoothed back the hair that had flopped down onto his forehead. The tender gesture was almost his undoing. His eyes stung. He swallowed hard to clear his clogged throat.

"Sweetheart,," she said, "you're not okay. Normally I see your jaw tighten maybe once a month. Lately it's more like once or twice a day, and some days it's clenched nonstop. You need a break from all this, and another round of being hounded by the paparazzi strikes me as an excellent excuse for all of us to get out of town for a while."

Skip gave in, mainly because he didn't want to cause her more stress from worrying about him. "Okay, you talked me into it."

~~~~~~~~~

They arrived home to discover that the fresh deluge of paparazzi had not yet materialized.

Kate had hoped to get everything packed that evening so they could get away early the next day. But by the time she'd called her clients to reschedule appointments and had gotten the kids' things packed up, it was bath and story time.

Skip had been unnaturally quiet all evening. He'd called around and found a bed and breakfast in Thurmont—a town in the foothills of the Allegheny Mountains in western Maryland—that had a family cancel on them for that weekend. He'd reserved the two adjoining rooms with private bath.

But other than reporting his success to her, he'd said very little.

While he was tucking the children in, Kate pulled suitcases out of the back of their closets. She tossed a few things in them, then went into the bathroom to pack her toiletries.

When she came out, Skip was lying on top of the comforter on his side of the bed, his forearm draped across his face. She knelt beside the bed and kissed his elbow. He didn't react. "Sweetheart," she said softly. "I think we deserve an early bedtime tonight. I can finish packing tomorrow after I get home."

She expected him to make some suggestive comment, or at the very least turn his head and grin at her, but he just nodded without moving his arm from his eyes.

Kate went to check on the children and secure the house for the night. When she came back, Skip had dropped his clothes on the floor and had slid between the sheets. His eyes were closed but she knew he wasn't asleep. She quietly got undressed and slipped in beside him, turning onto her side and gently nudging his hip with her butt. As she expected, he turned and draped an arm around her waist, pulling her snug up against him.

They lay there, spooned together, for several minutes. When he made no further move, she listened for his breathing to slow into the pattern of sleep.

It didn't. He was still awake.

Finally she turned over to face him. "Skip–"

"Sh, sh, it'll be okay." He kissed her forehead. "The dust will have probably settled by the time we get back on Sunday."

But that wasn't what she was worried about.

She ran her hand down his side, sliding past the ticklish spot just above his hip. His skin quivered slightly but still he made no move to kiss her. She considered tickling him, but was afraid to find out that this wouldn't solicit the normal response either.

"I'm okay," he said, reading her thoughts. "I just need to get some sleep."

No you're not okay, a voice screamed inside her head. She'd never seen him withdraw into himself like this.

But there was no point in pushing him to talk. There was nothing either of them could do to rid themselves of the cause of the problem, at least not tonight.

Rolling back over, she snuggled against him again.

He wrapped his arm around her waist and pulled her close.

A long time later, she felt the arm relax and heard his breathing slow.

But the knowledge that her husband was clinically depressed kept Kate awake for another hour, before fatigue finally overrode anxiety.

CHAPTER TWENTY-ONE

Skip kept his mind occupied the next morning with the need to tie up loose ends at work so he could leave early. At eleven-ten, he was staring at the application form for the renewal of the agency's license, trying to decide if it could wait until next week.

Rose appeared in his office doorway. She had papers under her arm and the grimmest look he'd ever seen on her face.

Her back-up slipped past her into the office. Dolph settled into the visitor's chair. Mac moved over to lean against the opposite wall.

"I've got four of our men headed for the house and Ben's been alerted," Rose said.

Skip sat back in his chair and stared at the ceiling, gritting his teeth. They couldn't even get out of town before something else happened.

"Tell me," he said, without lowering his eyes.

Rose didn't answer him right away.

"Just tell me, damn it."

"Pics of you and Cherise at the farm, outside as we were leaving. Her grabbing your arm as you're turning away. Her air kiss, that looks like she's trying to kiss you and you're pulling back. Then when she ran toward the truck to rescue the kittens. Together, looks like the two of you are having a lovers' spat. Story to match."

Skip stared at the ceiling for another moment. The thoughts tumbling through his mind, thoughts of doing violence–to the paparazzi, to himself–scared him. Leaning forward, he carefully removed his gun from its waistband holster with two fingers and set it on his desktop, then gave it a push. It skittered across the surface in Dolph's direction. "Hold on to that for the time being," he said to the older man, then crossed his arms on the desk and lowered his head onto them.

After a minute, he said, without raising his head. "Call Cherise. Tell her not to try to fix it. Who knows how they'll twist whatever she says."

"Mac," Rose said softly. Rustling as he left the room, no doubt to make the call.

Rose's hand on his shoulder. "I'm driving you home."

Skip didn't bother to protest. It would take too much energy. He pushed himself to a stand and moved toward the door.

Dolph stood to one side, his hand wrapped around Skip's gun barrel, the butt dangling toward the floor.

"You and Mac bring his truck to the house," Rose said quietly as she passed the older man. Dolph nodded.

"Take me to Kate's office first," Skip said. "I need to tell her about this myself."

~~~~~~~

The paparazzi were now out in force. They descended on the Expedition when it pulled up in front of the house with Mac at the wheel.

Dolph parked his own car behind him.

They'd briefly discussed strategy before leaving the office. Dolph had pointed out that Mac was putting his license to carry a gun and maybe even his private investigator's license in jeopardy, especially since he was still in the two-year provisional period required of anyone who was not previously in law enforcement.

Mac's reply had been that he didn't give a damn. He wasn't going to allow those asshole reporters to upset Kate and the kids.

They joined the two big men standing guard at the front of the property. The other two were behind the house, making sure no reporters tried to sneak across a neighbor's yard.

Mac raised his arms in the air. The crowd gradually fell silent, as one by one, they noticed the Glock in one of his hands.

Dolph saw vans from the mainstream media, Channels 2 and 13, pull up. This was not good. Mac was going to suffer for this for sure, but he decided to stand with the man. Hell, he always had his police pension to fall back on.

"Listen up," Mac yelled. "Official press release. The Canfields are going on vacation." He lowered his voice and growled, "Turn off the mikes and cameras. Now." After a long pause, the reporters nodded to their assistants and camera people.

"This is off the record," Mac said. "The first finger twitches on a mike or camera switch while I'm saying this, my finger's gonna twitch. First asshole who yells anything to any member of the family coming out of that house, my finger's gonna twitch even worse. And anybody who tries to jump in their vehicle and follow the Canfields when they leave, they're gonna mysteriously have four flat tires real quick."

~~~~~~~~~

When Kate came out of her session, she startled a little at the sight of him once again sitting in her waiting room. She said goodbye to her client and came over to sit beside him. "What's the matter, sweetheart?"

Skip opened his mouth but nothing came out. He dropped his head into his hands.

"Did something else happen?" Kate asked, anxiety in her voice.

He nodded, but still couldn't find the words to tell her that it had gone from bad to worse–much worse.

She reached for the folded sheets of paper sticking out of his back pocket. She let out a small groan when she saw the pictures, then dropped the pages on the floor as if they were scalding hot.

Skip dropped to his knees on the carpet in front of her. "Kate, can you ever forgive me for this?"

She didn't answer immediately.

Her silence terrified him. Unable to continue to look into her washed-out eyes, he buried his face in her lap.

"This isn't your fault." Her voice was gentle. She stroked his hair.

"Yes, it is. I brought this down on us, and now I can't make it go away."

Skip felt the ground shift under him. Everything he had, everything he was–it was disintegrating. He couldn't protect his family, end the harassment. He was still that scrawny teenager being terrorized by bullies, and nothing he tried would make them stop.

"No," Kate said more emphatically. "You're not responsible for this."

He shook his head without looking up at her. "Yes, I am. A man's supposed to protect his family. That's what my Dad..." His voice broke. He stopped and sucked in air. "He always told me, 'Take care of your family, son. Keep them safe, no matter what.'"

"And you do that. We're all safe. You're a good man, Skip. A great father." Her voice sounded far away.

Memories flooded back. Being mocked for his goofy nickname, and when he tried to stand up for himself, they'd gang up on him, beat him up, then walk away laughing. Again and again. They wouldn't stop.

Fingers dug into his shoulders. Kate forced him to sit back on his heels and look at her. "Skip Canfield, you are the best husband a woman could ever ask for. You didn't make this happen, and we'll get through it, together."

He stared at her, struggling for an emotional foothold. Embarrassment scalded his cheeks. He shoved himself to a stand and moved a few feet away, his back to her.

Rustling, then Kate's hand lightly touched his back. "Sit down and try to relax for a minute, sweetheart. I've got a client I need to call before I can leave, okay?"

He nodded without turning around.

~~~~

Kate went into her office and closed the door, but the call she planned to make had nothing to do with clients. Kate held her breath until Rob answered his cell phone.

"Franklin."

Kate poured out the story as quickly as she could, fighting back tears. "I'm worried about him, and I'm not sure how to deal with this. He thinks he's less than a man because he can't protect his family."

"Where are you? At home?"

"No, at my office, but we're headed home. We were planning to go away for the weekend anyway, before this new development."

"I was on my way out to grab some lunch. I think I'll swing by your house to see you off."

She breathed out a sigh. "Thank you."

When Kate came out into the waiting room, Skip was sitting in a chair, his head resting back against the wall, eyes closed.

He sat up when he heard her door close. Glancing furtively at her, he said, "I'm sorry."

She knew this time he was apologizing for losing control. She sat down next to him and took his hand in hers, not sure what to say. Finally, she settled on, "It's okay to be human, sweetheart."

~~~~~~~~~~

The relief in Kate's voice when Rob had volunteered to come by the house had spoken louder than her "Thank you." He'd decided to call in reinforcements. As he hurried to his car, he phoned his wife at her office.

When Rob got to Kate's house, there was no sign of her car, although Skip's Expedition was parked at the curb. Mac and Dolph stood nearby, between the mob of paparazzi and the house.

Rob stepped out of his car and started toward the front porch.

"Hey, there's the wife's lover," a reporter yelled out.

Rob glanced back over his shoulder without turning around. Mac was waving his hand in the air, making a lazy circle. The crowd of paparazzi edged back a bit.

With a jolt, Rob realized the hand held a very big pistol.

"I'd behave if I were you, ladies and gentlemen," Dolph called out in a conversational tone.

Despite the gravity of the situation, Rob chuckled under his breath.

Maria let him in, then slammed the door shut behind him. Fear dominated her broad face but her mouth was set in a firm line. It dawned on Rob that this whole mess was probably reminiscent for her of even more dangerous situations in her native Guatemala.

"It'll be okay," he reassured her. "These clowns can't do any real harm."

"They already do plenty harm," she said. "I get kids ready." She turned and headed for the stairs.

Rose rounded the corner from the laundry room on the back of the house, Skip and Kate trailing behind.

"Liz and I figured we'd see you off," Rob said. "She'll be here soon to help Kate pack." He tilted his head slightly toward the bedroom.

Kate took the hint and headed that way.

Rob gave Skip's shoulder a friendly pat and maneuvered him toward the kitchen. "I thought I'd make some sandwiches for all of us."

Standing at the counter, Rob put together sandwiches and listened as Skip told him what had happened, pretending he hadn't already heard the story from Kate.

"Shit, Rob. I'm six-five and weigh two-fifty. There isn't much in this world I'm afraid of, but I'm developing a phobia of Rose showing up in my office doorway, with those fax sheets under her arm."

"It's frustrating as hell," Rob said, "that nothing we've tried seems to be stopping these assholes for good."

Skip dropped into a chair and ran a hand through his hair. "I feel so damned helpless."

Rob abandoned the sandwiches and took a seat at the table across from him. "Skip, we do our best to take care of our families, but we can't always protect them from everything."

"I know that, intellectually. But my daddy's voice keeps echoing in my head, 'Protect your family, son.' It's..." Skip shook his head. "I feel like... like I'm letting him down, as well as Kate and the kids."

Rob stayed silent, giving his friend the space to vent.

"He was a great dad," Skip said after a moment. "I always figured, if and when I had a family, if I could be just like him..." He trailed off, his Adam's apple bobbing in his throat as he swallowed hard.

After a beat, Rob quietly said, "If your father were alive today, what would he tell you about all this?"

Skip stared into space for a minute. Finally, he said, "He'd recite the Serenity Prayer to me."

Rob nodded. "Control the things you can. Accept the things you can't. Your dad was a wise man." He rose and went back to the sandwiches.

Ten minutes later, Liz came into the kitchen. "Where's Skip?"

"Checking on the kids." Rob held up a big paper bag. "I decided to pack their lunch for the road," he whispered. "The sooner they get out of here the better."

Liz nodded. "I added a little something to Kate's suitcase." She stood on tiptoe and Rob leaned down. She whispered in his ear.

He smiled. "That should come in handy."

Suddenly the mischievous light went out in her eyes and her mouth set in a grim line. "Isn't there anything we can do to make this stop?" she said in a low voice.

He gave a slight shake of his head. "I wish there were, but any protests at this point will just fan the fire."

She nodded and sighed.

He wrapped his arms around his petite wife and rested his chin on her head, blinking hard to get the gritty feeling out of his eyes.

~~~~

Rose came out of the house carrying two suitcases. She headed for the red van.

"Hey, is Mrs. Canfield leaving her husband?" one of the reporters yelled.

Just couldn't resist, could you? Dolph thought.

Mac waved his gun in the air.

Out loud, Dolph said, "She's a member of the family."

A car pulled up and parked behind his own. A black woman got out and walked briskly across the lawn, the stark white of her clerical collar standing out between mocha skin and black blouse, under a tailored gray suit.

A reporter opened his mouth.

"She's a family member too," Dolph said pleasantly.

"She's not coming out of the house," the reporter muttered.

"That, sir, is a technicality."

The female reporter from Channel 2 smiled at him. "The Canfields have a very diverse family, it seems."

Dolph winked at her.

~~~~

Skip raised his head as Kate escorted Elaine Johnson into the living room. "Mary Peters saw the tabloid at the grocery store," Elaine was saying. "She called me. I've been trying to get through, but I guess you have the phone off the hook."

Skip started to push up off the floor where he'd been sitting, the kids playing around him.

Elaine waved a hand at him. "Stay put. I just came by to check on you all."

"We're getting out of town for the weekend," Kate said.

"Good idea." Elaine gestured to the children. "Come climb on your daddy's lap, and I'll bless your mini vacation."

The children complied and Elaine raised both arms in the air.

"Dear Lord Jesus," her voice rang out as if she were addressing the whole congregation. "Hold this family in Your hands as they travel the roads on their journey this weekend, and as they travel the path of their spiritual journey. Protect them, Lord, and give them the strength to endure whatever crosses their path."

She suddenly leaned down and used her thumb to sketch a cross on Skip's forehead. Lowering her voice, she said, "The Lord be with you, Skip Canfield. The Lord *will always* be with you."

He stared up at her.

She raised her arms again and boomed out, "Dear God in Heaven, protect these fine people and give them strength. In the name of the Father, the Son and the Holy Spirit. Amen."

The children had already lost interest. They scrambled off their father's lap to go back to their toys.

Skip was still trying to process what just happened. Something had shifted again. He wasn't sure just what.

Elaine, who was half his weight, reached out a hand as if to help him to his feet. He snorted softly to himself and pushed himself to his feet. Then he took her hand.

She wrapped both of hers around his and squeezed. "You and your family have a grand little vacation now."

He smiled down at this woman who kept showing up just when he needed a kick in the butt. "Thanks for coming, Elaine."

She grinned back at him. "You're welcome." She turned on her heel and left.

Skip and Kate herded the children to the van and got them buckled into their car seats. Rob passed the bag of sandwiches to Kate and they exchanged hugs and handshakes all around.

The crowd of paparazzi rustled.

Mac barked out, "My finger's gettin' twitchy."

Skip hid a smirk as the photographers lowered their cameras again.

Rose carried her cousin's overnight bag outside and put it in the trunk of her car. Maria followed and climbed into the passenger seat. The plan was that she would spend the weekend with Rose's parents.

But Rose had insisted that she was going to follow the red van for a while, to make sure no press tried to tail them.

Skip waited for her to flash her lights, indicating she was ready to go. Then he started the van and pulled away from the curb.

He looked up in the rearview mirror. The Franklins were waving from the front yard. Under Mac's and Dolph's watchful gaze, the crowd of media dispersed to their vehicles. But none made a move to follow the red van.

Skip smiled as he turned the corner.

~~~~

No one had noticed the remaining reporter standing across the street–a tall, thin man, with salt and pepper hair. He tapped the fat envelope in his shirt pocket, the added incentive he'd received to stir this story back to life.

CHAPTER TWENTY-TWO

On Saturday, the Canfields poked around the small town of Thurmont, then hiked one of the trails in the foothills surrounding it. Billy's short legs gave out quickly. Skip swung him up onto his shoulders. When Kate noticed her daughter's feet were also beginning to drag, she took Billy from her husband. Skip stooped down so Edie could clamber onto his broad back. She rode piggyback the rest of the way.

They returned in the late afternoon to their B and B, tired but refreshed. The children were nodding off over their mac and cheese at the family-style restaurant where they ate dinner.

As Skip was doing story time with the kids, Kate rummaged through her suitcase, looking for some hand lotion she could have sworn she'd thrown in there. What she found instead was an object she knew she hadn't packed. The baby monitor from Billy's room.

Kate grinned. "Thank you, Liz," she whispered under her breath.

Slipping into the children's room, she kissed them goodnight and set the little transmitter on the table between the twin beds. Once out of the room, Kate held up the receiver and said to Skip in a low voice, "Let's see if this thing works out on the front porch."

Sure enough, they could hear little rustling noises coming from the small plastic box, even on the porch. They settled into rockers and watched the summer sunset turn the sky brilliant. The mountains were silhouettes of deep purple against slashes of gold, pink and violet.

Skip sighed and reached over for Kate's hand. "Rob has some jimdandy ideas sometimes."

"We're so blessed to have their friendship," Kate said.

"I'm blessed to have you." Skip's voice was thick with emotion as he squeezed her hand.

Kate looked over at him in the gathering dusk. "Skip Canfield," she said with mock sternness, "I have something to say to you and I don't want any back talk."

"Uh oh, what'd I do now?"

"I got the better end of this deal, and don't you ever forget it."

He grinned at her. "My daddy used to say that a good business deal was when both parties believed they had gotten the better end of it."

Kate's heart did a funny little flip at the sight of that grin.

Skip sighed again. "What could be better than sitting on a porch in the clean mountain air, sharing a sunset with the woman you love?"

Kate waited a couple of minutes as the last of the colors drained from the darkening sky. "Sharing a big feather bed with her, maybe," she finally answered him.

Skip stood and pulled her to her feet. He grinned down at her. "Yup. That could be better."

~~~~~~~~~

Rose called Kate's cell phone at noon on Sunday. "Coast is clear. You can come home whenever you want." There was a chuckle in her voice.

"What's going on?" Kate asked.

"Media did the right thing for a change. The mainstream media that is. Two TV stations were there Friday, covering your departure. Only their spin was how horrible it is that the tabloid press are harassing an everyday family. Just because the husband and father happened to cross paths with a celebrity in the line of his work."

"Seriously?" Kate was having trouble digesting this turn of events.

"Seriously. My guess is there's no love lost between the mainstream press and the tabloids. The latter give the more legitimate journalists a bad name. No mention of Mac brandishing his Glock, thank God. But one channel said, and I quote, 'armed guards were necessary to keep the overzealous tabloid media at bay.' The follow-up stories last night showed footage of your house. There were flowers and notes all over the front yard. Went by this morning and gathered up the notes. Want me to open them?"

"Yeah, do that," Kate said.

Rustling for the better part of a minute, punctuated by a couple of soft grunts.

Finally Rose cleared her throat. "About twenty-five or so here. Skimming through them, they're all sympathetic, except one lady who calls Skip an evil man and encourages you to divorce him."

"Trash that one."

"Already did," Rose said.

Kate thanked her, then turned to tell Skip what had happened.

After lunch, they packed up their family and went home.

~~~~~~~~

Rose was quite satisfied with how her own weekend had gone.

She'd tripled the guards at Cherise's farm, fearing the paparazzi would descend there, even though the article on Friday hadn't mentioned the address. She'd sent Ben to supervise the men, while Skip and Kate were out of town.

But all had been quiet in Howard County. If the reporter who'd written the lovers' quarrel article was hanging around, he was staying well out of sight. And he was apparently keeping the knowledge of Cherise's address to himself. No doubt that would be next week's juicy story.

On Saturday, Rose had spent some quality time with her man. They'd had a long talk that morning, which was saying something, since neither of them was really what you'd call a talker. At noon, they'd headed for Towson Town Center to grab some lunch, and then check out jewelry stores.

As she drove to Howard County early Monday afternoon, Rose turned her left hand on the steering wheel to admire the small ruby—her birth stone—surrounded by tiny diamonds.

They had decided not to tell anyone, just see how long it took for people to notice the ring. So far no one had. She wasn't surprised by Dolph's obliviousness this morning. She would have been by Skip's, if he weren't still recuperating from the emotional wringer he'd been through the last few days.

She grinned. Once he did notice, she was going to enjoy ribbing him about how long it took the big, bad detective to detect that his partner was engaged.

She'd spent the morning checking out local security companies. She had two possibilities and the owner of the most promising one was meeting her at four this afternoon at Cherise's farm. Tom McPherson had said he would need to see the property before he could give her a detailed proposal and firm price.

In the meantime, Rose was headed to Johnny Troop's apartment to interview him.

Troop lived in a building overlooking Lake Kittamaqundi, in the center of the planned city of Columbia in Howard County. Rose discovered why Troop had turned down their offers of a bodyguard. The building had state-of-the-art security. The staff stopped just short of a full body pat-down.

She got into a verbal tussle with the concierge over whether she could "retain her sidearm while on the premises"–his fancy-smancy words. She was about to tell him where he could retain a large stick, when a girl-next-door type stepped off an elevator and approached the desk.

"It's okay, Frank. I'll take our guest up now," the wholesome-looking young woman said.

"Yes, ma'am." The concierge's tone was now deferential.

The woman turned to Rose and held out her hand. "Sharon Millington. I'm Johnny's fiancée."

Rose took the proffered hand. It was slender, cool and dry. "Rose Hernandez."

They made small talk, awkwardly, as the elevator rose smoothly to the tenth floor. Millington led the way into a surprisingly modest-looking apartment.

Rose had only met Johnny Troop once before, at the concert at Merriweather. Today he seemed much smaller and less impressive than he had on stage. He was about five-seven, slender and pale, his straight dark hair tied back in a ponytail. He looked the part of the poet/songwriter.

His fiancée, a brunette with big brown cow's eyes, was not a particularly large woman, but she had an inch on him and probably outweighed him by twenty pounds or so.

No wonder he sits on a stool while performing, Rose thought, as Millington introduced her.

Troop just nodded.

Once they were all seated on the plain beige sofa and brown leather recliner in the living room, Rose was at a bit of a loss as to where to start. She hadn't anticipated interviewing Troop in front of his fiancée.

Start at the beginning, with the basics. "Private Investigating 101," Skip had called it when Rose was in training.

"As you know, Mr. Troop, Cherise Martin has been getting weird, and sometimes threatening, anonymous notes for some time. My partner and I have not only been providing bodyguard services for her, we've also been investigating the source of those notes."

"I thought you'd figured out who was doing it and had scared him off," Troop said, opening his mouth for the first time.

"We had and did. But there have been some new notes. Cherise didn't tell you about them?"

"Johnny communicates as little as possible with Cherise," the fiancée said, "outside of their work together." Her tone was cool.

"We're pretty sure the notes up through the box with the dog head in it were sent by one of Cherise's ex-boyfriends, Kirk Thompson."

Troop's face had gone even paler at the mention of the decapitated dog. Millington showed no reaction.

"Thompson's taken off," Rose said. "But these recent notes sound different from the previous ones, so we're working under the assumption that they're being sent by someone else."

Sharon Millington narrowed her big brown eyes at her. "And this has what to do with us, Ms. Hernandez?"

Rose was beginning to think the woman's looks were deceiving. Sweet girl next door she was not.

"Well, that's what I'm here to find out."

Millington bristled. Troop looked confused.

Damn!

Rose wished she'd asked Skip to come with her. She knew her own strengths and weaknesses, and tact was not on the former list. "Please don't take this the wrong way," she said. "We have to investigate all possibilities."

Millington's eyes were now slits. "Cut to the chase, Ms. Hernandez."

"There are some indicators that the new notes could be coming from you, Mr. Troop. Are they?"

Johnny threw up his arms and jumped up out of the recliner. "That woman is a pain in the arse." He stuffed his hands into the pockets of his jeans and paced the length of the living room.

Rose wasn't all that comfortable sitting while he was standing. But she couldn't see how she could get up, not without making the situation more confrontational.

"And these indicators are?" Millington's tone was icy.

"The note sender is now referring to Cherise as 'my love,' as Mr. Troop did during their fake romance." Rose was watching Troop's expression and body language as he paced around the room.

"You said indicators, plural," Millington said.

"Lots of things point to the probability that this guy knows Cherise. It's not just some random fan, and the latest note implied she should be able to figure out who he is."

"You keep saying he, Ms. Hernandez," Millington said. "Have you eliminated the possibility that the note sender could be a woman? Personally, I think that Sarah what's-her-name's a bit creepy."

"What makes you think it could be Sarah?" Rose asked.

"She gives Cherise little adoring looks all the time. Maybe she's a closet lesbian who's fallen in love with her boss."

"Or maybe she's just a bit star-struck."

But, Rose admitted to herself, the woman had a point. They hadn't really looked at Sarah all that closely, other than the routine background check they'd done on all of Cherise's employees. They'd found no police record, not even a traffic ticket. Googling her name had produced no hits that had anything to do with this particular Sarah Hamilton. The woman seemed to have led a very unexciting life.

"Cherise is setting me up," Johnny Troop abruptly announced, as he marched back over to perch on the edge of the recliner. "That bitch is setting me up."

Rose stared at him. "In what way, Mr. Troop?"

"She told you she thinks it's me, didn't she? She's using these damn notes to screw with me, as payback."

"Why would she do that?" Rose asked.

"Because the last few months, when we were supposed to be play-acting that we were lovers, she was making it quite clear to me, and to Sharon–"

"*Especially* to me," Millington said with venom in her voice. "Cherise wanted the fake romance to be a real one."

"I told Jim Bolton I was done pretending to be her boyfriend," Troop said. "She was all over me every time we went anywhere."

"Which explains why Bolton jumped on the story about Cherise and my partner as an excuse to announce that you two had broken up."

Troop nodded.

"Do you think she'd really fallen for you?" Rose asked. "Or did she just want the forbidden fruit?"

"More likely the latter," Troop said. "Cherise has trouble believing that any man can resist her charms. I think she saw me as a challenge. The more I didn't want her, the more she had to have me."

Rose resisted the temptation to nod and agree with his assessment. Cherise, after all, was their client.

"Did she ever date married men?" Cherise had claimed she didn't but Rose wasn't sure she trusted that. "Maybe there's a jealous wife out there, who's trying to mess with her?"

Troop shook his head. "No, her old man ran around on her mother, and she hated him for it. I think that's why she's so screwed up when it comes to men. But she has a strict rule. No married men."

Rose breathed out a quiet sigh. Standing up, she said, "Thank you for your time, and congratulations on finally being able to announce your engagement."

Sharon Millington rose from her seat. "This isn't for public consumption yet, but Johnny and I were married in Bermuda two weeks ago."

"Does Cherise know that?" Rose asked.

"No, but feel free to tell her." For the first time, Sharon Millington-Troop smiled.

It was not a nice smile.

As Rose drove to Cherise's farm, she mentally scratched Johnny Troop off her suspect list, and added Sarah.

And Troop's new wife for good measure.

That malicious smile had made the hair stand up on Rose's neck.

CHAPTER TWENTY-THREE

Harry Bailey was more than happy to show Tom McPherson and Rose around the farm. He was obviously proud of what they had accomplished in the four years Cherise had owned the property.

"This was all overgrown with bushes and weeds when Ms. Martin bought the place." He gestured across the rolling hills of green grass. "Now we got six acres in pasture, a paddock, a riding ring. The barn's been refurbished. We grow hay, oats and corn on the rest of the land. I mix our sweet feed myself. Ms. Martin likes it that everything the horses eat is grown here. Says she likes to be in complete control of their diet."

Why am I not surprised? Rose thought.

"Seems like a lot of trouble and expense for just four horses," McPherson said.

Bailey shrugged. "She's got the bucks, and she pays well for Bobby's and my time."

"Is there enough to do, to keep both of you busy?" McPherson asked.

"Sure is. Bobby also does most of the maintenance on the buildings. He's pretty handy. He helps me with the crops some too. I'm only part-time. Retired actually. Worked at Beth Steel for forty years. I was gettin' bored and cranky hangin' 'round the house all the time. The wife tossed me out one day, sayin', 'Don't come back 'til you've got a part-time job.'" Bailey chuckled.

"This is a damn fine part-time job, too," McPherson said. "You get to be the boss, do the things you like to do, delegate the rest."

"Well, now, I ain't nobody's boss. The staff, we all have our own little niche, answer directly to Ms. Martin, each of us does."

McPherson changed the subject. "How often does she trail ride?"

Rose was warming up to this guy. He was asking all the right questions. She may have hit pay dirt on the first try. They were slowly walking the outer perimeter of the property while they talked. Rose hung back a little, not saying anything.

"She hasn't been out on the trail at all lately," Bailey said as they turned a corner and headed across the back property line. "The one mare just foaled and the other's about to drop hers any day now. Gelding's still nursing an injury from a few weeks ago, and the two-year-old's just green broke. Ms. Martin's been working with him in the ring."

Rose hid a grin at the look of relief on McPherson's face. Providing security for a woman on a horse in the woods would be a total nightmare. She dropped back a little further, looking around. She'd never been up to this part of the property before. It bordered woods and was kind of pretty back here.

Her phone buzzed in her pocket. She pulled it out and checked caller ID, then let the men get a few more paces ahead before answering it. The signal was poor. She thought she heard Dolph say that Judith Anderson had picked up Kirk Thompson. Sticking a finger in her other ear, she lowered her head to concentrate on Dolph's voice that was cutting in and out.

A cracking sound startled her, just as someone grabbed the bun on the back of her head and gave it a vicious tug. Yelping in pain, she whirled around to face her attacker.

Nobody was there. Her scalp stung like hell. She reached up and touched the disheveled bun. Her hand came away wet and sticky.

The men were running back toward her. "Get down!" McPherson yelled.

Rose turned toward him, and felt air movement next to her cheek as she heard another cracking sound. She hit the ground.

A third crack, and dirt and grass sprayed over her. She rolled toward the nearby woods as she heard McPherson yelling into his cell phone, "Somebody's firing on us–"

The rest of what he was saying was drowned out by a fourth crack, and splinters of bark flew off the tree under which Rose had just rolled. She scrambled behind the tree.

The two men dove into the woods beside her. "Damn freakin' hunters!" Bailey growled.

McPherson duck-walked over to where Rose was crouched. "Let me see your head."

"I'm okay."

"Uh, no you're not. You've got blood running down your neck and there's a nice neat little hole right through your bun."

Rose held up the hand with which she'd grabbed her hair. It was covered in blood, and there was dirt and gore all over her shiny new ring. She swore under her breath.

"Let me see," McPherson said. He started poking at her scalp. "You're lucky. Just nicked you, but head wounds bleed like a son-of-a-bitch."

They could hear sirens in the distance. "I suppose this means you won't be taking the job?" Rose said as she saw Cherise bolt out of the back door of the house and run toward them. Sarah was on her heels.

"Hell no, I like a challenge," McPherson said.

"Good, then go tackle your new charge before she gets herself shot."

Forty minutes later, two Howard County officers were taking a statement from Bailey in the living room, having already written down what McPherson and Rose had to say. Rose sat at the kitchen table, her hair loose, cascading down her back. She winced as a paramedic cleaned the wound on the crown of her head.

Dolph hovered nearby, looking anxious. When his call to Rose had been so abruptly interrupted, he'd raced out to the farm, beating the cops there by a few minutes.

But there had been no more shots. The shooter had apparently taken off.

"Just a surface wound, ma'am," the paramedic said, his tone indicating his frustration that she refused to go to the hospital. "I need to shave the hair around it, so I can bandage it properly."

Rose twisted her head around and glared up at him. She wasn't a vain person, but the one exception was her hair. "Has it stopped bleeding?"

"Mostly. It's seeping a little."

"Then we're done. Thanks for your help."

The young man shrugged and started packing up his gear. McPherson touched Rose's shoulder and tilted his head toward the dining room. Dolph followed them.

Once out of earshot of the others, McPherson said, "I'm assuming you know that July is not hunting season around here."

"That wasn't a hunter. One shot's an accident. Four is on purpose," Rose said.

"And the shots weren't coming from the woods," McPherson said. "I walked back up there. The angle the bullet went into that tree," he dropped his voice to a whisper, "it came from the direction of the buildings."

Rose turned and looked through the doorway into the living room, where Sarah hovered solicitously at her employer's elbow.

"Shot didn't go in very deep, but it made a mess of the wood," McPherson was saying. "Low caliber, hollow point bullet would be my guess."

Rose digested that. Hollow points fragmented upon contact with a target. Even at low caliber, they did a lot of damage inside a human body.

"So *not* just trying to scare me off," she said.

"Kirk Thompson's in custody," Dolph said. "So this has to be a copycat."

Rose nodded.

And whoever it is wants Canfield and Hernandez out of the way badly enough to kill.

Rose was still staring at the computer monitor in her office at seven that evening, absently fingering the tender spot on her head. She'd completed a thorough background check on Sharon Millington and then had moved on to Cherise's PA.

Hell of a way to treat her new fiancé, but she wanted to get this done tonight. Mac would understand. He was the same way–strong sense of duty and fiercely loyal to those he loved. They were like two peas in a pod, even though they seemed so different on the surface.

They'd waited a long time to make this decision. He'd been married twice before so of course he was gun shy. And she'd never planned to marry at all, couldn't handle the thought of some man trying to take care of her or control her. But Mac knew she could take care of herself, and he'd no sooner try to tell her what to do than he'd try to fly to the moon.

Rose shook her head, then winced at the tug of the new scab on her scalp. Why was she sitting here daydreaming when she should be finishing up so she could go home.

She clicked keys on her keyboard, glared at the screen, then closed that window. Okay, let's try something else. She went to another website. Hit computer keys a few times, moved the mouse, clicked, clicked again. Shook her head. Nope, nothing there either.

Rose blew out air. After an hour of searching, all she had was a Record of Live Birth, with the correct Social Security number, issued September 20, 1978, in Talbot County, Maryland.

Okay, begin at the beginning. School records. More tapping and clicking. Nothing.

What was it with this woman? Squeaky clean was one thing, but she had to have gone to school somewhere?

A possibility dawned on her. Rose exited that website and surfed on over to another. After searching for a few minutes, she found what she'd suspected.

Sarah Hamilton, Social Security number 555-84-4691, had no police record, not even a traffic ticket, had never had her name in the paper, never chatted with friends on Facebook or My Space as a teenager. Indeed, she had never gone to school, not even elementary school, because Sarah Hamilton had died of crib death when she was four months old.

CHAPTER TWENTY-FOUR

Bright and early the next morning, Rose went into her partner's office and closed the door.

Skip's face blanched. He reared back in his chair.

"No, it's okay." She held out her empty hands. "No new articles. See no papers under my arm, nothing up my sleeve." She started to grin at him, but the seriousness of his expression stopped her.

"Damn," she said as she flopped into his visitor's chair. "Now you're like Pavlov's dogs, only instead of salivating, you freak out every time I come into the room." That worked. Now he was smiling a little.

She put both hands on his desk, giving him a perfect opportunity. Her new ring sparkled in the light from the florescent fixture overhead.

Skip ran a hand down his face. "Sorry. I'll try not to act like you're the grim reaper coming to get me."

Okay, he'd had his chance. Rose retracted her hands.

"I came in and closed the door because I didn't want the whole crew hearing this. I'm beginning to think Cherise's new stalker is an inside job." She filled him in on what she'd found, and failed to find, on Sarah Hamilton.

"I'm going out there and have a little chat with Miss PA right now," Rose concluded.

"I'm going with you, as back-up."

"Good. You can probably charm the truth out of her better than I can."

As they climbed into Skip's truck, he said, "I got something else to discuss with you, partner. I met with yet another potential new client yesterday."

"Yippee," Rose said.

He started down the street, checking his rearview mirror for unwanted tag-alongs. "Well, maybe. I need to get a proposal to them by the end of the day. I'm hesitating because we really are getting spread too thin. Even with McPherson taking over most of the security at Cherise's, that only frees up bodyguards. We still don't have enough investigators. Dolph's started on the Paterson case today, which is gonna keep him tied up for a while. And with Mac and Ben guarding my family... Maybe that isn't really necessary now. The paparazzi have backed off, and Thompson's in custody."

Rose looked over at her partner. He'd said that getting away for the weekend had done him a lot of good, but his face was tight. And there were new worry lines etched into his skin that hadn't been there a few weeks ago.

"Let's leave that be for a few more days, considering what happened yesterday. We don't know for certain that Thompson was the one who messed with the van. Better to make sure Kate and the kids are safe. So what's the new case you're debating about?"

"Insurance fraud, straight-forward surveillance. But they want fast results. We'd need to put somebody on starting tomorrow."

"Go ahead and take the case. With any kind of luck, we'll wrap up Cherise's stalker soon, one way or the other. I'll start the surveillance myself in the morning. I'll see if Ben's willing to work overtime, to do the evening shift. Did his paperwork come through yet for his provisional license?"

"Yeah, just yesterday. I'm glad he finally decided to start training," Skip said. "He's smarter than he gives himself credit for. He's been wasting himself just using his muscle as a bodyguard."

"Yup, but now he's got a bright future with Canfield and Hernandez, and this week he'll get his first official investigating gig."

For the rest of the ride, as was their habit, they bounced ideas off each other about their cases.

~~~~

As Skip pulled into Cherise's driveway, Rose sat up even straighter than her normal erect posture. "I just thought of something.

Sarah might not be our stalker after all. She could be using a false identity because she's running from the law."

"Or an abusive boyfriend or husband," Skip said. He didn't want to get the young woman fired if she had good reason to be hiding from somebody. "I don't think we should tell Cherise that Sarah isn't who she seems, at least not until we can get the woman alone to question her."

Rose nodded.

Manny answered the door. As they entered the vast living room, Cherise came out of the kitchen. "Uh, oh. Last time you both showed up, you tried to get rid of me as a client."

Skip gave her his most disarming smile. "Not our agenda this time. We actually wanted to talk to Sarah."

"Afraid you're out of luck. She's not here. Why do you want to talk to her?"

"Just wanted to touch base with her about a few things regarding the notes," Rose said. "Where is she?"

"I sent her home. She was sniffling and I can't afford to catch a cold. I have a performance coming up soon." Cherise gestured toward the white leather sofas. "What things about the notes?"

Skip ignored the question as they all sat down. "Where does she live?"

"Honestly, I don't know. She seems to move every three or four months. Can't seem to find an apartment that really suits her, I guess. I stopped trying to keep track of her address over a year ago."

Skip and Rose exchanged a look. Moving often would fit with running from an abusive spouse or boyfriend.

"How long has she worked for you?" Rose asked.

"A little over two years."

"How well did you check her out when you hired her?" Skip asked.

"She had a good resumé, came highly recommended. She had a letter from her previous employer, a bigwig producer in Hollywood."

"Did you call this producer to verify that the letter of recommendation was real?"

"Well, no. I figured I'd take her on for a trial run, and if she didn't work out, I'd let her go. But she did work out. She does a great job. Why all the questions about Sarah? What's going on?"

"Just a minor discrepancy we need to ask her about. It's not a big deal," Skip said.

Cherise looked at him skeptically.

Rose pushed up from the sofa. "I'll come out tomorrow to talk to her."

"She probably won't be here tomorrow. I told her to stay home unless she was totally okay. Like I said, I can't afford to catch a cold right now."

"Okay, just give us a call when she does come back to work," Skip said as he stood up.

Cherise also rose. "I don't like this, Skip. If there's something off about Sarah, I want to know what it is."

"It's not a big deal," he repeated.

"Then why are you *both* here?"

"We were headed to D.C., to talk to a new client," Rose said. "Figured we'd stop off here on our way. The bosses showing up unannounced now and then tends to keep the men on their toes."

Skip hid a smile. Rose was getting really good at lying.

Cherise shuddered and moved toward him. "The shooting yesterday was so scary. I'd feel a lot safer if you were here." She glanced at Manny across the room, and lowered her voice. "Manny's a nice guy, but he's not you, Skip."

"Cherise, we've already told you we're stretched thin." Skip tried to keep the impatience out of his voice.

I used to be a patient man. What happened to that? Oh, yeah, Cherise happened to that.

"Manny's a bodyguard but he's not an investigator. I've got investigations to run. He can't do that, but he can guard you. And besides, I can't be here 24/7. I have a family."

"I know, I know." She stepped closer to him, sliding her arms around his waist. He caught her hands in his own, just before she made it to his gun.

What is this woman's fascination with my gun anyway?

Strike that.

He knew some women were turned on by firearms, or more precisely by the idea of a big, strong man using a big, powerful gun to protect them.

Has to be a phallic thing. He made a mental note to ask Kate about it.

Strike that!

No way was he going to mention to Kate that this woman kept hugging him and trying to stroke his gun.

Holding Cherise's hands between his own, he pumped as much sincerity into his smile as he could manage. "Believe me, Cherise, you're safe. Everything's under control."

"I believe you," she said.

Skip let go of her hands and moved toward the door. She followed him, then stood on tiptoe and gave him a peck on the cheek.

"Thank you, for still being so kind to me after all this case has put you through. You're a good man."

This time Skip's smile was more genuine. "Thanks, Cherise. You just made my day. You have a good one now." He backed out the door that Rose was holding open behind him.

As he and Rose walked side by side out to the driveway, she made gagging noises in the back of her throat.

"Behave yourself, partner. At least, until the client is no longer watching us," Skip said softly.

"Ack, ack," was Rose's response.

"Ya got a hair ball yer tryin' to hack up there, Rosie?" Skip drawled.

She flashed him a smile, then punched him in the arm. "Don't call me Rosie."

CHAPTER TWENTY-FIVE

It was still dark when Rose left her apartment the next morning. She wanted to be in position before the subject she would be watching, one William Crawford, came out to get his morning paper. After a minor car accident, he was claiming that he could no longer bend at the waist and he was in excruciating pain most of the time.

She had all her paraphernalia spread out on the passenger seat next to her. Two digital cameras, one still, one video, with extra battery packs, binoculars, small digital recorder so she could dictate her surveillance log, a bag of pretzels, the egg and salsa burrito she'd whipped together for her breakfast, and a small battery operated fan so she didn't have to keep the car running to use the air conditioning.

On the passenger floor was a small cooler with energy drinks and a sandwich, in case she was still here at lunchtime. Beside the cooler was a plastic bucket she was hoping she wouldn't have to use.

Lack of appropriate bathroom facilities was the only thing Rose didn't like about surveillance work. Most detectives, private or in law enforcement, were not particularly fond of the assignment. It was the ultimate definition of tedium. But Rose didn't mind it. Being the quintessential introvert, she enjoyed any time when she could be alone with her own thoughts.

Nonetheless, she would be happy if Mr. Crawford came out on his front porch soon, stretched and then bent over to pick up his morning paper.

One small problem. When the delivery guy drove slowly down the street, tossing papers out his window, he didn't throw one on Crawford's porch. Damn, the man didn't take home delivery of the newspaper.

Rose picked up the napkin-wrapped burrito and settled in.

Her mind turned to Cherise's case. She'd left two phone messages on Sarah's cell phone voicemail, but the woman hadn't called her back. The address on her driver's license records was for an apartment complex in Mt. Airy, a town on the border between western Howard County and Carroll County. A call to the management office had netted the information that Sarah had moved out without notice and without leaving a forwarding address, seventeen months ago.

Rose doubted the woman's failure to update her address with the motor vehicle administration had been an oversight.

She sighed. They'd just have to wait to question the PA until she returned to work.

~~~~~~~~~

Kate got up earlier than usual, as she had every morning this week, to help Maria get the children ready. This week was vacation bible school at church and the youth director had decided to include the preschoolers in the program. Maria had graciously volunteered to help out with the little ones.

The kids were having a blast. They were so excited that they were more than their usual handful in the mornings.

Kate looked across the breakfast table at her son, as he sniffled for the third time. Was his little face just flushed from excitement or did he have a fever? Maybe she should keep him home. It wasn't fair to the other kids, and their parents, to spread germs.

He was bouncing up and down in his chair, singing one of the songs he and his sister had learned that week. Kate hated to think what his reaction would be if she told him he couldn't go today.

While the kids ate their breakfast, Kate picked up the phone to call her office answering machine for messages. The first one was her ten o'clock appointment, cancelling because she was achy and feverish. The second message was her nine o'clock person with similar complaints, also cancelling. While Kate listened to the woman's sniffling voice asking her to please call her back to reschedule, she walked around the table and used the time-honored maternal thermometer, a hand on the child's forehead.

Hmm, not cool but not particularly warm either. She should go get the real thermometer to be sure. Kate's hand was still against

Billy's forehead when he started singing and bouncing in his seat again. She almost poked him in the eye.

Hell with it.

If there was something going around, which her client cancellations certainly indicated, everybody's kids would eventually get exposed to the germs anyway. She wasn't going to disappoint the little boy.

Kate suddenly remembered she didn't have a client scheduled in the eleven o'clock time slot. She'd planned to catch up on paperwork. But she wasn't going in just for that. She'd meet Rob for lunch and then go in for her afternoon clients, assuming they weren't all sick as well.

Oh, happy day, a whole morning to herself! How often did that happen?

Ben. She'd better head him off before he left home to pick her up for the office.

Kate called his cell phone. "Hey, Ben. I've had a rash of cancellations this morning. But I am meeting Rob at noon, and then hopefully I'll have some afternoon clients. Seems to be some bug going around."

"I hope I'm not coming down with it," Ben said, his voice more gravelly than usual. "Tonight's my first official investigation assignment."

"Oh, yeah. Congratulations! It's probably just as well then that you can take the morning off and rest up some."

"Thanks. I'll come at eleven-thirty, to pick you up for your lunch with Rob."

"See you then." Kate smiled as she disconnected. Skip had been bugging his friend for a year now to get his PI license. They needed another investigator and, as Skip had put it, he knew Ben could do much more with his life than just stand around looking scary.

~~~~~~~~~

At ten-forty, Skip was just putting the finishing touches on the agency's license renewal application when his cell phone rang.

He checked caller ID and groaned softly. It was Cherise.

"Skip," she whispered urgently when he answered, "Sarah showed up just a little while ago, and I think she's the one who's been sending the notes. She was rummaging in the fan mail sack that came yesterday, and I could've sworn I saw her putting a letter in rather than taking it out. When she left the room, I looked in the sack and found a letter with no return address. I ran back here into my bedroom and locked the door." Her voice squeaked with fear. "It says, 'This is your last chance, my love. If I can't have you than nobody will.' Oh, Skip, I'm so scared."

Skip jumped out of his chair. "Where's Manny?"

"Out there in the living room with her. I can hear them talking."

"You stick close to him. Rose and I are on our way." He was out the door, his cell to his ear calling Rose, as he took the stairs three at a time and then sprinted across the parking lot to his truck.

Rose's car was halfway down Cherise's driveway when Skip turned in. Manny's was the only car parked by the house. That gave him a real bad feeling.

He skidded the Expedition to a stop, slammed it into park and jumped out. Rose was already knocking on the front door.

There was no answer. Skip banged on the door and called Cherise's name while Rose jogged around the corner to the back of the house.

Skip joined his partner in the back. No answer at that door either.

He spotted Manny standing beside the barn with Harry Bailey, Bobby Hall and what had to be one of McPherson's men. He pointed in their direction and he and Rose sprinted over to the men.

"Where's Ms. Martin?" Skip said.

"Out on the trail," Bobby Hall answered. "She insisted on taking Joey out, even though he's not one hundred percent healed yet."

Bailey spoke up. "She was going on and on about something to do with Sarah, and said she just had to get on a horse and ride, be by herself so she could sort out her feelings." The man gave a little eye roll.

"Where's Sarah?" Rose asked.

"She left a little while ago," Manny said.

"Did one of the other men go with Ms. Martin?"

McPherson's man answered, "No, sir, she wouldn't let us. My guys are walking the perimeter of the property like we're supposed to, though I'm not real sure what or who we're protectin' at the moment."

"When did they leave?"

"Sarah, about forty minutes ago," Manny said. "Ms. Martin, about ten, fifteen minutes after that."

"Why'd Sarah leave?" Rose asked.

"Ms. Martin sent her home," Manny said. "Bawled her out first, for coming to work when she was still sick. Told her not to come back until she was healthy again."

Skip was looking at his watch, calculating. All this had gone down just after he had talked to Cherise. The woman must have lost her mind. First she yells at her PA, who could very well be the one who's been making threats, and trying to shoot people. And then she goes off in the woods by herself?

He could hear Rose grinding her teeth beside him.

To buy time while he decided what to do, he asked, "Where's Ms. Martin's car?"

Manny shrugged.

Bobby Hall spoke up. "She had me drive it up the street to some guy's place last night. Said he was gonna take a look at it for her today, because it was makin' funny noises."

Rose was looking up at Skip. She gestured with her head and they moved out of earshot of the others.

"What do you want to do, partner?" she asked.

"Besides strangle Cherise with my bare hands?" Skip said, jamming those hands into his pockets. "Go look for her. She's pretty vulnerable in those woods by herself."

Rose thought for a second, then shook her head. "Somebody shot at me last time I got near those woods. I may be brave but I'm not crazy. We aren't going in there. She knew the risks and took off on her own anyway."

"We could take MacPherson's men as back-up?"

Rose thought about that. She shook her head again. "Don't really have the right to ask, since they don't work for us. And safety in numbers didn't do me much good on Monday."

"So what do you want to do?" Skip asked.

"I'm thinking that she broke her word and slipped off the leash again, so if and when she comes out of those woods, we tell her we're done. I'll call MacPherson on the way back to Towson and see if he wants to take over the case completely. We give the Howard County police what we have on Sarah, and let them check it out."

A little bubble of joy started forming in his chest as Skip nodded his agreement.

They walked over and said goodbye to the men, then Rose gestured for Manny to come with them.

Halfway to the house, Rose said, "Don't let on we were here. Just call me as soon as Cherise comes back."

"Okay." Manny headed for the house.

Once he was out of earshot, Rose started chanting under her breath, "Free, free, dear Lord, we're free at last."

"Try not to break out in a happy dance 'til we're 'round the corner, partner," Skip drawled quietly, but he could feel a big grin spreading across his own face.

CHAPTER TWENTY-SIX

Ben arrived promptly at eleven-thirty. Kate took one look at him–red nose, watery eyes, drooping shoulders–and tried to send him home.

"No way," he said. "I like my job. Skip would skin me alive, and *then* he'd fire me."

Kate smiled at him. "My husband does tend to be a bit over-protective sometimes." She made a mental note to call Skip, once she was at Mac's Place and out of Ben's earshot, and insist he let the poor man go home and rest. After all, there hadn't been any paparazzi hanging around this week.

"Have a seat. I'll be ready to go in a few minutes."

Ben gratefully sank down on one of the living room armchairs. His eyelids drooped closed.

Kate shook her head. He was in no shape to be working.

She was headed down the hall toward the bedroom to finish getting ready when the doorbell rang. She changed course and turned the corner back into the living room.

Ben was hunched down, peering through the peephole that had been installed at her eye level. He straightened and unlocked the door. Opening it, he said, "Hi. What are you doing here?"

Kate couldn't see past his bulk. "Another letter came this morning." A woman's voice. "Skip wanted me to drop it off. Uh, can I trouble you for the use of a bathroom? It's a long drive from Howard County."

Kate glanced at her watch, trying to hide her annoyance.

Why would Skip have the letter brought to the house?

But they still had a few minutes before they had to leave to meet Rob. She nodded at Ben.

He stepped back to let the woman walk past him. "Bathroom's down the hall," he said.

~~~~~~~~~

Rob was heading out of his office to meet Kate for lunch when Fran flagged him. She pointed to the blinking light on her phone console. "It's Mr. Hastings. Says it's urgent."

He groaned. Hastings was too important a client to ignore. The problem was Bartholomew T. Hastings, the fourth, knew he was important, and he rarely let others forget it for very long.

Rob stood beside Fran's desk and lifted the receiver of her phone as she punched the blinking button. "Hi, Bart, what's up?" he said, in as cheerful a voice as he could muster.

"Damn lawsuit, that's what's up. Just got served. The Light Street warehouse. Kids broke in, had a party, one of them fell down the stairs, and now somehow that's my fault."

"Fax the papers over to Fran and I'll take a look at them this afternoon. Doesn't sound like they've got much of a case."

"I need you over here now. Gotta get this resolved. That property's for sale and I've got a potential buyer lined up. This suit could screw things up royally."

Rob tried not to sigh into the phone. He thought about arguing that a few hours would not make or break the property deal. Might as well save his breath with this client.

"Where are you?" he asked. Bart, the fourth, had three residences scattered around the region.

"At the country house. Half an hour."

Just great. All the way up in the northern part of the county.

"It'll take me at least forty-five minutes." He realized he was talking to himself. Bart, the fourth, had disconnected.

On the way to his car, he called Kate's office. Her answering machine picked up right away. She must still be in session. "Hate to do this to you but I've got an emergency meeting with a very annoying but also very important client, so I can't make lunch. Hope you get this before you leave your office."

He called her cell phone. After four rings it went to voicemail. "Hey, Kate. I'd hoped to catch you before you left the office. Got an emergency meeting and I won't be able to make it for lunch. Give me a call and maybe we can make something happen on Friday."

Once in the car, Rob decided to call her office again, just in case she didn't check her messages before she left to meet him.

He tried to remember which sequence of buttons he needed to push to activate his hands-free car phone. Liz had programmed it for him, but he could never remember which button was which, and they were labeled with obscure symbols rather than words. Finally he heard a dial tone coming from the speaker.

As he started his car, he was trying to recall the speed dial number for Kate's office. It was five on his cell, but which one was it on the car phone? Pulling out of the parking lot, he hit the five button.

"Jimmy's Auto Shop," a disembodied voice said.

"Sorry, Jimmy, pushed the wrong number."

Okay, which sequence of buttons disconnects this thing and then gives me a dial tone again?

And this was supposed to be less distracting while you were driving than just using your cell phone? Of course, for most people it probably was, but for some reason technology stymied him. And by the time he figured out the latest new way to do things, it had all changed again.

Six? Was that the number for Kate's office? He hit the six button.

"Hi, you have reached the psychotherapy office of Kate Huntington. I'm not available at the moment to take your call. Please leave a message after..."

Rob zoned out until he heard the beep. "Hey, Kate. I'd hoped to catch you before you left. Are you there? Maybe standing next to that antiquated answering machine of yours to see who it is before you pick up." He was half expecting her to answer and razz him, the technophobe, for calling *her* answering machine antiquated. When she didn't, he added, "Guess you're already gone then. I'll try your cell again."

He figured seven was the speed dial number for her cell phone, and he was right. But he got her voicemail again.

That's weird.

If she'd left the office she should be answering her cell phone now. As he drove, he couldn't shake the nagging feeling that she should be answering her phone *somewhere*.

There was a virus going around. Maybe one of the kids was sick and she'd stayed home this morning. He glanced at his watch. It wasn't quite noon. Might as well try there on the off chance. Although if she was tied up with a sick child, she probably would have called him by now.

He punched the buttons to get a dial tone.

Hey, this might be the day I do this enough times to actually memorize how it's supposed to be done.

He hit eight, hoping that was the right number for Kate's house. The phone rang six times and went to voicemail. He left a message.

Might as well try her cell again. Better than thinking about how pissed I am at Bart, the fourth.

He went through the sequence to get a dial tone and punched seven again. Her cell phone rang four times and went to voicemail.

At the next traffic light, Rob struggled to get his own cell phone out of his pocket. He checked to see if he had a message from her.

Nope.

He glanced at his watch. Only two minutes after noon. She wouldn't necessarily be calling to see where he was. He wasn't that late yet.

But why isn't she answering her cell phone? Or some phone somewhere?

He was starting to get a bad feeling about this and couldn't quite figure out why. He tried to talk himself out of the bad feeling. Bart, the fourth, was going to be royally pissed if he didn't get there soon.

He was just being paranoid. He'd been a bit spooked about her safety ever since he'd heard about the van being sabotaged. She and the kids could have all too easily been killed.

Okay, that probably wasn't the best thing to be thinking about. The bad feeling was now worse.

What was it Kate had said one time about gut feelings? Trust them until you have more information, one way or the other.

Rob pulled over onto the shoulder of the road. He called Mac's Place.

The new manager answered. He came back after a couple of minutes and said, no, there was no Kate Huntington in the restaurant.

Ben! He's chauffeuring her around these days. Do I have his number?

He scrolled through his contacts in his cell phone until he came to Ben Johnson. He pushed the send button.

Rang six times and went to voicemail. Rob didn't bother to leave a message. He disconnected and pocketed his cell.

Office or house? House is closer.

He made a U-turn.

Bart, the fourth, be damned!

CHAPTER TWENTY-SEVEN

Rose hadn't done a happy dance with her feet, but once she was in her car, she'd let her fingers do one on the steering wheel before she started the engine. They were working on day three, and Skip *still* hadn't noticed her ring. Oh, man, she was going to have so much fun razzing him. Her mentor, the man who taught her how to be a detective, and he couldn't even detect what was right under his nose.

She was grinning from ear to ear as she drove back to her insurance fraud surveillance. Way her day was going so far, ole Willie would probably be roller-skating on the sidewalk when she got there.

She couldn't believe they were actually shuck of Cherise and her crazy stalker. Of course the woman might try to damage their reputation, but Rose couldn't get too worked up about that right now.

"Free, free, free at last," she sang out as she turned onto Willie's street.

~~~~~~~~

Rob's bad feeling escalated when he saw Kate's Prius parked in front of her house.

If she's here, why isn't she answering her phone?

The dark sedan behind the Prius he thought belonged to Ben. But the red minivan wasn't there.

As he hurried up the sidewalk and onto the porch, Rob tried to convince himself that they'd all gone somewhere in the van and were just running late.

And cell phones don't always ring when they're supposed to, he told himself. *Maybe hers is malfunctioning and sending calls to voicemail without ringing.*

Rob knocked on the front door. The first contact of knuckles against wood pushed the door open. It hadn't been latched.

He looked down at the doorknob. It was smeared with a bright red substance.

Fear clamped around his heart. He shoved the door open and rushed into the living room, then froze.

Ben Johnson was sitting in an armchair, facing him. His head was flopped down on his chest, as if he were asleep. But his beard was wet and rust colored. The front of his white shirt bore a spreading red stain.

Rob fought down nausea as he fumbled his cell phone out of his pocket and dialed 911. Drops of red on the floor led around the corner toward the kitchen and the hallway to the master bedroom.

The 911 operator was talking in his ear but his mind couldn't process her words. Fear had closed his throat.

A lucid part of his mind reminded him that this was a crime scene. Trying not to step in the blood, he edged cautiously around the corner and looked in the kitchen.

His heart stopped.

Kate lay on the floor, her back to him. Blood pooled around her. A knife protruded from her shoulder.

"Ambulance, fast. Two people knifed. 2610 Linden Lane," he croaked into the phone as he raced across the room.

Dropping to his knees beside her, Rob felt Kate's neck. Her skin was clammy. Relief washed through him when he found a pulse, weak but there.

The 911 operator was still talking in his ear, demanding his name. "What the hell does that matter," he screamed at her. "My friend has a knife in her. Send the ambulance. Now!"

"*Don't* pull the knife out, sir," the operator said.

Rob's hand froze halfway to the hilt. That was exactly what he'd been about to do.

"Ambulance and police are on the way," the 911 operator said. "Is the assailant still on the premises?"

That possibility hadn't even occurred to him. "Uh, I... I don't know," he stammered. "I don't think so. She's bleeding. What should I do?"

"How much is she bleeding?" The woman's voice was firm but calm.

"Not much now. It's kinda oozing around the knife. There's a lot of blood on the floor. She has a pulse but it's weak."

"What about the other victim, sir?"

"I haven't checked, but I think he's dead." Tears blurred Rob's vision. He swiped his jacket sleeve across his face. "Should I check him? I didn't want to disturb a crime scene."

"No, sir. Go outside and watch for the ambulance. They should be there any second now."

"I can't *leave* her," Rob cried into the phone.

"Do it, sir. It's the best way to get her help quickly. Stay on the line with me, until the paramedics or police get there."

Rob scrambled up off his knees and staggered backward a few steps, then turned and ran for the front door, the sirens in the distance finally registering in his mind. By the time he was on the porch, the ambulance was turning onto Linden Lane. He raced down to the street and waved frantically.

Rob and the female paramedic were back inside the house in less than thirty seconds. They'd left the young woman's partner pulling equipment out of the side compartment of the ambulance.

She headed for Ben, but Rob grabbed her arm and dragged her toward the kitchen. "Take care of her. I think he's dead."

When the other paramedic joined his partner a few seconds later, he concurred. "Guy's throat's been slit."

Rob's knees gave out and he sat down hard on the floor several feet from where they were now working on Kate.

The young woman's fingers deftly inserted an IV needle in Kate's arm while her partner packed bandages tightly around the knife to keep it from moving and to stop the bleeding. "Get the gurney," the woman told her partner.

Rob followed the paramedic as he moved quickly out of the house, talking into his radio as he went.

"Second ambulance is on its way, sir." In response to Rob's confused look, he added, "To transport the other victim."

The muscular young man was no doubt capable of managing the collapsed gurney by himself, but Rob, desperate for something to do, helped him carry it up the porch steps.

The paramedics gently lifted Kate's unconscious body, stomach down, onto the gurney. They strapped her securely, then rolled the gurney out of the house, Rob following close behind.

"Police'll want to talk to you, sir," the young woman said over her shoulder.

"I'm going with... my wife," Rob said. He wasn't taking any chances. There was probably some damn rule these days about only relatives in the ambulance. He was going to the hospital with Kate if he had to stand on the back bumper, hanging onto the door handles.

The paramedic shrugged as if that's the answer she'd expected. They race-walked the gurney toward the ambulance.

Just before the ambulance's siren blasted, Rob caught the sound of another siren. He glanced through the small window in the back door of the ambulance. A police cruiser had just rounded the corner.

He heard the young woman up front key her radio, then the words *Greater Baltimore Medical Center*.

The paramedic hooked a bag of clear fluid attached to Kate's IV tube onto a bracket above her head. Rob took her limp right hand that was dangling off the side of the gurney.

Tears blurred his vision. "Hang on, Kate," he whispered, "Don't leave us."

~~~~~~~~~~

Skip laid on his horn and made a U-turn in the middle of Towsontown Boulevard. Fortunately no one was coming the other way.

His stunned mind replayed the brief phone call from Rob, telling him his wife was in the emergency room at GBMC, the victim of a stabbing.

His luck held at the light at Charles Street. It was just turning yellow when he got there. He took the turn fast, his tires squealing in protest as he accelerated up the hill.

At the front entrance of the hospital he abandoned his truck with the motor still running. Let the asshole who was yelling, "Hey, you can't leave your vehicle there," move it.

He raced into the building and desperately charged down corridors, searching for the ER.

CHAPTER TWENTY-EIGHT

"Rose, are you there?"

"*¡Dios mio!*" Her voice was barely above a whisper.

"The kids may be in danger," Rob said into his cell phone.

A garbled sound that could have been her clearing her throat, or a stifled sob. "I'll call Mac. Have him take them and Maria to our place. I'll be there in–"

"There's nothing really you can do here. They're taking her into surgery now."

"Okay, I'll go to the house. Give the police the background on all this. Keep me posted."

"I will." Rob disconnected and then punched in the number for his wife's office as he walked toward the elevators.

Skip rounded a corner down the hall and sprinted toward him.

Rob aborted the call and pocketed his phone. He grabbed the big man's arms to stop his momentum. "We're going upstairs. They just took her to prep for surgery." He turned Skip toward the elevators and managed to get an arm around the taller man's shoulders.

Maneuvering him into one of the elevators, Rob repeated what the paramedic had said in the ambulance. "He told me he wasn't supposed to say anything about her condition, but he thought the knife had missed her heart. She's going to be alright." He was trying to convince himself as much as the man next to him.

They rose toward the third floor. Tears streamed down Skip's cheeks. Rob handed him his handkerchief, then swiped his suit jacket sleeve across his own face.

"Where was Ben?" Skip demanded. "How the hell did he let this happen?"

Rob froze. His stomach clenched as his mind scrambled for words. But there was no good way to say it.

"Ben... He's dead."

Skip's angry face went blank, then twisted into anguish. He turned away and banged his fists against the side of the elevator. "Noooo!" he screamed, just as the doors slid open.

Two people waiting to get on took several steps backward when they saw a man the size of a small mountain banging on the elevator wall and yelling.

Rob grabbed his friend and dragged him into the hallway.

By the time they'd found the surgical unit's waiting room, Skip was somewhat under control. Rob led him to two chairs, as far away as he could get from the other people waiting for news of their loved ones.

Skip sat and leaned forward, his elbows on his thighs, staring at the floor.

Rob put his hand on the man's back. Quietly he said, "Mac's taking Maria and the kids to their apartment, and Rose is headed for your house, to fill the cops in."

Skip nodded without raising his head.

Several minutes passed. "By the way," Rob said, "we're going to have some explaining to do at some point. I told them I was her husband so they'd let me ride in the ambulance and authorize her surgery."

Skip sat up. He looked around.

Rob realized his handkerchief had gotten lost along the way.

Skip fished out his own, wiped his wet face, then turned to Rob. "Yeah, that could definitely take some explaining." His voice was shaky.

"It was someone they knew," Rob said. "Someone they trusted. Ben was sitting in an armchair in the living room and Kate was stabbed in the back. No sign of forced entry or a struggle."

Skip stared at him for a beat, then nodded. He looked off into space, his eyes glazing over. His lips moved soundlessly.

Rob slipped quietly from his chair and went out to the hallway to call his wife.

An agonizing hour and a half later, a doctor with an inscrutable expression on his face came into the waiting area. "Mr. Franklin?" he called out, looking around the room.

Both Rob and Skip jumped up.

The doctor closed the gap between them and motioned them back into their seats. "And you are?" he said to Skip.

"I'm her husband," Skip said.

The doctor did a double-take.

Rob silently cursed the HIPPA rules that kept doctors from giving out information to worried loved ones, unless they were next of kin or designated medical surrogates. "I'll explain in a minute," he growled. "Right now you'd better tell us how she is."

"She's in guarded condition," the doctor said, then hesitated, looking from one big, scowling man to the other.

Rob gritted his teeth. "I'm the family lawyer. There won't be any lawsuits over privacy issues."

Again, the doctor looked back and forth between them.

A rumbling noise came from low in Skip's throat.

The doctor's shoulder twitched in a half shrug. "She's lost a lot of blood, but I'm fairly confident she'll be okay. I was afraid the knife might have nicked her heart, but it hadn't. She's very lucky."

Rob's own heart raced as he realized just how lucky. The assailant must have assumed the job had been accomplished. Otherwise a second blow would have surely followed, and Kate would be dead now.

His eyes stung.

"Whichever one of you actually is her husband, you can go in to recovery to see her," the doctor was saying.

Skip was on his feet. "Where's recovery?"

The doctor pointed to a door. "Nurses will get you gowned and gloved. Gotta be careful about post-op infections."

As Skip loped across the room, Rob opened his mouth to explain about the husband issue.

The doctor held up his hand. "Quite frankly, it's the end of a very long shift and I'm too damned tired to care. You'll need to get it straightened out on her records though." After a beat, he added in a quieter voice, "I can understand your motivation, but in emergencies, we can operate without next-of-kin authorization."

"Yeah, but I didn't know if they'd let me ride in the ambulance with her." Rob's voice broke. He swallowed, then whispered, "And keep telling her to hang on."

The doctor stood and rested a gentle hand on his shoulder. "It was good you were there." His voice was low. "She could've slipped away from us." He turned away and trudged toward the door to the hallway.

Rob took a moment to compose himself, then followed. Out in the corridor, he started making calls to let the others know that Kate was still with them.

The police detective had come and gone with her questions, when a nurse finally informed Rob that Kate had been moved to a regular room and he could go see her now.

As he stepped into the doorway, his breath caught in his throat. Kate was so pale and still, he thought for a moment she was dead.

But Skip wouldn't be calmly sitting there next to the bed, stroking her forehead, if she'd stopped breathing. His other hand was awkwardly holding the limp fingers hanging out of a sling-like contraption, that was no doubt designed to keep her injured shoulder immobilized. The big man still wore a paper gown over his clothes, but he'd removed the rubber gloves required in recovery.

Rob dragged a chair over to the other side of the bed and sat down. He put his hand on Kate's uninjured arm, just above the IV tube taped to the back of her hand. "Has she opened her eyes at all?"

Skip nodded without taking his gaze off his wife's face. "Briefly, in the recovery room."

After another moment, Skip's face contorted. Rob realized he was struggling not to cry.

"Thank you," the big man whispered. "If you hadn't gotten there when you did... I couldn't live without her."

A week ago, Rob would have denied the truth of that statement, believing Skip would go on for the sake of his children. Now, he wasn't so sure. This strong man's only weakness was the woman lying so deathly still on the bed between them.

Finally Rob stated the simple truth. "You don't have to. She's still with us."

~~~~

They sat quietly for a long time. Skip started massaging the cold, limp fingers of Kate's left hand, trying to rub some warmth into them.

Rob pointed to her empty ring finger. "I have her diamonds, including your mother's ring."

Skip nodded, although even the diamond that had adorned the left hands of three generations of Canfield wives was of little importance to him right now. He brushed his thumb over his wife's pale cheek and willed her to open her eyes.

"Detective Anderson said she'd be back later to talk to you," Rob said.

Skip lifted his head. "Judith Anderson?"

"You know her?"

"She's Dolph's former partner. Seems like a good cop."

The sat in silence again for a few minutes.

Finally Rob asked, "Does this make any sense to you?"

Skip shook his head. He'd been trying to sort it out, but anxiety kept derailing his thought process. All he knew was that it couldn't be a coincidence. Somehow it was related to all this crap with Cherise and her stalker. "Two notes ago, the message was that the stalker was going to get rid of, quote, 'those people who are keeping us apart.' Rose and I assumed that meant us and her bodyguards. Rob, I almost pulled..." He stopped and stared at the ceiling, swallowing hard. "I almost pulled Ben off of Kate yesterday." He shook his head again, not sure what difference that would have made in the outcome.

His eyes stung when he realized the main difference. Ben would still be alive.

"It doesn't make any sense," he said after a moment. "Our strongest suspect at this point is Cherise's personal assistant. We think she may have some kind of crazy crush on her boss. But Sarah wouldn't have any reason to go after Kate."

He went back to massaging his wife's limp fingers. His hands stilled as a thought struck him. "Unless... Cherise yelled at Sarah this morning and sent her home."

Anger flared at the prima donna's stupidity and selfishness. If she'd bothered to call him back before she took off on that horse, he wouldn't have been in Howard County when...

He would've been at the office instead, not home. He still wouldn't have been there to protect his wife from her attacker.

He pulled his mind away from the shoulds and coulds and refocused it on solving the puzzle. "If Sarah sees me as competition for Cherise's affections, as the reason why Cherise rejected her, then Sarah may have come looking for me. And Ben would have let her in if she'd had some plausible explanation, that she had a message from Cherise or was bringing us the latest note. The note that Cherise said she saw Sarah put *in* the mail sack this morning. It said, 'This is your last chance. If I can't have you, nobody will.'"

"Shit," Rob said. "Did this woman seem that crazy to you?"

Skip didn't answer him. If it was Sarah, she had to be crazy. There was no sane reason for her to go after Kate.

He let go of his wife's fingers for a moment to scrub his hand over his face. Suddenly he was exhausted. He was trying to capture the random thought that was skittering around in the back of his head.

"Skip!" Rob's eyes were on Kate's face.

Her eyelids fluttered and her lips moved. Both men leaned in closer, Skip's ear practically touching her lips.

"Kids," she whispered.

"They're safe, darlin'. They're with Maria and Mac, at his a-partment." Skip kissed her cheek. Then she mumbled something else.

"What was that, sweetheart?" Rob said.

But Skip had heard her. He jumped to his feet, ripping off the paper gown. "Take care of her, Rob." He strode toward the door.

Judith Anderson was blocking his way.

"Ben?" The faint voice from the bed. Skip turned back around.

Rob stared helplessly up at him for a beat, then he patted Kate's arm. "Ben's fine, sweetheart," he lied in a choked voice.

Red-hot anger seared through Skip's chest. He shoved past Judith and took off down the hospital corridor at full speed.

"Wait!" the detective called after him.

He kept going.

CHAPTER TWENTY-NINE

Agonizing worry and blinding rage rode shotgun as Skip drove to Howard County. He punched the speed-dial number on his cell for Rose and Mac's apartment. When Mac answered, he told him not to let anyone at all near his children until further notice.

"What's going on?" Mac said. "How's Kate? Rob said she was outta surgery."

"She just woke up. The doc thinks she'll be okay. I'll call you later." Skip disconnected.

When he stopped the truck at Cherise's farm, he took two deep breaths before getting out. He had to stay calm.

Cherise opened the door.

Skip looked her over carefully. Her hair was damp. Her face, free of make-up, looked fresh and innocent. She was wearing clean jeans and a loose-fitting shirt. Her feet were bare.

"Excuse my appearance," she said. "I just got out of the shower."

Then his expression must have registered. "What's the matter, Skip? You look like you've seen a ghost." She took his hand.

"Long time to be out on the trail with a lame horse," he said, as he let her lead him into the living room. He tugged his hand free and stepped away from her, moving toward the fireplace.

"I just walked him."

Skip turned back toward her. "Where's Manny?"

"On the back patio. I told him I needed to be alone for a while. What's the matter?"

He narrowed his eyes at her. "You didn't happen to find out Sarah's address, by any chance, before you threw her out of the house? After I'd told you to sit tight, that we were on our way to question her."

"I'm sorry, Skip." She dropped her gaze in an imitation of remorse. "You're angry with me and you have every right to be. I just freaked after I got off the phone with you. I couldn't stand having her here another minute. Then I had to get away, get my head straight. Am I forgiven?"

She took two steps toward him before the cold look in his eyes stopped her.

"Kate was attacked," he said. "She almost died."

Cherise put both hands over her mouth, a look of horror on her face. "Oh my God! Is she going to be okay?"

"Doctor thinks so."

Cherise took another step toward him. "I'm touched, Skip, that you rushed out here to make sure I was safe." Then she made the move he'd been waiting for. She rushed to him and slid her arms around his waist. He clamped a hand down on top of hers before it got to his gun butt.

Cherise relaxed her hand and gave him a comforting squeeze with her arms, then leaned back. Resting her other hand on his chest, she looked up at him. "That must've been horrible for you to come home and find her lying there like that."

Skip waited a beat. "I never said where she was attacked, Cherise."

She froze.

Then the hand he didn't have control over was sliding under his shirttail, fumbling for the pistol. He had anticipated the move, but not her speed and dexterity. Wrapping long fingers tightly around her wrist, he forced her hand out to the side, the gun pointed away from them.

"Stop! You're hurting me."

"Then let go of my gun," he growled, clamping down harder. The gun clattered to the floor. He let go of one of her wrists as he leaned down to scoop up the pistol. She twisted the other arm free and ran away from him.

Skip retrieved his gun and straightened up, just as Cherise whirled back around to face him.

She was holding a .22 long-barreled revolver. A drawer in the cabinet behind her stood open. "Don't move. This is loaded with hollow points. The caliber may be low, but at this range, they'll rip a hole right through you."

"You know your guns, Cherise," he said, almost conversationally. "Is that the one you tried to shoot Rose with?"

"Yeah. I had to get the little dyke out of the way, so you'd take over my case again."

"Who'd you hire to sabotage the van? Can't see you getting grease under your fingernails," he said, stalling, distracting, as he slowly eased his gun hand up.

"I'm a country girl, Skip. Helped my daddy fix the tractor more than once. You need to stop underestimating me, my love."

"Yeah, I definitely have been doing that. So there wasn't any note this morning, was there? That was all just to make sure I wasn't around. How'd you know Kate was at home?"

"Went by her office first," Cherise said, then laughed. "And you still don't get it, do you? Those notes, the recent ones, those messages were from me, to you. And they kept you coming back, didn't they?"

Skip was digesting the horrible thought that his kids could have all too easily been at home this morning.

Cherise suddenly braced herself and extended both arms, finger tightening on the trigger of the .22. "Drop your gun, Skip. Right now, or I swear I'll shoot you."

He stopped moving. "I thought you loved me?" He let his hand droop at the wrist, the pistol pointing toward the floor, as if he had no intentions of using it.

"I do, with all my heart." Tears pooled in her eyes. "This is your last chance. Either you leave her and marry me, or I'll kill you. And then I'll go finish off your little family." She curled her lip.

Skip realized she was truly crazy. Did she think they could just ride off into the sunset together, and live happily ever after? She had killed a man–his friend–and had almost killed his wife.

Watching her closely, he tried to look like he was thinking about those choices. A part of him was tempted to confront her about the roses, the bogus e-mails, the paparazzi she had stirred up every time they had lost interest. But confrontation was probably a bad idea–one that would most likely get him shot.

"Where would we go, Cherise?" he said instead. "They're going to be looking for you."

"Ah, but that's the beauty of my plan. I didn't send Sarah home because she had the sniffles. She told me a long time ago that she was running from her ex-husband. He used to beat her. I took her aside, told her a man had come looking for her last night, real angry. She ran out the front door, and I yelled after her, 'Don't come back until the risk is over.' Manny thought I meant the risk of catching her cold."

"So how's that going to keep the police from coming after you?" Skip asked, once again easing his gun up.

"She's long gone by now, and she'll probably change her identity again. The police will believe us when we tell them she was the stalker. She went after Kate for some crazy reason. That'll buy us some time to get away."

Skip struggled to school his expression into one of calm interest. This woman was planning to frame her innocent assistant, who had served her diligently for two years. Frame her for murder.

"You haven't answered my question, Cherise. Where did you have in mind that we would go? It should be out of the country."

Cherise smiled, relaxing her grip on her gun. "I've got just the place. A little island in the Caribbean. They'll never find us there."

She hesitated. He knew she was considering lowering the gun and rushing into his arms. He willed his body not to move. Now he didn't want to distract her from those thoughts, her struggle to believe he truly loved her, when they were standing there holding guns on each other.

"You have to promise me," she said, "that you'll never abandon me. I love you so! I thought I was in love with Kirk, but that wasn't anything like this."

He started slowly moving his hand again.

"I realize now that I haven't been able to love before. I was too afraid. But I'm not with you. You're so reliable, so strong. You'll always protect me, love me. But you have to promise you'll never leave me. I need to hear the words. Know that you mean them."

"Why are you so afraid of abandonment, Cherise? It seems to me that you're usually the one who throws guys out of your life."

"I have before, but I won't with you. Those others, they let me down. Pretended to love me, but then they'd do things that hurt me."

Skip considered pointing out that humans did that to each other sometimes, hurt each other, usually without meaning to. He certainly knew that for a fact after the last few weeks. But this wasn't a philosophical discussion about love. Easing his hand up another fraction of an inch, he decided that once his gun was high enough, he wasn't going to order her to drop her weapon. He knew she wouldn't do it, and warning her he was about to shoot could be fatal.

"They were like my father. He was a charmer. All the women loved him." Cherise's voice dropped, her eyes softening into a far-away look. "I adored him when I was a kid. My big, handsome, funny daddy."

Skip's hand edged a little higher.

"Until he destroyed my mother." Her eyes were still staring past Skip's shoulder, but now they were hard with anger. "She was weak. She kept letting him hurt her."

"So that's why you won't put up with men hurting you," Skip said softly.

"No, I won't. I'm not weak like her. She let him destroy her. And then he left me with her, that shell of a woman who had once been my mother." Her eyes refocused on his face. "That's why I need you to promise me, Skip. Promise you'll never leave me."

He opened his mouth, but he couldn't say the words, not even as a lie to keep her talking. He edged his pistol a bit higher and snugged his finger against the trigger.

His voice gentle, he said, "I already made that promise, Cherise, to my wife."

Her face contorted with hurt and fury. Her hands tightened around her gun.

The back screen door slammed. "Ms. Martin?" Manny's voice. Footsteps on the kitchen's hardwood floor.

Cherise's eyes skittered toward the doorway between the two rooms.

Skip squeezed the trigger. Two shots roared in rapid succession. But he was already on the floor.

Manny came around the corner fast, his gun drawn. "Shit!" He bolted across the living room.

CHAPTER THIRTY

Rose stood by the fax machine waiting for it to spit out the last pages of the follow-up story on the Cherise Martin case. The police department in Walton County, Georgia, according to the article, had reopened the investigation into the house fire that had killed Cherise's mother. The fire marshal had apparently suspected arson at the time, but hadn't been able to prove it.

Rose looked across the bullpen. It was cluttered with desks and chairs, used by the bodyguards and investigators when they were in the office, but on a Saturday morning, she was alone.

Her gaze landed on the desk in the corner, where Ben had sat to fill out reports and his time sheets. Manny Ortiz had shared it with him. On Thursday, Manny had quietly removed his own things from the drawers, and put them in another desk.

Rose swallowed hard. She grabbed the last page and tucked the article under her arm, then glanced at her watch. She was running late. Kate was coming home from the hospital today.

The kids had planned a little party for her, complete with a homemade 'We luv u, Mommy' banner and cupcakes Maria had helped them bake. They wanted their Aunt Rose and Uncle Mac to be there.

Those kids had been through enough lately. Rose wasn't about to disappoint them.

~~~~~~~~

Kate was being wheeled out of the hospital. She tried to distract herself from the dull ache in her chest, despite the 800 milligrams of Motrin in her system. She'd resisted the stronger pain killer the nurse had offered, not wanting to be doped up in front of the kids.

Her mind veered toward thoughts of Ben and tears welled in her eyes. Best not to go there.

She focused instead on the question of why hospitals made discharged patients ride to their cars in wheelchairs. There was nothing wrong with her legs.

The automatic doors swished open. Liz jumped out of the driver's seat of the Expedition and came around to open the passenger door.

But the man pushing Kate's wheelchair beat her to it. "Where's Rob?" he asked, pausing with the door halfway open.

Liz tilted her head toward the driveway leading down the hill to Charles Street, where the Franklins' car was idling. "We were going to follow you back to the house. Help you get the patient settled."

"That'd be great. It's not gonna be fun running the gauntlet of reporters in front of the house."

Liz snorted. "This time it's real news at least, not some invented fantasy."

"Thanks for bringing the truck around," Skip said.

Kate had been looking up at them, swiveling her head back and forth. "Somebody going to help me out of this contraption?" She struggled to push herself upright with one hand but the footrest was making it difficult to find the ground with her feet. "Or are you two gonna chat all day while I get a crick in my neck?"

Liz smiled down at her. "The patient is grumpy." She sketched a little wave at them, then jogged off toward Rob's car, calling back over her shoulder, "See you at the house."

~~~~

Skip helped his wife into his truck, then went around and climbed in the driver's seat. He threaded her seat belt under the sling on her left arm and buckled it.

She grinned at him. "I wasn't real sure which of my husbands I was going to be riding with today."

He grinned back and started down the drive, Rob and Liz falling in behind them. "I'm not sure we've gotten that mess straightened out yet."

Kate snickered a little. Then her expression grew serious. "There's something I need to say before we get home."

He glanced her way, then looked back at the road as the traffic light at Charles Street turned green.

"Skip, you broke a promise to me."

"I did? Not that I know of." He turned onto Charles Street. "What promise?"

"The last time you had to use your gun..." She trailed off.

His own mood sobered. The last time he'd fired his gun at a human being, he'd been forced to kill.

"You promised me, afterward," she said, "that you wouldn't hesitate to use it again, to protect yourself."

He glanced her way as he made the right turn onto Towsontown Boulevard. She was looking at him with worry in her eyes.

He took one hand off the wheel to pat her knee. "Darlin', I remember the promise but other than that, I have no clue what you're talking about."

"You've told me, and so have Rose and Mac, that if you have to shoot somebody to defend yourself, you aim for the chest or stomach because it's the bigger target, even though there's a greater risk you'll kill the person that way."

He glanced her way again, still confused. Then understanding dawned.

He pulled onto a side street and stopped at the curb, lowering his window as Rob pulled up beside him. "Need to make a stop. You guys go on to the house. We'll be along in a minute," he said to the Franklins, by way of explanation.

When Rob had pulled away, Skip put the truck in park and turned to his wife. "Darlin', I wasn't aiming for her thigh." He paused to choose his words carefully. "It's a little hard to hold a gun totally steady while you're shooting it and diving to the floor at the same time."

Kate's worried look shifted to relief. "Are you sure you weren't hesitating?"

"Not for a second."

The truth was he hadn't gotten his gun all the way up. He'd had to take the best shot he could get, then drop to the floor and roll. A moving target was harder to hit. He'd expected Cherise to fire a second shot. But she hadn't. She'd dropped the revolver, then crumpled down next to it.

She'd tried to pick her gun up again, but her hands were slick from clutching at her bleeding thigh. Manny had wrestled the pistol away from her without much difficulty.

But Skip wasn't about to tell Kate all that. He didn't want to worry her more by painting too vivid a picture of that scene in Cherise's living room. He reminded himself again that he needed to talk to Rose about giving Manny a raise.

Taking his wife's face between his hands, Skip kissed her gently. Her lips parted and he nudged his way a bit further in. She moaned softly.

Oh, yes! So much better than those chaste pecks in the hospital room.

They came up for air a few minutes later. His hands still bracketing Kate's face, Skip said, "That woman had just killed a friend of mine and had almost killed you. I didn't have any qualms about shooting her, and I still don't."

Kate smiled up into his face, love and relief in her eyes.

A less-than-Christian part of him wished he had killed Cherise. He shook his head. "Her trial is going to be a three-ring circus."

"Will we have to testify?" she asked.

"Most likely, but there's a lot of forensic evidence against her. She'll be convicted."

"What evidence?"

"A partial print on one of the later letters, and one of her hairs in the envelope." He opted not to mention the traces of Kate's and Ben's blood the crime scene techs had been found in Cherise's shower drain.

"Won't she just say that she handled it after it came?"

"Sarah found it in the mail bag and gave it directly to Manny."

He stroked his thumb gently over her soft lips. "You know, darlin'," he drawled. "I haven't been able to kiss you proper like that for a whole four days now. I think I'm a little out of practice."

Those luscious lips curled up a bit on the ends. "Hmm, it didn't seem that way to me. But maybe you ought to do it again, so I can tell for sure."

A minute later, she broke away from him, gasping. "No, I think you're as good as ever. But we ought to head home now. Everybody will be wondering where we are." She gave him a mischievous grin and tapped her sling with her right hand. "Besides, making love is going to be awkward enough with this thing, without trying to do it in the front seat of your truck."

He caught her hand before she could return it to her lap. "Something tells me we'll figure it out, darlin'." Turning her hand over, he kiss the palm.

She sucked in her breath.

"I, for one," he whispered, his mouth lingering over her palm, "am looking forward to the challenge." Then he kissed the sweet spot on the inside of her wrist, just to hear that sharp intake of air again.

He let go of her to put the truck in gear and head for home.

Kate fluttered her hand over her chest in an exaggerated be-still-my-heart gesture. "Guess we should talk about other things, to get ourselves settled down before we get there."

He just shot her a grin.

"So has Rose said anything to you about a date yet?" she asked.

"Date for what?"

"For the wedding. Have she and Mac settled on when they're getting hitched?"

Skip almost drove off the road.

~~~~~◇~~~~~

AUTHOR'S NOTES

If you enjoyed this book, please take a moment to leave a short review on Amazon and/or other retailers. Reviews help to sell books and sales help to keep the series going! You can readily find the links to these retailers at the *misterio press* bookstore (http://misterio press.com/misterio-press-bookstore/#kassandra-lamb).

We at *misterio press* pride ourselves on producing top quality mysteries. Each book is proofread several times by several sets of eyes. But proofreaders are human. If you found errors in this book, please e-mail the author at lambkassandra3@gmail.com and let her know. Thanks!

Just a few quick expressions of gratitude and random comments, and then I will give you a synopsis of the next adventures in the lives of Kate and her friends and family.

I have a wonderful group of beta readers who helped me polish this book. My husband, who never reads fiction except when coerced to do so by me, actually volunteered to read the first draft two summers ago. When he said he 'really liked it' I knew I had a winner, but there were still many months of refining to come. A huge thanks to Angi, Sue, Ralph, and Ann who critiqued it for me at various points along the way (some of them reading it more than once). And a special thanks to my cohorts at *misterio press*, JoAnn Bassett, Kathy Owen and Kirsten Weiss, who each contributed tremendously to the quality of this book, and especially to my co-founder of *misterio*, Shannon Esposito, who has become a dear friend.

Also, I am always grateful to the other wonderful people in my life who support and encourage me in my writing career. You know who you are. God bless you!

One of the things about writing that never ceases to amaze me is how the characters will sometimes take over and write much bigger parts for themselves than I ever intended. This first happened with Rose Hernandez in Book 1, *Multiple Motives*. She was supposed to be a bit player, with just a few short lines. Next thing I knew she'd become this rather complex character with a fierce and idealistic sense of right and wrong and she'd joined the investigation.

Likewise, Skip Canfield was never intended to be any more than a minor character in the first book. He came into the investigation late and provided a bit of a sounding board for Kate and Rose. Since then the man has managed to woo both Kate and myself into letting him become a main character in her life and the series.

Celebrity Status ended up being Skip's story, but the original premise was to explore what would happen to a fairly average middle-class family if they suddenly became the targets of the paparazzi. How do celebrities deal with that pressure and scrutiny day in and day out? I know that I couldn't take it!

I've received some feedback that Skip's emotional reactions are too intense in this story. To that criticism I offer two pieces of evidence in my defense. One, my brother–who is both quite psychologically astute and also a fairly macho guy–thought Skip's reactions were on target.

Two, scientific research on the topic has found that male and female *internal* emotional reactions to various situations tend to be quite similar. The gender differences only become apparent regarding *if* and/or *how* the emotions are expressed.

In other words, men and women experience the same emotions at the same level of intensity. But socialization dictates how much and in what ways we express those emotions to the outside world.

I was further intrigued by the development of the relationship between Rose and Skip in this story, both as business partners and as friends. Again, somewhere along the way, Rose has moved into a much more central role. The theme of her and Mac Reilly as extended family is further developed in *Collateral Casualties* and *Zero Hero*. Indeed, Rose really shines in *Collateral Casualties*.

To some extent, Kate takes a backseat to Skip and Rose as an investigator in these earlier stories. But don't worry, she grows into her role as amateur sleuth as the series progresses, and becomes downright kickass in *Zero Hero*.

So without further ado, here are previews of *Collateral Casualties* and *Zero Hero*.

COLLATERAL CASUALTIES
A Kate Huntington Mystery (Book 5)

When a former client reaches out to psychotherapist Kate Huntington and reveals a foreign diplomat's dark secret, then is found dead of "natural causes" just days later, Kate isn't sure what to think. Had the man been delusional or has she been made privy to dangerous information?

As Kate connects the dots between a series of seemingly unrelated events, she realizes that Miller Dawson was totally sane... and he was murdered. Now she and everyone she loves are at risk. Someone is trying to eliminate anyone and everyone whom she or Miller might have told.

Her family and her friends, including the Franklins, are forced to go into hiding. As the body count rises, Kate and her husband, Skip Canfield, struggle to put aside grief and guilt in order to focus on discovering who is trying to kill them. Along with Skip's business partner, Rose Hernandez, and the operatives of their private investigating agency, they race against time to stop an unknown but ruthless assassin.

Skip and Rose are good investigators, but this time they may be in over their heads. Kate is terrified that they will all drown in a sea of international intrigue.

ZERO HERO
A Kate Huntington Mystery (Book 6)

First responder Peter Jamieson saved many lives on 9/11, including several children. For the next ten years, the reserved firefighter pursued the only career he had ever wanted.

Then on the tenth anniversary of 9/11, the media replays the videos again and again–the smoke against the blue sky, the towers coming down, the aftermath at Ground Zero–and Pete starts having nightmares and flashbacks. His world quickly spirals out of control as he turns to drugs and alcohol in an attempt to block the images and feelings. He hits bottom when he is suspended from the job he loves.

Seventeen months later, Pete is slowly recovering the life he once had when the insurance companies cut him off.

Psychotherapist Kate Huntington is afraid that her lawyer friend, Rob Franklin, has lost his professional objectivity with regard to Pete's case. Are the *pro bono* client's symptoms stirring up Rob's memories of his own past struggles with PTSD? When she meets Pete, she soon finds herself sucked in as well. How can they not do everything possible to help this man who risked his life to save others?

Pete's circumstances go from bad to worse when he is accused of murdering his best friend and former drug dealer. As Kate and her P.I. husband set out to clear him of the charges, they are thrust into a deadly world of drugs, prostitutes and hired killers, and end up questioning who they are and what it means to be brave.

ABOUT THE AUTHOR

Kassandra Lamb has never been able to decide which she loves more, psychology or writing. In college, she realized that writers need a day job in order to eat, so she studied psychology. After a career as a psychotherapist and college professor, she is now retired and can pursue her passion for writing.

She spends most of her time in an alternate universe with her characters. The portal to this universe, aka her computer, is located in Florida, where her husband and dog catch occasional glimpses of her. She and her husband spend part of each summer in her native Maryland, where the Kate Huntington series is based.

Kass has completed seven books in the series, plus three *Kate on Vacation* novellas (lighter reads along the lines of cozy mysteries). She is currently working on Book 8, *Suicidal Suspicions*, and the next Vacation novella.

To read and see more about Kate Huntington you can go to http://kassandralamb.com. Be sure to sign up for the newsletter there to get a heads up about new releases, plus special offers and bonuses for subscribers.

Kass's e-mail is lambkassandra3@gmail.com and she loves hearing from readers! She's also on Facebook (https://www.face book.com/kassandralambauthor) and hangs out some on Twitter @KassandraLamb. She blogs about psychological topics and other random things at http://misteriopress.com.

~~~

Please check out these other *misterio press* series:

Karma's A Bitch
The Pet Psychic series by Shannon Esposito

Multiple Motives
The Kate Huntington series by Kassandra Lamb

Maui Widow Waltz
The Islands of Aloha series by JoAnn Bassett

The Metaphysical Detective
The Riga Hayworth series by Kirsten Weiss

Dangerous and Unseemly
The Concordia Wells series by K.B. Owen

Murder, Honey
The Carol Sabala series by Vinnie Hansen

**Plus even more great mysteries/thrillers in the
misterio press bookstore.**

Made in the USA
Columbia, SC
20 September 2018